Welcome to Smoky Point

Welcome to Smoky Point

Al Lamanda

Encircle Publications
Farmington, Maine, U.S.A.

Encircle editor: Cynthia Brackett-Vincent

Book design by Deirdre Wait

Cover design by Christopher Wait
Cover photograph © Getty Images

Published by:

Encircle Publications
PO Box 187
Farmington, ME 04938

info@encirclepub.com
http://encirclepub.com

Prologue

THE DARKNESS OF HER CONFINEMENT was as if she had suddenly gone blind; it was that dark.

The first instinct was to panic. No amount of training can overcome that initial response. What the training does, however, is help you fight through the panic and allow clear thinking to emerge.

She could feel the sides of her confinement with her hands. They were made of wood. The air was damp and smelled stale. She slowed her breathing to sips because she didn't know how much air was available and needed to conserve what there was or risk suffocating.

She reached up and touched the ceiling. It was also made of wood and maybe a foot above her face.

She swallowed the terror in her chest and tried to remember how this came to pass and couldn't. The last thing she remembered was…

Her utility belt, it was still around her waist.

She felt for her weapon in the holster on her right hip. On her left hip was the two-battery Maglite she always carried and she withdrew it from the sheath. Her hands shook a bit as she clicked it on.

Immediately, she recognized her confinement.

She was inside a cheap pine coffin.

Jesus Christ, she had been buried alive.

Chapter One

AS SHE RODE THE FERRY back to Newport, Claire Evergreen replayed the job interview in her mind and decided that she wouldn't get the position.

The mayor of Smoky Point, Carl Walker, who also served as town manager, a squirrelly little man who reminded Claire of the pointy haired office manager in the Dilbert cartoon didn't like her. She could see it right off, the way he looked at her with disdain that he was going to be a problem.

The other four members of the town council seemed fine with her, but she could tell Walker was going to do his best to poison their votes.

She caught the ferry out of Newport and arrived at Smoky Point thirty minutes early. She wore a pants suit and flats, the flats because at five foot nine and one half inches tall, she could appear overpowering in two-inch heels.

It was just her luck Walker stood five foot four inches tall. She could see he would have an immediate problem with her height. The other members of the council seemed to like her well enough though, so maybe she had a shot after all.

The interview took place in the town hall, a small building where public meetings were held.

Each member of the council had her resume and cover letter.

Walker opened the interview.

"Miss Evergreen, thank you for coming and for being prompt," he said. "I know you came a long way to be here this morning."

The five members of the council sat at a long table. Claire sat in a chair facing them. It was awkward to say the least.

"Now then, as you are aware, the position you are interviewing for is sheriff of Smoky Point. Our previous sheriff, Matthew Holt retired after eight years of loyal and distinguished service. When you spoke with Mrs. Maxwell, you told her you were interested in one year of employment. Is that correct?"

"Yes, that's correct," Claire said. "My suspension with the Rhode Island State Police is for one year. I would like to return to work after that if possible."

"Perhaps you see this position as a fill-in, something to do while you wait to return to the Rhode Island State Police?" Walker said.

"I didn't say that and I certainly don't," Claire said.

Perhaps she had said that a bit too harsh, but she was not about to have this squirrelly little man put words in her mouth.

"But you have no plans to make this position your career," Walker said.

"No," Claire said. "I do not. I specifically stated my intent of one year employment in the position while I wait for my suspension to conclude."

"And if we're to hire you, in one year, we would be right back where we are now, seeking a suitable sheriff for our town," Walker said.

"Not necessarily," Claire said. "If during my one year tenure I was able to elevate one of the three deputies and get him or her ready to assume the role of sheriff, you would have a ready-made replacement for when my time is up."

Claire could see the other members of the council, especially Mitzi Maxwell, the lone woman on the council, appreciated her remark.

Walker wasn't sold.

"In which case we would be short one deputy, and right before the season," he said.

4

"I would think it easier to find a qualified deputy than a sheriff, especially if I were to begin accepting applications for one month before my departure," Claire said.

Walker glared at her.

Well, fuck him, Claire thought.

"Miss Evergreen, it is Miss, isn't it?" Walker said.

"Yes," Claire said.

"Would you explain to us how your suspension came about?" Walker asked.

"I explained all that in my letter," Claire said.

"I know, but I was wondering why a state trooper assigned to homicide was making a traffic stop," Walker said.

"Because I'm in homicide doesn't mean I should ignore all other facets of the law," Claire said.

"Yes, but please elaborate for us on what happened," Walker said.

Claire stared at Walker for a moment, analyzing his 'gotcha moment' and then decided screw it and said, "I just worked a double shift on a particularly gruesome murder investigation. A woman in Cranston put her baby in a pillowcase and smashed him against the side of a building, so I was not in a good mood to begin with. It was after midnight and I was driving home on 95 when a drunk driver cuts me off and waltzes across four lanes. I hit the wailer and…"

"Wailer?" Walker said.

"The siren and lights," Claire said. "And I pull him over. He blows a 2.4 and is staggering drunk. He resisted arrest and grabbed my right tit and insisted I perform oral sex on him. When I went to put the cuffs on him he tried to bite me on the neck so I tazed him and threw him in the back of my car."

"That seems a bit excessive to me," Walker said.

Enough with this twerp, Claire thought. "I take it that you've never had a drunk grab your tit, call you a bitch and ask you for a blowjob then."

Mitzi Maxwell all but burst out laughing and the other three men on the council had to hide their smiles.

"Miss Evergreen, your language," Walker said.

"If I offended I apologize," Claire said.

"Could you...?" Walker said.

"Miss Evergreen, are you prepared to start work immediately?" Mitzi asked.

"I am," Claire said. "I have a tenant ready to sublet my apartment for one year standing by. I could be ready by next Monday."

"Your qualifications speak volumes," Mitzi said. "I for one have little doubt you would make an excellent sheriff of Smoky Point."

Walker seemed highly annoyed and glared at Mitzi.

"Miss Evergreen, were you aware at the time that the man you tazed was a Congressman home from Washington on a two-week break?" Walker asked.

"I was not," Claire said.

"Should you have been?"

"New York State has twenty-seven Congressmen and two Senators; would you recognize every one of them on a dark highway especially if they were drunk?" Claire asked.

"Probably not," Walker said. "In your opinion was your suspension due to excessive force or because the Congressman pulled some strings to have you punished?"

"My captain said it was because I showed poor judgment in how I handled the situation," Claire said.

"In what way?" Walker said.

"My captain said I should have given him a blowjob," Claire said.

Mitzi and the other three men burst out laughing.

"I think we're done here," Walker said.

"May I say something?" Claire asked.

"Go ahead," Walker said.

"I suppose I could ride out my suspension, collect unemployment, maybe even take a few college courses," Claire said. "But I feel the genuine need to protect and serve. That is my calling if you will. I am very good at my job or I wouldn't have made homicide before the age of thirty-five. Had I known the Congressman was a Congressman, it wouldn't have made any difference. The man was drunk on a public highway and could have killed himself or worse, somebody else. Ask yourself if you would tolerate that in Smoky Point."

"Thank you, Miss Evergreen," Walker said. "That will be all for now."

So when she finally arrived back in her apartment just before midnight, the last thing Claire expected to hear on her voice mailbox on her home phone was Mitzi Maxwell offering her the position of Sheriff of Smoky Point.

Chapter Two

"WHAT'S A SMOKY POINT?" CAPTAIN Dugan asked when Claire told him the news.

"It's a small vacation town on the tip of Long Island in New York," Claire said.

"Sounds exciting," Dugan said.

"I didn't ask to be suspended on a bullshit charge trumped up by some drunken Congressman," Claire said.

"Do you know how much punch a twelve-term Congressman who sits on five Congressional committees has?" Dugan said.

"Enough to blow three times the legal limit on I-95 and get away with it," Claire said.

"He didn't… he hasn't gotten away with anything," Dugan said.

"Has he been suspended from Congress for one year?" Claire asked.

Dugan looked at her.

"Call me if you need help?" he said.

"In Smoky Point, help with what?" Claire asked.

*   *   *   *   *

Claire packed all of her clothes into several large boxes that fit into the back seat and trunk of her car. She left all furniture and appliances as is for her sublet tenant, a businessman on a one-year job transfer.

Her seven-year-old Angora cat Snowball didn't like being placed into a carrier but having two legs instead of four made Claire the boss.

Snowball meowed her annoyance the first hundred miles of the drive. At a pit stop in Hartford, Claire decided enough was enough and let the cat out and Snowball slept peacefully on the floor in back the rest of the way.

She reached the George Washington Bridge around five in the afternoon and skirted her way onto the Grand Central Parkway and onto Long Island where she found out just how long of an island it really was.

One hundred and eighteen miles long to be exact and much of it at bumper-to-bumper. The last ten miles on a state road before a sign greeted her with *Welcome to Smoky Point*.

It was eight o'clock in the evening when Claire parked in front of a small office on Main Street. 'Mitzi Maxwell, Real Estate Agent' the letterhead on the door read. Besides being the only real estate agent in town, Mitzi was also the Town Clerk at the town office where Carl Walker's office was located.

Mitzi was a firecracker of a woman, around fifty with burning red hair and a plump, appealing figure.

"A long drive," Mitzi said when Claire entered the tiny office.

"Very," Claire said.

"Sit for a minute and we'll talk," Mitzi said.

Claire took the chair opposite Mitzi's desk.

"The vote was four to one to hire you," Mitzi said. "Walker being the lone no."

"I figured," Claire said.

"Don't let it bother you. Carl hasn't been laid in years since his wife ran off with an interstate trucker," Mitzi said. "It made him distrustful of women."

"Sure," Claire said.

"Do you want me to fill you in on your staff or wait and see for yourself?"

"Wait and see."

"Okay, let's go," Mitzi said. "Follow me to the house I told you about on the phone."

*   *   *   *   *

Claire followed Mitzi's Town Car for about a mile where the house for rent overlooked the ocean.

"It's small," Mitzi said as she unlocked the front door. "Two bedrooms, kitchen, living room, one and a half baths and two-car garage."

"My apartment back in Providence is small," Claire said. "To that this is a castle. What is the rent?"

"How much is the rent on your apartment?"

"Nine hundred a month."

"And you sublet it for what?"

"Twelve hundred."

"The rent is three hundred a month," Mitzi said.

"How is that possible?" Claire asked.

"I own this house," Mitzi said. "The rent is what I say it is."

"Okay then, deal."

"Good. You'll find coffee and fresh milk in the kitchen. I'll make some while you bring your stuff in and we can chat for a bit."

*   *   *   *   *

"You see dear, it may not look like much right now, but come Memorial Day when the boardwalk and amusement park opens and the charter fishing and beaches kicks in, Smoky Point will explode and it will stay busy right up to Labor Day and beyond to Columbus Day. After that we get a lull until leaf peeping starts and we hop again for another two weeks. Come November we return to our cocoons until spring. In four weeks, twenty-one B&Bs will open as well as four motels by the ocean and one resort. Shops, stores and places to eat will triple. We have eleven bars that stay open year-round on what we call Alcoholics Alley, but that number will double. In short, you will earn the thirty-eight-thousand a year we're paying you."

Claire sipped her coffee.

Snowball jumped onto Mitzi's lap and Mitzi said, "And who is this gorgeous creature?"

"Snowball," Claire said.

Mitzi stroked Snowball and said, "Divorced, huh?"

"Twice."

"Ouch. I'm a three-timer myself. First thing a divorced woman does is get a cat and buy a copy of *Bridget Jones's Diary*."

Claire grinned and sipped more coffee. It was fair to say that she liked Mitzi Maxwell from the start.

"What about uniforms?" Claire asked.

"Your predecessor wore plain clothing," Mitzi said. "As sheriff, you have that option."

"I'll order a few sets and keep them in the rotation," Claire said.

"Well, it's late and I have a dozen rental properties to show to tourists jump-starting the season," Mitzi said. She stood and Snowball jumped off her lap. "Good luck and call if you need anything."

"I do need one thing," Claire said. "Where is the Sheriff's Department located?"

* * * * *

11

After choosing the smaller of the two bedrooms because it had the full bathroom and more comfortable bed, Claire unpacked her clothing and made the bed with fresh linen she found in the linen closet.

There was an alarm clock on the bedside table and she set it for six even though she knew she wouldn't need it.

Then she filled a glass with water and set it by the clock.

Claire hated the idea of pajamas and wore usually just panties and a tank top to sleep in, even on the coldest winter nights. Tonight was no exception even though the temperature had dropped considerably since sundown.

She cracked the window for the fresh air and also for the sound of the ocean.

Then she removed her Glock .40 pistol from its holster and set it under the second pillow as was her custom.

From where Snowball came Claire couldn't say, but the moment she turned off the light and got into bed, there she was by her side.

Claire rubbed her ears for a few seconds and Snowball purred loudly.

"Like our new home?" Claire asked.

Snowball curled into a ball and closed her eyes against Claire's stomach.

"Me, too," Claire said.

Chapter Three

CLAIRE WORE DARK BLUE JEANS, a gray T-shirt and a corduroy sports jacket to conceal her utility belt when she left in the morning and drove around town for a daylight look-see at the what's-what.

She found a donut shop on the main drag and stopped for a large container of coffee. She took it to the beach and parked in the lot to watch the sun rise slowly over the ocean.

It was a chilly morning around forty-five degrees. Fog rolled in off the ocean creating a hauntingly beautiful picture.

When she finished the coffee, Claire returned to her car and after a few wrong turns, found the Sheriff's Department on Elm Street next door to the library.

Two white cruisers and a Volkswagen sedan were parked out front.

Claire parked next to the Volkswagen and sat for a few minutes.

Hardly anyone was on the streets, but it was just past seven in the morning so what did she expect? Even Providence was no hot spot of activity so early in the morning.

She watched a man walking his dog and a woman walking her dog and a newspaper delivery truck go by and then another woman and dog.

A few kids walking to school passed by and then a school bus stopped to pick them up.

At seven-thirty Claire left her car with her briefcase and entered the office.

There were three desks in the main room of the department. A separate office with a glass window and door was directly behind the last desk.

At the closest desk sat a deputy in his mid to late forties.

"You must be James Turley," Claire said to him.

At the second desk sat a deputy in his twenties.

"And you're Roger Knox, but I was told you like to be called Shortstop," Claire said.

Claire looked at the woman at the third desk. She was in her mid-forties.

"And you have to be Rose Bailey," Claire said.

"And you are?" Turley asked.

"Your new boss," Claire said.

Knox appeared stunned.

Rose smiled.

Turley looked at Claire as if he'd just seen a ghost.

"I assume that's my office so one at a time, let's go get acquainted," Claire said. "Who wants to go first?"

* * * * *

Rose had made a pot of coffee and Claire found a clean mug on her desk with the inscription Smoky Point Sheriff's Department inscribed in gold lettering on it. She sipped from the mug as she read Turley's file.

Turley sat in a chair and quietly watched her read.

Finally Claire closed the file and looked at him.

"I was wondering why a forty-seven-year-old man was content to be a deputy in a small town, but I understand after reading your file," she said. "Tell me about the shooting. How did it go down?"

"It was a routine traffic stop on the LIE," Turley said. "Night shift, one in the morning, the driver of an SUV is doing eighty-five in a construction site posted for fifty. I approached the vehicle and the man behind the wheel shot me in the right knee with a .22 caliber pistol and then drove away."

"Sixteen years with the state police, rank of sergeant, six commendations and it's over in the blink of an eye," Claire said.

"I was in rehab for a year," Turley said. "The knee was shattered and replaced, but I walk with such a limp I was forced to take a disability pension."

"I didn't see much of a limp when you walked in here," Claire said.

"I wear a brace under my pants," Turley said.

Claire nodded. "How did you wind up here?"

"I sat around for a year doing nothing," Turley said. "I decided to get back into the game, work if I could and contribute to my pension for as long as possible. I really loved being a trooper. I don't love being a deputy, but at least my hat is still in the ring."

"Can you pull your weight?" Claire asked.

"I've lasted five years," Turley said.

"Okay," Claire said.

*   *   *   *   *

"Why are you called Shortstop?" Claire asked.

"I played shortstop in high school and college," Knox said. "Tore my rotator cuff in my third year and that was that. Nobody wants a shortstop that throws like a little girl."

Claire looked at Knox.

"Oh, no offense," Knox said.

"None taken," Claire said. "I don't throw like a little girl."

Knox grinned.

"Three years with Smoky Point, you're only twenty-eight, why are you still here?" Claire said.

15

"I'm waiting to be called by the state police," Knox said. "Probably next year, and in the meantime, I keep a foot in the door as a deputy."

"What if you don't get called?" Claire asked.

"Why wouldn't I get called?" Knox said with a grin.

He was boyishly handsome with blue eyes and sandy hair, tall and fit and probably scored well with the women, Claire assessed.

"How did you score on the tests?" Claire asked.

"Good," Knox said. "Not great but good. I figure another year in the Point."

* * * * *

"Twelve years as an EMT, what made you switch over?" Claire asked Rose.

"My husband left me for a younger, prettier woman," Rose said. "I needed a job with a more regular schedule. I took the 120 hours at the academy and Sheriff Holt was kind enough to give me a chance."

"Seven years in?"

Rose nodded.

"You're only forty-five, Rose," Claire said. "You have a long way to go. Are you happy being a deputy in a small town or is there more below the surface?"

"My oldest is in college. My middle daughter is a senior and the youngest is a freshman," Rose said. "I got the house and child support. The child support ends when my youngest graduates college. Ask me that question again in seven years."

Claire picked up her briefcase and removed a folder and set it on the desk.

"That's my file," she said. "I'd like the three of you to read it carefully and then ask me anything you'd like."

* * * * *

Claire gave them fifteen minutes and then returned to the squad room, filled her mug with coffee and looked at her three deputies.

"Well?" she asked.

"Well what?" Knox said.

"Questions," Claire said. "For me."

"Did you really taze a Congressman?" Knox asked.

"I did."

"I remember seeing that on the news," Turley said. "As I recall he would have dropped charges if you apologized."

"Why would I apologize for enforcing the law if that's what I'm paid to do?" Claire said.

"You only plan to do one year?" Turley said.

"Unless the Rhode Island State Police for some reason fires me after my suspension is up," Claire said. "In which case I'll probably stay a while longer."

"Five shootings in fourteen years is a bit high, isn't it?" Turley said. "I never drew my gun once in the line of duty."

"Somebody shoots at me, I shoot back," Claire said.

"What about policy and schedules?" Knox asked.

"How do you work it now?" Claire asked.

"Two of us works days, one of us works nights and Rose works dispatch unless needed in the field," Knox said.

"Who is on tonight?" Claire asked.

"Me," Knox said.

"I suggest you go home right after this meeting and get some sleep then," Claire said.

"Who has the VW?" Claire asked.

"I do," Rose said.

"Have a radio and wailer?"

"It does."

"One thing we need to be clear about," Claire said. "You're all going to want to make helpful suggestions on how we do things. Give me advice on what works and what doesn't. Please don't. Turley, you have dispatch. Rose, you come with me."

* * * * *

"What goes on around here, Rose? What am I up against come Memorial Day?" Claire asked.

"A lot of drunk and disorderly on the beach, a lot of bar fights especially when the motorcycle enthusiasts show up and more than our fair share of drugs," Rose said. "Sometimes Sheriff Holt would ask for help from the County Sheriff or State Police and sometimes he would even get it."

"Take me to Alcoholics Alley," Claire said.

About a mile from the office, Rose turned down a side street, made an immediate left and parked at the corner.

Claire counted twenty-three bars that lined both sides of the street.

"Next?" Rose asked.

"Boardwalk and amusement park and stop at the donut shop, I want to grab some coffee," Claire said.

* * * * *

They sat on a bench a hundred feet from the ocean. A stone wall a mile long was at their backs. Every thirty feet there was a break in the wall allowing access to the sand. A quarter mile on their left the amusement park was quiet and isolated. A stiff breeze off the water made the fifty-five degree temperature feel like forty.

They sipped coffee from donut shop containers.

"Aren't you cold?" Rose asked as she turned up the collar of her uniform jacket.

"I don't think about it," Claire said.

Rose sipped some coffee. "It's freezing. It's not supposed to be this cold this close to May."

"How often do you go in the field, Rose?" Claire asked.

"Not as often as I'd like to," Rose said. "Maybe a dozen times over the course of the summer."

"Unless it's all hands on deck, count on none," Claire said.

"I don't understand. I'm competent enough to…"

"Our budget doesn't allow for a detective," Claire said. "So from now on you are my investigator. If, in the course of an investigation you need to go out, go. But no more sitting on your ass waiting for the phone to ring. Agreed?"

"Agreed."

Claire sipped some coffee.

Rose sipped some coffee.

"What are you going to tell Turley and Shortstop?" Rose asked.

"Turley is a field man," Claire said. "I doubt he would have ever made detective. Knox is one step away from being a security guard at a bank. I'll tell them you're my investigator and that's that."

"How did you make detective in homicide at so young an age?" Rose asked.

"By working harder than anybody else," Claire said. "Why do you think I'm divorced twice by the age of forty?"

"Anyplace else you want to see?" Rose said. "Because I'm freezing my ass off."

"Let's drive around," Claire said. "I want to feel the town."

* * * * *

19

"Tell me about Holt," Claire said as Rose drove around town.

"Matt was... I mean is a good man," Rose said. "I don't know if you read his file, but he quit the New York City Police Department after twenty-two years when his wife died. He sat around for two years raising his two sons and then came aboard eight years ago as sheriff after they were grown."

"Why did he quit?"

"He said thirty years was enough," Rose said. "He said he wanted to enjoy his pension while he was still young enough to spend it."

"Let's grab some lunch and then head back," Claire said.

*   *   *   *   *

Turley was on the phone when Claire and Rose returned to the office.

"Yes, I realize I'm not Rose, Mr. Cassedy," Turley said into the phone. "But is there something I can help you with?"

Rose went to her desk.

Claire stood beside Turley's desk.

"No, sir, I don't think it's possible that Rose could call you back to say hello, but I'll tell her," Turley said and hung up.

"And that was about?" Claire said.

"Mr. Cassedy is eighty-seven years old and is in love with Rose," Turley said. "He calls every day to hear her voice."

"Cute," Claire said. "Rose, bring me everything."

Claire went into her office and sat at her desk.

Rose appeared in the doorway.

"What do you mean by everything?" Rose asked.

"Start with all arrest reports from last year," Claire said.

*   *   *   *   *

Claire read arrest reports cover-to-cover until, at five o'clock, Turley knocked on her door.

"It's five o'clock," he said. "I've been here ten hours. Unless you need me I'm clocking out."

Claire nodded.

"Rose?"

"She stays until six when Short comes on."

"Goodnight then," Claire said.

After Turley left, Claire stood and went to the squad room where Rose was at her desk writing a report.

"Do you usually stay until six?" Claire asked.

Rose nodded. "Until the night watch shows up. That way he can work until at least two."

"And from two until eight?"

"Whoever worked the day shift takes the call at home."

Claire sat on the edge of Rose's desk.

"Last summer there was an average of two arrests a day for drunk and disorderly on the beach, one bar fight a night and at least two arrests a week for drug possession," Claire said. "Not pot but cocaine and heroin. The bar fights usually are between motorcycle gangs. Are they responsible for the drugs?"

"Holt believed so but was never able to make a case against them," Rose said.

"I want you to start an investigation tomorrow," Claire said. "I'd like you to go back five years and check for priors on all motorcycle gang members arrested for drugs. Possession and intent to sell. Somebody is bringing drugs to the beach and it's up to us to stop it. Build me a case, Rose."

Rose looked at Claire.

"My fingerprints are in my file," Claire said. "Tomorrow get me a license to carry permit. The sheriff should be able to legally conceal, don't you think?"

Rose nodded.

"Go home," Claire said. "I'll stick around and wait for Short."

* * * * *

Claire was still reading the arrest log when Knox arrived at five to 6:00. He had a paper bag and a Thermos of coffee and set them on his desk.

Her door was open and he poked his nose in and said, "Where's Rose?"

"I sent her home early," Claire said. "Short, sit for a minute."

There was a small sofa against the wall, and Knox sat there rather than the hard chairs opposite the desk.

"Hey, do you know why they named it Smoky Point?" Knox asked.

"Because when the fog rolls in off the ocean at sunrise, it resembles smoke," Claire said. "Just a guess."

Knox looked at her.

"A lot of drug related arrests last summer," Claire said.

"It's to be expected with so many college kids and teenagers around the beach and park," Knox said.

"What did Sheriff Holt try to do about it?" Claire asked.

"Name it and he tried it," Knox said. "Parked cruisers at the beach and amusement park, traffic stops, investigations into motorcycle gangs, had us walking the beach in uniform, even borrowed a couple of female deputies from county to work undercover. Like I said, we tried everything. Nothing worked."

"Do you know where Holt is? I'd like to give him a call."

"He lives near Wading River on the beach," Knox said. "His address and number are in the files."

"I'll find it," Claire said. "I'm going to read a while so go about your business."

22

Knox stood up and turned to the door, hesitated and looked back. "What should I call you? I mean Sheriff Holt preferred to be called Matt."

"Claire. Call me Claire."

Knox nodded. "Okay, Claire. I'll be at my desk."

Claire read for another hour before calling it a night.

Knox was on the phone when she entered the squad room.

"Mrs. Parker, your son is twenty-seven years old, I don't think we can actually say he ran away from home," Knox said. "If he doesn't show up in twenty-four hours you can file a missing person's report. Yes, I'll keep an eye out for him. Goodnight."

Knox hung up and looked at Claire.

"She calls once a month when her son goes off on a bender," he said.

"Is there a market I can pick up some things at?" Claire asked.

"Two blocks east and one block to the north is Food City," Knox said. "It's open until midnight."

"Thanks."

Claire went to her office for her jacket and as she returned to the squad room, Mitzi Maxwell was coming through the door.

"I was driving by and thought I recognized your car," Mitzi said.

"I was just heading out," Claire said. "To the food market, actually."

"Well, as long as I'm here why not have dinner?" Mitzi said. "You can hit the market on the way home."

Claire slipped on her jacket. "Let's go," she said.

Chapter Four

MITZI HELD UP HER GLASS of white wine and said, "Cheers."

Claire lightly touched Mitzi's glass with her own and each woman took a small sip of wine.

"The council agreed to give you a few days burn-in time before calling a meeting," Mitzi said.

"Make it sooner than later," Claire said. "I'd like to discuss budgets and a few other things."

"I'll talk to Carl tomorrow," Mitzi said.

"Thank you."

"So what do you think of your staff?" Mitzi asked. "Be honest."

"I don't know them yet, know their capabilities," Claire said. "Ask me that again in two weeks and I'll be able to provide an honest answer."

"Fair enough," Mitzi said.

A waiter approached the table. "Have you decided yet?" he asked.

"Walter, bring me the house salad," Mitzi said. "You know how I like it."

"And the lady?"

"Walter, this is Claire Evergreen, our new sheriff," Mitzi said.

"A pleasure," Walter said.

"I think I'll go with the same," Claire said.

"Very good," Walter said and left the table.

"So Claire, what is the origin of your name?" Mitzi asked.

"Evergreen is such an unusual name. I don't think I've ever heard it before."

"As the family story goes, my great-grandfather came over from Scandinavia in 1911 and when he went through Ellis Island no one could pronounce his name," Claire said. "To the clerk checking him in it sounded like the word evergreen so that's what he wrote on my great-grandfather's papers."

"What a wonderful story," Mitzi said. "Any idea what it really is?"

"Something I can't pronounce," Claire said.

"And the house is?"

"Perfectly fine," Claire said. "I slept like a baby listening to the ocean."

Mitzi smiled. "Good."

Walter returned with the salads.

"Save room for dessert," Mitzi said. "They have a wonderful cheesecake here."

"Can you tell me something?" Claire said. "Off the record if you'd like."

"If I can."

"What was Sheriff Holt like?"

"In what way?"

"As a sheriff and as a person."

"I'm afraid Carl is the one to ask about his duties as sheriff," Mitzi said. "The sheriff reports directly to the town manager. I thought he was highly competent if not a little bored there at the end. He's a big fisherman and if you ask me would rather be on his boat fishing than anyplace else."

"My dad is like that," Claire said. "After my mom passed, he moved down to the Keys and bought a little charter boat and takes guests out fishing almost every day."

"Sounds like your dad and Matthew would get along just fine,"

Mitzi said. "And the first dinner is always on me."

* * * * *

Claire walked through her front door carrying two large shopping bags. Snowball was already in place and waiting to greet her.

Claire put down the bags and picked up the cat. She gave Snowball several kisses and scratched behind her ears and then set her down.

"To the kitchen," Claire said.

At the counter, Claire unpacked the groceries. Cat litter, cat food, milk, coffee, eggs, butter, bacon and bread.

After filling Snowball's food bowl and changing out her water, Claire went to the bedroom and took a twenty minute, blazing hot shower, something she did even on hot summer days.

Afterward she put on shorts and tank-top and a lightweight robe.

Snowball was already on the bed waiting.

Claire propped up the pillows and allowed Snowball to take up residence on her stomach.

Stroking Snowball's ears, Claire said, "I'm not so sure about this place."

Snowball purred and began kneading Claire's stomach.

"Why?" Claire said. "Because one deputy walks like a duck, another is one step above brainless and the third is a middle-aged woman who probably never fired the gun she doesn't wear."

Snowball rubbed her face against Claire's hand.

"Oh, that's right. We're women too, aren't we?" Claire said.

Snowball turned over and Claire rubbed her back.

"Well, I am anyway," Claire said. "You've been spayed, although for all the action I've been getting lately I might as well be, too."

Claire gently moved Snowball off her stomach and stood up. "Be right back," she said.

She went to the kitchen for a glass of water and set it on the nightstand. Then she placed her Glock .40 under the spare pillow and turned off the lamp.

Claire and Snowball were asleep within minutes.

*   *   *   *   *

Before the alarm went off at 6:00 a.m., Claire was out of bed and in the kitchen making coffee.

While the coffee brewed, she returned to the bedroom, dropped to the floor and did thirty-five push-ups. She rested for two minutes and then did another thirty-five. Immediately, Claire turned and did thirty-five sit-ups, followed by thirty-five stomach crunches and then held a plank for a count of one twenty. Then she did another thirty-five sit-ups and thirty-five crunches.

Snowball, as she usually did whenever Claire went through this routine, watched quietly from the bed.

When she finally stood up, Claire went to a cardboard box against the wall and removed the pull-up bar that attached to a door frame and hung it on the bathroom door.

Then she went to the kitchen and poured a cup of coffee and took it to the backyard where a small table and chairs faced the ocean. It was a chilly morning and she had to wear a robe, but the fresh, cold air along with the caffeine was the jump-start she needed to go on to stage two.

Coffee finished, Claire slipped into a jogging suit with well-worn running shoes and walked down to the sand. The waves crashed as fog rolled in. She checked her watch and started a twenty-minute run at waters edge.

After twenty minutes, she turned around and ran home.

The procedure ended at the bathroom where she stripped down

and did three sets of ten reps of pull-ups on the bar. After the final rep she jumped into the shower.

Claire performed this workout three times a week without fail.

She felt she owed it to the tax payers that paid her salary to be able to, if necessary, outrun the bad guy.

After dressing in jeans, dark blue denim shirt and steel-toe boots, Claire fixed some toast with scrambled eggs and ate at the kitchen table.

She left fresh food and water for Snowball, slipped on her holster and left for work.

Chapter Five

ROSE AND TURLEY WERE ALREADY in the office when Claire arrived.

Rose had a stack of reports on her desk and was making notes on a pad.

Turley was reading a copy of *Newsday*.

"Morning Claire," Turley said.

"Morning," Claire said.

"Short brought in a drunk last night," Turley said. "He's in the cage."

"Show me," Claire said.

Turley stood and Claire followed him to the door next to the bathroom. He opened the door and down a short hallway was the 'cage.' Large enough to hold a dozen, the cage was basically one large jail cell with six bunk bed type cots.

A middle-aged man was sleeping in one of the lower cots.

"Deputy Turley, can you run on that leg?" Claire asked.

"Can I... how do you mean?" Turley asked.

"I mean if you had to chase a suspect, can you do it? Can you run?"

"Well I don't... I mean I've never tried," Turley said.

"So if you and Short were on foot and chasing a suspect you believed to be armed you wouldn't be able to pursue the suspect and Short would be on his own," Claire said. "Facing a possibly armed and dangerous suspect."

Turley looked at Claire.

"I didn't ask to get shot," he said.

"I didn't ask you if you asked to get shot," Claire said. "I asked you if you could run."

Turley sighed. "No, probably not."

"How many more years did you figure on working?"

"Three. At least three."

"I'll get you the three, but on my terms," Claire said. "Agreed?"

Turley nodded.

"Now what do we have for weapons around here?" Claire asked.

Opposite the cage was a locked closet. Turley used a key to unlock the door.

"Four pistol grip shotguns and two vests," Claire said. "Anything in the cruisers?"

"No."

"From now on one shotgun for each cruiser," Claire said. "Fully loaded and extra ammunition in the glove box."

Turley removed one shotgun and a box of ammunition from the closet and locked the door.

Rose still had her nose dug in reports when they returned to the squad room. She looked up and watched Turley leave the building with the shotgun.

"Rose, do you own a gun?" Claire asked.

"I do."

"Where is it?"

"Home."

"What is it?"

"Smith and Wesson .40."

"Last time you fired it?"

"Who said I fired it?"

"From now on you wear it at all times while on duty."

Turley returned and Claire looked at him.

"What range do you practice at?" she asked.

"Suffolk Rod and Gun Club," Turley said.

"What time will Short be here?" Claire asked.

"Usually around two after a night shift," Rose said.

"Do we have petty cash?" Claire asked.

"About one hundred dollars," Rose said.

"At noon, I want the both of you to head over to the range and fire a minimum of one hundred rounds," Claire said. "More if you have to, but you don't come back until Rose can put seven out of ten in the black. Take what you need for practice ammo from petty cash."

"What about calls?" Turley asked.

"I think I can handle a few hours alone," Claire said.

*   *   *   *   *

At her desk, Claire studied budget reports for several hours. Forty thousand dollars was allocated for summer manpower.

She called Rose to the office.

"Last summer there were five part time deputies," Claire said. "Call over to the police academy and see if you can line up four top-class graduating deputies who wouldn't mind making ten grand for three month's work."

"Just four?"

"I'd rather pay a bit extra per man and get a better quality deputy."

"I'll make the calls," Rose said and returned to her desk.

After closing the files, Claire dug out the phone number left for Matthew Holt. She dialed the number and he answered after three rings.

"Matt Holt," he said.

"Mr. Holt, this is your replacement calling, Claire Evergreen."

After a short pause, Holt said, "It's snowing in hell then."

"I... excuse me?" Claire said.

"Carl Walker approved a woman as sheriff," Holt said.

"Yes, yes he did, but it was a four to one vote," Claire said.

"Should I guess who the 'no' was?" Holt said.

"No need," Claire said. "So why I'm calling is I'd like to know if you have some free time tomorrow. I'd like your input on a few things if you wouldn't mind."

"Do you fish?"

"No, no I don't."

"Do you eat?"

"Yes, yes I do."

"Make it around one. Know where I live?"

"I have the address. I'll find it."

"One o'clock then."

"I'll be there."

Claire hung up just as Rose knocked on the open door and entered. "It's noon. Jim and I are headed over to the range now. I took fifty from petty cash for practice ammo. Also, I put in a call to the academy."

"Get receipts," Claire said. "Oh, who delivers?"

* * * * *

Claire was eating noodles with chicken dumplings from The China Rose restaurant a few blocks from the office when Knox reported for his shift.

Claire met him at his desk.

"I cut your drunk lose with a desk appearance ticket for court," she said.

"Where are Rose and Jim?" Knox asked.

"I sent them to the range so Rose can practice," Claire said.

"Rose?"

"She's a deputy, isn't she?"

The phone rang and Knox answered it.

Rose returned to her desk and a few seconds later, Knox stuck his head in the door.

"Bar fight at the Palace," he said.

"It's three in the afternoon," Claire said.

"It's Dwayne and his wife," Knox said. "He's a..."

"Tell me about it on the way," Claire said.

"You're going with me?" Knox said.

*　*　*　*　*

The Palace was anything but. One of the eleven bars open year round, it was a dark and gloomy dive of a place.

Dwayne Haywood was beating the crap out of the bartender when Claire and Knox arrived.

A woman sat at a table with a bloody lip and a quickly closing black eye.

Otherwise the place was empty.

Knox grabbed Dwayne from behind and yanked him off the bartender and the bartender fell to the floor.

"Get the fuck offa me!" Dwayne yelled.

"Dammit, Dwayne, this is the third time this month you..." Knox said.

Dwayne, a former semi-pro football player and a good 250 pounds shoved Knox backward.

Knox grabbed Dwayne and they started wrestling against the bar.

Claire looked at the woman. "Who are you?"

"I'm that idiot's wife."

"He do that to you?"

The woman nodded.

"He thinks I'm having an affair with the bartender."

"Are you?"

"It's his first day."

Claire looked at the fallen bartender. He was a bloody mess. "Probably his last, too," she said.

Dwayne had Knox in a headlock and was screaming, "Nobody fucks my wife but me. Nobody."

"Every town has one," Claire said.

She tapped Dwayne on the shoulder and he released Knox and turned around. The second Dwayne was facing her; Claire kicked him in the balls with her right steel-toe boot.

Dwayne gasped, grabbed his sack and slumped over to the floor.

Knox and Dwayne's wife stared at Claire.

"Cuff this asshole and toss him in the cruiser," Claire said.

*   *   *   *   *

"You're going to need medical attention," Claire said to Dwayne's wife.

"I'm alright. He's done it before. He'll do it again."

Her name was Sally and she was the waitress at the Palace. She was seated on the sofa in Claire's office.

"Not this time," Claire said. "And not anymore."

"You don't understand how mean Dwayne can get," Sally said.

"How long have you been married to this idiot?" Claire asked.

"Since we graduated high school ten years ago," Sally said. "Dwayne was going to be a big football star. Had a tryout with the Jets over at Hofstra. He blew out his right knee and that was that."

"Well, Dwayne is going to jail," Claire said.

"What for?" Sally asked.

"Domestic violence, assault and battery for openers," Claire said.

"Dwayne can't go to no jail. He has a job."

"I hope they hold it for him," Claire said. "He'll be gone for at least one year."

"A year?" Sally said. "Dwayne can't do no year. I won't press charges."

"That's not up to you," Claire said. "That's up to me."

Knox tapped on the door and opened it.

"Claire, county boys are here for Dwayne," he said.

"I'll be right out," Claire said.

She stood and said, "Sally, you wait right there."

Claire went to the squad room where two county deputies were talking to Knox.

"Transport to county," one of the deputies said.

"In the cage," Claire said.

"I'll get him," Knox said and opened the door to the backroom.

"You're new," one of the county deputies said.

"Claire Evergreen. Sheriff Holt's replacement," Claire said.

Knox returned with Dwayne in cuffs.

"I want a lawyer," Dwayne said. "This fucking bitch kicked me in the balls."

"Twice," Claire said and kicked Dwayne in the balls again.

"Jesus," Knox said.

As the county deputies and Knox carried Dwayne out to their van, Claire returned to her office.

"The bartender is really hurt," Claire said. "I wouldn't count on seeing Dwayne for a year or more. Go home and tend to those bruises."

"What about... what do you call it... bail?" Sally said.

"Tomorrow, if you'd like, drive to the county sheriff's department and when he's arraigned ask his lawyer if he can post bail," Claire said. "I wouldn't count on it though."

"Did you have to kick him again?" Sally asked.

"No," Claire said. "It just felt like the right thing to do."

*   *   *   *   *

Claire was engrossed in writing her report and didn't notice Rose and Turley until she heard their voices and looked up from her desk.

She grabbed her empty mug and went to the squad room and filled it at the coffee maker. "How did it go at the range?" she said.

"Sixty-four out of one hundred in the black," Turley said.

"Good enough, but keep practicing," Claire said to Rose. "And from now on you wear your piece on duty."

"Short tells us you took down that idiot Dwayne at the Palace," Turley said.

"Twice," Rose said.

"His wife will stick by him though," Claire said. "She doesn't know any better."

Claire sat on the edge of Rose's desk.

"Last summer the majority of the arrests for drunk and disorderly and drugs came between four in the afternoon and ten at night," she said. "Something like eighty percent."

"That's when the beaches, amusement park and bars are at the busiest," Turley said. "The amusement park closes at midnight and most of the beach crowd leaves at dark. The bars give us most of the trouble."

"They usually do," Claire said. "Alcohol and stupidity don't mix."

The phone rang and Knox answered the call.

"Rose," Claire said as she returned to her office.

Rose followed Claire and Claire closed the door.

"I noticed that quite a few arrests at the bars came from out of town bikers," Claire said as she sat behind her desk.

Rose took the sofa. "Drunken bar fights and bikers are synonymous," she said.

"That's true everywhere," Claire said.

"Even in small towns," Rose said.

"I wonder if you noticed that the out of town bikers always seem to get arrested around the first of the month?" Claire asked.

"I… no, I didn't," Rose said. "I'm still doing research."

"It just strikes me odd that gangs from Rhode Island and Massachusetts always seem to be around the first of the month and then disappear," Claire said. "They must ride the ferry down for a good time, blow off steam and then head back."

"Must," Rose said.

"Why the bother?" Claire asked.

"I don't follow."

"There are dozens of towns in Rhode Island and Mass where these assholes can go to let off steam. Why bother with a long, boring ferry ride to a nowhere town on Long Island?" Claire said. "And why the first of the month all summer?"

"Maybe that's when they get their checks?" Rose said.

Claire grinned.

"Keep up the research," she said.

Rose stood and returned to the squad room.

A minute later, Rose poked her head in the door.

"Mitzi Maxwell on line one," she said.

Claire picked up her phone.

"This is Claire," she said.

"The council wants to meet at ten tomorrow morning. Okay?" Mitzi said.

"I'll be there," Rose said.

"We serve bagels and coffee," Mitzi said.

"Not donuts?"

Mitzi laughed and then hung up.

Claire went out to the squad room. Turley and Knox were on a call. "I'm meeting with the town council tomorrow at ten. After that I'll be meeting with your former boss at one. I probably won't be in the office until four. Take down my cell number and give it to Turley and Short when they return."

"Are you taking off?" Rose asked.

"I am," Claire said. "Who covers tonight?"

"Turley."

"Are you free for dinner?" Claire asked. "I'd like to talk to you away from the office."

"I'm free."

"Make it seven-thirty." Claire said.

Chapter Six

ROSE RANG CLAIRE'S DOORBELL EXACTLY at seven-thirty. She had gone home, taken a shower and changed, picked up a bottle of wine and even wore her weapon under her blazer.

From inside, Claire yelled that the door was open.

Rose opened the door and entered the living room. She was immediately struck with the aroma of something wonderful cooking in the kitchen. She followed her nose.

Claire was in the kitchen stirring something in a large Wok with a wood spoon. A pot with boiling water was on a back burner.

"Smells good," Rose said.

"White or red?" Claire said as she looked over her shoulder.

"White."

"Good. Open it and pour us a glass," Claire said. "Dinner in five minutes."

* * * * *

Claire made a stir-fry of chicken, beef, several different vegetables and brown noodles and all of it was delicious.

"I'm stuffed," Rose said. "And is your cat eating noodles?"

"Yes. She loves noodles," Claire said. "And boiled potatoes for some reason."

"So we talked about the weather, life on Long Island, why you became a cop, my divorce, your two ex-husbands and how much you enjoy cooking but don't do enough of it unless you have company," Rose said. "You're taking the long way around the barn getting to the point."

Claire took a sip of wine, set the glass aside and tapped her lap. Immediately, Snowball hopped on and began to knead.

"Cut that out, it hurts," Claire said. She looked at Rose. "When you work homicide you develop a certain flair for details that doesn't go away when you stop chasing murderers."

Snowball rubbed Claire's stomach and Claire scratched her ears. The cat purred loudly and settled in.

"Details are always at the forefront of every murder investigation," Claire continued. "And every other type of crime you can think of. It always comes down to the details. So... when I see arrest reports on Rhode Island and Massachusetts motorcycle gangs in Smoky Point my details meter goes off. I know those gangs and some of the members. They are hard-core to the bone. Drug runners, killers for hire, gun smugglers and a host of other suspicions. I ask myself what in the world are these bad-ass bikers doing in Smoky Point?"

"I don't... I have no answer," Rose said.

"Me neither," Claire said. "That's the problem."

"I can continue with the stats report and see where that goes," Rose said.

"I want you to and more," Claire said. "I want to know what these assholes are doing here and why the first of the month."

"Why couldn't you tell me this at the office?" Rose asked.

"You're doing this quietly," Claire said. "Not that I don't trust the boys, but I don't trust the boy's egos so to speak."

Rose nodded. "Men and their fragile egos," she said.

"I'll be making some changes and I don't want to damage the egos anymore than I have to. Agreed?"

"What changes?"

"I'm not sure yet," Claire said. "Some will depend on how things go at the council meeting. Others will depend on what kind of deputies you can get me from the academy."

"Maybe I'll take a drive there instead of waiting on a call?" Rose said. "Do some recruiting in person."

"Good. Do it. Tomorrow."

"What shall I tell the egos?"

"Nothing. That's my job," Claire said. "Head over to the academy in the morning and I'll be in the office by nine."

Rose nodded.

"Do you really think something is going on with those bikers?" she asked. "Other than them being biker assholes I mean."

"I doubt they come down for the amusement park," Claire said. "Details and gut instinct, Rose. It always comes down to that."

*   *   *   *   *

Rose drove home somewhat in a fog. She was used to pretty much being ignored by Holt, Short and Turley and now she had more responsibility in two days than all her previous years combined.

The question rolling around in her mind was a coin toss. Was this newfound confidence in her abilities the result of Claire being biased toward women, or actual belief in her as a deputy?

She should have asked Claire point blank.

The thing was she was enjoying the confidence Claire placed in her. If the answer was biased, maybe she didn't really want to know.

*   *   *   *   *

Claire finished the last bit of the wine Rose brought while she soaked in a hot tub full of bubble bath.

Snowball watched her from the closed lid on the toilet seat.

Claire sipped some wine and looked at Snowball.

"I'm sure you have an opinion on all this," Claire said.

Snowball yawned.

"Yes, I agree," Claire said.

Chapter Seven

AFTER HER MORNING WORKOUT, CLAIRE showered and wore dark jeans, a paisley shirt and a lightweight blazer to conceal her Glock pistol.

She left for the office at eight-thirty and arrived at a quarter to 9:00.

Knox was at his desk manning the phones.

"Morning Claire," he said. "Rose isn't here yet and she's usually in at eight-thirty."

"I sent Rose to the academy to recruit some deputies for the summer," Claire said.

"Matt usually did that," Knox said.

"I have a meeting with the town council at ten so I sent Rose," Claire said.

She went into her office and returned with her mug and filled it and then sat on the edge of Knox's desk.

"I need you to step up your game, Short," she said.

"How do you mean?" Knox asked.

"Is Turley due in?"

"Any minute."

"We'll have a meeting when he gets here," Claire said.

She went to her office and closed the door. Before she could take her chair, her cell phone rang and she removed it from her belt and checked the number.

It was Captain Dugan.

She hit talk and said, "This is Claire."

"Hey kiddo, how are you doing?" Dugan said.

"Settling in."

"Got some news."

Claire waited, then said, "And?"

"Jeez, you're no fun. You're supposed to get all excited and ask what it is."

"Well good golly Miss Molly, what's your news, Cap'in?" Claire said.

"I got you an appeal," Dugan said.

"When?"

"Scheduled for the day after Labor Day."

"That's almost four months."

"Best I could do. Take it or leave it."

"Shit."

"You're welcome."

"Oh, fuck off."

"That's no way to speak to a superior officer."

"I'm on suspension, remember. I can speak any way I want."

"Keep in touch, kiddo," Dugan said and hung up.

Claire set the phone aside. "Damn," she said.

Knox tapped on her door and opened it. "Turley's here," he said.

Claire went to the squad room. She sat on the edge of Rose's desk and looked at Turley and Knox.

"Resist the temptation to interrupt or offer advice," Claire said. "This isn't a democracy, it's a sheriff's department and I'm the sheriff. Come Memorial Day, Turley, you are dispatcher full time and will only go out as backup when needed. That means when Rose or I are unavailable. Short, you will assume command of the summer deputies and all calls will be answered in pairs."

"What does Rose do if Jim is dispatcher?" Knox asked.

"Rose will serve in two capacities," Claire said. "She will act as department investigator and also partner up for calls when needed."

Turley glared at Claire.

"You object?" Claire said.

"I have ten times the experience Rose does," Turley said.

"Yes, you do," Claire said.

"It's my leg, isn't it?"

"Like you said, you didn't ask to get shot but shot you did get," Claire said. "I have to think of what's best for the department and best for the town."

"My experience doesn't count, huh?" Turley said bitterly.

"Tell you what," Claire said. "When Rose returns we'll have a foot race. You and her in the forty-yard dash. If you win, I'll reverse the order. Fair?"

"You know I can't outrun her with this leg," Turley said.

Claire nodded. "I told you I'd get you three years. I didn't say how."

She looked at her watch.

"I'll be back after the meeting with the town council," she said.

*   *   *   *   *

Claire sat in a chair facing the town council and sipped coffee from a deli container.

"This is ridiculous," she said.

"What is ridiculous?" Walker said.

"This," Claire said. "This setup. I'm sitting here as if this were the Nuremberg Trials. Can we please change the format to one less formal?"

"We've always had this format," Walker said.

"I happen to agree with the sheriff," Mitzi said. "It is a rather stuffy way to hold a meeting."

Walker looked at Mitzi. "And what do you suggest, the Knights of the Round Table?"

"Never mind, forget it," Claire said. "I'll stand."

She stood and looked at the five-person panel. "Let's make this simple," she said. "I'll tell you what I need based upon the statistics I've looked at and you tell me if it's feasible. Every year the traffic into the amusement park and beach increases and along with that the crime stats go up. I need an additional $10,000 allocated for summer deputies and another $2,500 for new shotguns. The ones we have are a decade old. In addition, I'd like another $2,500 for Kevlar vests for the deputies."

"That's $15,000," Walker said. "Of tax payer money."

"The arrest stats have increased twenty-five percent in the last six years while the budget to control crime has not," Claire said. "If you want a town full of drunks, dopers and bikers that's up to you, but expect a big drop in tourists as a result."

"Sheriff Evergreen, I'm not sure I appreciate your tone," Walker said.

"Oh Carl, she has a very valid point," Mitzi said. "We've all seen the rise in crime over the past several years. We don't want to lose our tourists to a bunch of drunks and dopers; it's our livelihood after all."

Walker sighed.

"We'll put it to a vote," he said.

*   *   *   *   *

Rose was at her desk when Claire returned to the office. Knox was on patrol and Turley was at his desk working on a report.

"The town council agreed to up our summer budget by $20,000," Claire said. "Turley, check around for police-grade shotguns, at least four and two additional Kevlar vests. Rose, how did you make out at the academy?"

"Found three graduates without a home, all with high marks,"

Rose said.

"Find one more," Claire said. "We might as well spend the extra money on something worthwhile. I'll be with Matthew Holt in a meeting if you need me."

* * * * *

Claire used her GPS to find Holt's beach house in Wading River. The rear of the house faced a narrow street. There was an un-worked flowerbed and a two-car garage. When she parked and got out Claire could see the ocean about a hundred yards away.

Matthew Holt opened the front door before Claire had the chance to knock.

"Heard your car," Holt said. "Chicken, fish or steak?"

"Excuse me?" Claire said.

"For lunch," Holt said.

"I dislike fish and would take a steak over chicken anytime."

"Good. Come in."

Claire entered the home. It was small and cozy in a guy way.

"My boat is docked at the beach. We'll have lunch there."

Holt was not what Claire expected. His file said he was fifty-eight, but he looked forty-five. At least six-foot-two, a solid 200 pounds, he had forearms like thick rope. His hair was mostly gray and streaked with the black of his youth. His eyes were a dark brown. Stubble covered his face and his skin was tanned like leather.

There was a large cooler in the kitchen and he picked it up and said, "Come on. If you get cold I have jackets on board."

He slid open the kitchen door and she followed him outside and he slid it closed.

"Are we going for a ride?" Claire asked as they walked down to the water.

47

"If you want," Holt said.

"Not really," Claire said. "I get a bit sea sick on small boats."

"No problem."

Holt's boat wasn't that small actually. Twenty-eight feet long and set up for deep-sea fishing.

"Next summer I plan to charter out," Holt said when they reached his dock. "Hop on."

Claire stepped onto the gangway and then onto the floor of the boat with Holt right behind her.

Besides the seats attached to the railings, there was a round patio table with a large umbrella for shade and four chairs.

"Make yourself at home while I get things started," Holt said.

Claire took a chair at the table while Holt removed the cover from a steel grill and turned on the gas-powered burners.

"If you go below you'll find a sack of baking potatoes," Holt said. "I'll get those started first."

Claire went below and found a large canvas sack of potatoes in the small galley. She dug out four and brought them topside to Holt.

"Put them on and if you'd like we can have a beer and talk," Holt said. "I have a fresh keg below."

Claire set the potatoes on the grill while Holt went below. She took a chair and within a minute or so, Holt returned with two frosty mugs of cold beer. He set them on the table and sat opposite Claire.

"So, why did you quit?" Claire asked.

Holt took a sip of beer and said, "Right to the point."

"No reason to beat around the bush," Claire said.

"No, no there isn't," Holt said. "Thirty years ago my priority list was as follows. My wife and family, the job and way at the bottom deep sea fishing. Now my wife is dead, my kids are on their own and I find deep sea fishing in priority one and police work at the bottom. The people you serve deserve better than the bottom. It's that simple."

I can't say I disagree with that," Claire said.

"Hold on," Holt said. He stood, opened the cooler and brought two steaks to the grill, then returned to the table.

"What I'm concerned about is the high number of arrests for drunk and disorderly and drugs," Claire said. "The town has a population of just 3,700, but the arrests speak of a town ten times as large. What do you make of that seeing as how you were at the helm for eight years?"

"The summer population adds another 2,000 residents," Holt said. "The beach is one of the best on the Island. It attracts thousands from all over the Island and even Brooklyn and Queens every day. So does the amusement park. Couple all that with two dozen bars and it's a cauldron of drunk and high people waiting to get arrested."

"I get the drunks and the bars, but what do you make of the drugs?" Claire asked. "Heroin and cocaine and every type of pill you can think of and nobody knows or sees a thing."

Holt sipped some beer. "I appreciate your attitude," he said. "I was the same way. After years of trying to uncover a local source, and believe me I tried everything, I realized the people bringing in the drugs were the same people using them. They weren't buying in town as I first suspected, but buying elsewhere and bringing the stuff with them. There is not a lot you're going to be able to do about that except arrest and get them off the beach and out of the park."

Claire nodded. "I'm afraid I have to agree with you on that. What do you…?"

"Hold that thought," Holt said.

He went to the grill, flipped the steaks and returned.

"Okay, what was that?" he said.

"I'm from Rhode Island," Claire said. "I recognize some of the motorcycle gangs that have been arrested in previous years, some even by individual names and I have to wonder why they would bother to take a long ferry ride to hang out at some dive bars in a small town at the ass end of Long Island."

"I wondered that very thing," Holt said. "So I asked."

"And?"

"Know what a pilgrimage is?"

"Yes."

"They have affiliate clubs on Long Island, Manhattan, Jersey and even Pennsylvania they visit in a spring get together ritual," Holt said. "On the return trip they hit Delaware, Connecticut and upstate New York. They save a lot of time on the road by taking the ferry directly to the Island to begin their pilgrimage. They do this the beginning of each month starting with June and ending in September or October."

"If that were true it actually makes sense," Claire said.

"I tried everything I could think of to make it not true," Holt said. "Bloody or well done?"

"Bloody."

Holt went to the grill and put steaks and potatoes on plates and carried them to the table. He grabbed steak knives, forks, butter, salt and pepper and napkins from the cooler.

"I contacted other cities and states about the clubs and from what I was able to find out they actually do make this spring to summer pilgrimage every year," Holt said. "Club business, they claim. Other than arrest them and fine them, there doesn't seem to be much to do about it. It's not illegal to belong to a motorcycle club and every one we pulled in has a valid license and place of residence. None we arrested was in possession of weapons except for legal folding pocket knives and multi-tools. Even the bar fights involved each other and no outsiders and they always pay for damages."

"This steak is wonderful," Claire said.

"The secret is not in the spices or marinade," Holt said. "The secret is to let the steak reach room temperature and rub a little butter on it before putting it on the grill."

"I'll remember that," Claire said. "So you think their trek on the ferry is what it appears to be, a spring ritual?"

"What I think and what I can prove are two different things," Holt said.

"What can you prove?"

"Not a thing," Holt said.

"What do you think?"

"You know, after you called me I did some checking on you," Holt said. "Seven solved murder cases in four years is pretty impressive. Six citations, promotion to homicide before the age of thirty-five, two failed marriages probably because you find home life boring and a year-long suspension because you lost your temper with a Congressman. That means…"

"Not true," Claire said. "Had I apologized the suspension would have dropped. I don't apologize when I'm in the right."

"That means you have a strong core of principals that you won't yield to," Holt said. "Me too. So what I think doesn't matter if I can't prove it."

"I relieved Turley of patrol duty and made him dispatcher," Claire said.

"He's an experienced cop," Holt said.

"Who can't outrun a child," Claire said.

"But still valuable."

"That's why I didn't retire him outright," Claire said. "I've assigned Rose to investigative work to free up Knox and the summer rentals and myself. She'll also serve as a backup on calls."

"I often thought that very thing," Holt said.

"You still have a lot of cop left in you," Claire said. "Want to come on as a summer deputy?"

"A woman rushed home all excited one day," Holt said. "She reaches home and says to her husband, I won the lottery. Pack a bag. The husband starts to pack and notices his wife isn't packing. He says, hey, how come you're not packing. She says I don't care where you go, just get out."

"Is that your way of saying when something is over it's over?" Claire asked.

"More or less."

"Would you mind a phone call or two if I should happen to need advice?"

"I wouldn't mind, but I doubt you'll need my advice. Coffee?"

"Yes, thank you. A splash of cream in mine."

"Be right back."

Holt went below and was gone for several minutes. He returned with two mugs of coffee and set them on the table.

"A word of caution on Carl Walker," Holt said. "The man is an excellent town manager and mayor, but he can be a bit bitter over losing his wife. I noticed a hostility toward women the last year or so."

"I'll take that under my wing," Claire said.

"Sure you don't want to go for a ride? I need to test the engine."

Claire looked at the rough waves crashing against the side of the boat and beach.

"Ask me that question on a calm, windless day," she said.

"I hope I've been some help to you," Holt said.

"Plenty," Claire said.

"When you're ready I'll walk you back to your car."

"Thought you wanted to take your boat out," Claire said.

"I do, but I figure I'll grab some rods from the garage and try my hand."

Claire and Holt left his boat and walked back to the house. He walked her to her car and when Claire was behind the wheel, Holt opened the garage door and she caught a glimpse of a dozen or more fishing rods along the back wall.

*   *   *   *   *

It was after four when Claire returned to the office. Knox was at his desk writing a report. He looked up when Claire entered the squad room.

"Got a kid in the cage," he said.

"For?"

"According to the girl's father, third degree rape."

"What girl and what father?"

"Mr. Percy Munn," Knox said. "His daughter is Scarlet. She's sixteen. The boy is Johnny Lind. Rose has Scarlet and her father in your office. Lind's mom is in the hallway talking to her son."

"Details," Claire said.

"Mr. Munn works in Nantucket as an insurance broker," Knox said. "He didn't feel well today and came home early and claims he found Johnny and Scarlet in her bed together. He called us and I went to the house and picked up the boy. Mr. Munn wants to press charges."

"Jesus," Claire said.

She went to her office and opened the door. Rose was at her desk. Mr. Munn and Scarlet were seated on the sofa.

Munn was around fifty years old, slender and balding a bit with glasses. Scarlet was small, with dark hair and eyes and more pretty than not.

"I'm Sheriff Claire Evergreen," Claire said.

"This is Mr. Munn and his daughter Scarlet," Rose said.

Munn stood. "I want to press charges against that... that...rapist and see he gets what's coming to him."

"Rape is a harsh word, Mr. Munn," Claire said.

"My daughter is sixteen," Munn said. "I caught that boy in bed with my daughter and they both were naked. Harsh word or not, what would you call it?"

Claire sat on the edge of her desk and looked at Scarlet. "Did you have sex with that boy?" she asked.

"Sheriff, for God's sake," Munn said.

Claire looked at Munn. "I'm talking to your daughter."

"That's right, she's my daughter and I don't appreciate your..." Munn said.

"Mr. Munn, be quiet," Claire said.

"What?" Munn said.

"I said be quiet," Claire said.

"I will not be quiet where my daughter is concerned," Munn said.

"Rose, please remove Mr. Munn from the room," Claire said.

Rose stood up.

"Wait, what is this?" Munn said.

"What this is Mr. Munn, is an inquest," Claire said. "And I'm the one inquiring. Now please shut up so I may continue."

"I want to press charges," Munn said.

"That's up to you, but one more word and I'll have Rose stick your ass in the cage with the Lind boy."

Claire looked at Scarlet. She had her head down.

"Scarlet, look at me please," Claire said.

Slowly, Scarlet looked up.

"Did you have sex with the Lind boy?" Claire asked.

A tear rolled down Scarlet's cheek. She nodded her head yes.

"How many times?" Claire asked.

"I don't know. Maybe six or seven," Scarlet said.

"Is he the only one?" Claire asked.

"Yes, of course," Scarlet said. "I'm not a slut. We love each other."

"Oh, please," Munn said.

Claire looked at Munn. "I won't warn you again to be quiet."

"We didn't do anything wrong," Scarlet said. "We love each other."

"Unfortunately it's not that simple," Claire said. "Rose, take Scarlet to the squad room so I can speak to Mr. Munn privately."

Rose took Scarlet by the arm and led her to the squad room.

"I want to press charges," Munn said as he stood up. "That boy is eighteen. That makes him an adult."

"It will ruin that boy's life forever," Claire said.

"He should have thought of that before he raped my daughter," Munn said.

"It was consensual."

"Not in the eyes of the law," Munn said. "And you know that as well as I do."

"Mr. Munn, how old were you the first time you had sex?" Claire asked.

"What does that have to do with anything?" Munn asked.

"How old?"

"That's none of your business and has nothing to do with this," Munn said.

"No?" Claire said. "Then answer my question, how old were you?"

Munn glared at Claire.

"Mr. Munn, the only difference I see between you and that boy is nobody put you in jail and labeled you a sex offender for the rest of your life," Claire said.

Munn slowly sat down on the sofa.

"He can't go unpunished," he said.

"Mr. Munn, I am sworn to uphold the law and I will do so without hesitation if a complaint is filed," Claire said.

"And if one isn't filed?" Munn asked.

"Maybe we can work something out."

"Like what?"

Claire went to the door. "Rose, bring the Lind boy, his mother and Scarlet in my office please."

A few minutes later Scarlet and John Lind sat in chairs facing Claire's desk. Mr. Munn and Mrs. Lind sat on the sofa. Rose stood beside the closed door.

"My son is no criminal," Mrs. Lind said.

"I do the talking and you do the listening," Claire said. "Unless I ask a question."

Rose looked at Claire and grinned.

"John, you are neck deep in a steaming pile of dog shit," Claire said.

Rose bit her lip and looked away.

"I know that, sheriff," John said. "And I'm willing to face the consequences."

"No you're not," Claire said. "You're a wet-behind-the-ears dumbass kid being led around by your dumbass teenage hormones," Claire said. "And your consequences could include prison time and a sex offender rap that follows you around for the rest of your life."

On the sofa, Mrs. Lind gasped.

"I'm going to propose the following instead of arrest and if both of your parents agree that will be the end of it," Claire said. "John, Scarlet, you are forbidden to see each other again until she turns eighteen and is of legal age. John, you will do one thousand hours of community service to the town during the next two years. The services will be what I say they are and your mother must agree to this or it won't work."

"Eighteen?" John said.

"That's two years before I'm eighteen," Scarlet said.

"I don't want to hear any I'm brokenhearted nonsense," Claire said. "You'll both forget about the other in a month. What do your parents say?"

"I want reports on the community service to make sure he's not slacking off," Munn said.

"Agreed," Claire said. "Mrs. Lind?"

"Yes, of course," Mrs. Lind said.

"Everybody go home," Claire said. "John, stay behind a second."

When it was just John and Claire in her office, Claire said, "Let me be clear about certain things. You report to Rose on Monday for your community assignment. I know a thousand hours sounds like a great deal, but spread out over two years it's twelve hours a week. If you fail to show up I will come get you and drive you directly to county prison where you will be charged with statutory rape. Are we clear?"

"Yes ma'am," John said.

"Rule number two. If you go near Scarlet before her eighteenth birthday, see rule number one. Clear?"

"Yes ma'am."

"Rule number three. Keep your dick in your pants unless you're sure the girl is eighteen and then we won't have to have this conversation again. Clear?"

John nodded. "Yes ma'am."

"Go home."

John stood, went to the door, opened it and left Claire at her desk.

"Jesus Christ," Claire sighed.

"I thought that went well," Rose said as she entered the office.

"Kids," Claire said.

"How did you make out with Holt?" Rose asked.

"He said the bikers use Smoky Point as a place to start their spring pilgrimage to visit other clubs in the Northeast," Claire said. "They do this several times over the summer as a way to keep in touch. We just happen to be a place to hang out after a long ferry ride."

"I've heard that story a dozen times," Rose said.

"Do you believe it?"

"I believe they use here as a starting point," Rose said.

"Pull all the names together of those arrested going back five years," Claire said. "If you can have it by tomorrow that would be great."

"I almost have it done now," Rose said.

"The fourth deputy?" Claire asked.

"I was going to take a run over to the academy in the morning," Rose said.

"Finish up your reports as best you can, leave it on my desk and keep your plans in the morning," Claire said.

Rose nodded.

"Listen, I know how you handled that was a bit unorthodox, but I think it was a good decision," she said.

"Good, since you're the one dolling out his punishment," Claire said.

"The kid doesn't know what he's in for," Rose said and returned to her desk.

Claire grabbed her mug and went to the squad room and filled it at the coffee pot.

Turley was at his desk, talking on the phone.

Claire sat on the edge of Knox's vacant desk and waited for him to hang up.

"Mossberg is sending us four police grade shotguns at twenty percent below costs and tossing in a case of ammo free," Turley said. "Two Kevlar vests will be here within a week."

"Good," Claire said. "You, Knox and Rose can train on them at the range as soon as they get here."

"What about the summer rentals?" Turley asked.

"They'll use what's available," Claire said. "Who covers tonight?"

"Me," Turley said.

"Night shift?"

"Knox."

Claire nodded. "We'll work on a new schedule as soon as our summer help is in place. Right now I'm going home to soak in a hot tub."

*   *   *   *   *

"Claire?" Dugan said.

Soaking in a hot tub full of bubble bath, Claire rested her head against the rim as she held her cell phone.

"Who is the liaison officer to the motorcycle clubs in Rhode Island?" she asked.

"Lieutenant Miller. He works out of Warwick."

"Can you give him a call and asked him to call me?"

"He's going to ask why?"

"He or you?"

"Both."

"About motorcycle clubs in Rhode Island, what else?" Claire said.

Chapter Eight

TURLEY WAS AT HIS DESK when Claire arrived at the office at nine in the morning.

"Coffee's fresh," he said.

She grabbed the mug off her desk and filled it at the pot and then sat on the edge of Knox's desk.

"Holt said you're a valuable and experienced officer," Claire said.

Turley looked at her.

"And I happen to agree with him."

Turley sighed. "I'm not exactly thrilled with being assigned desk duty, but I thought about it and in your place I would do the same," he said.

Claire sipped from her mug and nodded. "This won't be a walk in the park assignment," she said. "You'll be responsible for scheduling four summer deputies and Short. You'll handle all arrest reports, transportation to county when necessary and all in-coming dispatches. In a pinch, if Rose or I aren't available, you'll backup deputies if needed."

"Sounds like I should get a raise," Turley said.

"Sounds like," Claire said and went to her office where Rose had left a stack of reports.

Rose had also left a legal pad with hand-written notes.

Claire opened files and started to read. Two mugs of coffee later, Turley buzzed her phone.

"Claire, there's a Lieutenant Miller from Rhode Island on line one," he said.

She picked up her phone and said, "This is Claire Evergreen."

"Lieutenant Miller, Rhode Island State Police. Captain Dugan filled me in this morning," Miller said. "Tough break on the suspension, but I see you landed on your feet while you wait out the year."

"Thanks. Are you familiar with the Disciples?" Claire said.

"I am," Miller said.

"Who's the honcho?"

"Club president is one Randall Boyd," Miller said. "His veep is Arlo Tate. Captain Dugan told me they've caused some trouble in your town in the past. I wasn't aware of that."

"The story is Boyd and some of his minions take the ferry to Long Island and let off some steam in Smoky Point before riding into the sunset to visit charter gangs on the Island and south before riding north to do the same and then returning home. They claim the ferry ride saves them days of time on the road."

"I wasn't aware of that," Miller said again. "By let off steam you mean what exactly?"

"There's a street with almost two dozen bars on it," Claire said. "They get drunk, get into fights with another gang or each other, pay the fines and damages and go on their merry way."

"What other gangs?" Miller asked.

"Freedom Riders and the Sentinels."

"The Riders and Sentinels are rivals, but the Disciples are neutral," Miller said. "The Disciples are the largest club in the state, the Riders and Sentinels fight for pecking order. Do they all ride the ferry at the same time?"

"Probably not," Claire said. "The pattern seems to be they stay overnight, get drunk, get into fights, pay what they owe and leave and repeat the process a month later right up to Labor Day into October."

"Other than that?"

"There is no other than that."

"I'm failing to see your major concern, Sheriff."

"What are the Disciples suspected of?" Claire asked.

"Name what's illegal."

"So maybe that makes me a tad suspicious of their repeat behavior," Claire said.

"Maybe so, but if all you got is they get drunk in a public bar, have a few fights and pay for their own damages, what do you got?" Miller said.

"I don't know."

Miller sighed. "When do they usually show up?"

"Right around Memorial Day."

"I'll take a ride to Providence and have a chat with Boyd," Miller said. "I'll call you back in a few days."

"Thanks," Claire said.

"Welcome," Miller said.

She hung up and finished the last bit of coffee in her mug and went to the squad room for more.

Rose entered the squad room and walked to her desk. She had four file folders under her arm and handed them to Claire.

Claire nodded to her office and Rose followed her inside and closed the door. Claire went behind her desk while Rose took the sofa.

"Something stinks," Claire said.

"I showered this morning," Rose said.

"Einstein said… I think it was Einstein, that insanity is doing the same thing over and over again and expecting a different result," Claire said.

"I don't… what are you… you lost me here," Rose said.

"When do these four report for duty," Claire said and tapped the folders.

"When do you want them?"

"When do the beaches open?"

"Two weeks."

"What's today?"

"Friday."

"Monday morning. Set it up."

"Okay," Rose said.

"Rose, pull everything you can find on Randall Boyd and Arlo Tate," Claire said.

* * * * *

Randall Boyd was forty-seven years old. Born in Providence, he served three years in the Army and spent eleven months in Iraq during the first Gulf War. When he returned home he joined the Disciples, a motorcycle club with a long and storied history. It was unknown to the police how Boyd rose through the ranks to become club president, but his reputation as a fierce and deadly advisory was well known through the state and New England.

Arlo Tate was forty-eight years old and born in Warwick. He met Boyd while in the Army and they served together in the Gulf. It was unclear how Tate and Boyd wound up together as number one and two in the Disciples, but Tate's reputation was every bit as vile as Boyd's.

The only source of income came from three body shops the club owned in the greater Providence area. Club members skilled in body work worked at the shops. The club headquarters was an old candy store that was adjacent to one of the shops.

Boyd and Tate were suspected of assassination, murder for hire, extortion, arson, drug dealing, kidnapping, and car theft, operating a chop shop and running illegal guns.

Rose tapped on her door and opened it.

"We got a call and Short isn't due in for hours," she said.

"What's the call?"

"Another disturbance at the Palace."

"I'll go with you," Claire said.

*   *   *   *   *

As Rose stopped her car outside the Palace, a small crowd had already gathered on the sidewalk.

Claire and Rose left the car and approached the crowd.

"He's back, that lunatic," a man said.

"Who is back?" Claire asked.

Rose returned to her car and then rushed back to Claire.

"Dwayne escaped from the county courthouse through a bathroom window this morning," Rose said.

"That's what I said, that lunatic," the man said.

"Who's the bartender here?" Claire asked.

A man stepped forward. "Me."

"Is there a back door, a kitchen entrance?" Claire asked.

"Yes."

Claire looked at Rose. "Go in the front and keep his attention."

Before Rose could respond, Claire dashed away.

"Well shit," Rose said.

She walked to the front door of the Palace and cautiously entered. Except for Dwayne and Sally, the bar was empty.

They were directly against the bar. Dwayne had his left arm around Sally's neck and held a kitchen knife to her throat with his right hand.

"Aw, Jesus, Dwayne," Rose said. "There is no need for this."

"This whore has been spreading those skinny legs for every guy that walks in here," Dwayne said.

"No she hasn't," Rose said. "And unless you want to go away for life I suggest you put that knife down."

"Where's that bitch, the ball kicker?" Dwayne said.

"She isn't here," Rose said. "It's just me."

"I don't want to hurt you, but this stinking whore I'm married to has got to pay for her sins," Dwayne said.

"Sally isn't doing what you think, Dwayne," Rose said. "That's all in your mind."

"I saw her and that new bartender gazing into each other's eyes when I walked in here," Dwayne said. "What do you call that?"

"I lost a contact, Dwayne," Sally said. "He was helping me put it back."

"There, see," Rose said. "You're all worked up about nothing."

Dwayne pressed the knife tighter against Sally's throat.

"Dwayne, don't. Please," Rose said.

Silently moving along the hallway floor from the back door, Claire looked at Rose and nodded.

"Dwayne, put the knife down," Rose said. "Look at Sally's neck. You love her. You don't want to hurt her, do you?"

"I love her, this stinking bitch," Dwayne said.

"Then put the knife down if you love her," Rose said.

Claire disappeared behind the bar.

"You're cutting her neck, Dwayne," Rose said. "You don't want to do that. Hold her if you want to but put the knife on the bar."

"I put this knife down and you'll shoot me," Dwayne said.

"How can I shoot you with Sally in front of you?" Rose said. "Besides, I'm a terrible shot even from this distance."

Wayne lowered the knife and then set it on the bar.

"I'm holding onto Sally just in case you…" Dwayne said.

Claire came over the bar in one swift and silent motion. As she touched down behind Dwayne, her right arm encircled his neck while her left arm took hold of his right wrist and she squeezed tightly.

At the same time, she took two steps backward so that Dwayne's neck was bent and his chin nearly touched his chest.

Dwayne's hold on Sally released and she rushed forward to Rose.

Claire pressed her right thumb into Dwayne's artery and she took another step backward. He was strong as a bull and nearly broke the hold, but with oxygen and blood cut off he started to pass out.

"Don't hurt him," Sally cried. "Dwayne."

Dwayne sunk to his knees and then pitched forward unconscious.

Claire released her hold and slowly stood up.

"You killed him," Sally yelled, rushed to the bar and grabbed the knife and stabbed at Claire with it.

Claire blocked Sally's thrust with her left forearm and then punched Sally in the jaw with a stiff right hook.

Sally crashed against the bar and landed on top of Dwayne.

Claire looked at Rose.

"Call Turley and have him get county over here right away," Claire said. "Oh, and toss me your cuffs."

*   *   *   *   *

Six cruisers and twelve deputies responded. Once Dwayne was in the back of one cruiser and Sally in another, Sergeant Perry sat at a table in the bar with Claire and Rose.

"He leveled four deputies in the bathroom and two of them are in the hospital," Perry said. "And you took him alone?"

"She did," Rose said.

Perry looked at Rose.

"And you did what?"

"Watch," Rose said.

"Add the knife charge to everything else you're going to dump on

Dwayne and hit Sally with assault with a deadly weapon with intent," Claire said. "Maybe a year in county will wise her up some."

"I wouldn't count on it," Perry said.

*   *   *   *   *

Rose drove them back to the office.

"That was really quite amazing," Rose said.

"Now you know why I never do my nails," Claire said.

Chapter Nine

CLAIRE SOAKED IN A HOT tub full of bubble bath and salts to relieve the soreness in her neck and upper back caused by the strain of bringing down that oaf Dwayne.

She could have just tazed him but he had a solid hold on Sally and he could have injured her when he spasmed out from the shock.

Snowball watched her from the closed toilet lid.

On the floor beside the tub, Claire's cell phone rang. She scooped up the phone and answered the call.

"This is Claire," she said.

"Matt Holt. I heard about your little dustup with local moron Dwayne and his wife Sally," Holt said.

"It wasn't that big of a deal," Claire said.

"Reports say he put four deputies in the hospital and you put him out in under thirty seconds."

"Like I said, it wasn't that big of a deal," Claire said.

"I'm taking the boat out on Sunday for some fishing, want to go?" Holt asked.

"Are you asking me for a date?" Claire said.

"I'm asking as an old sheriff to a new sheriff if you'd like to drop a line on Sunday," Holt said.

"I already told you I don't like boats and I've never been fishing in my life," Claire said.

"I'll keep it open just in case," Holt said.

"Ever had a first-hand encounter with Randall Boyd or Arlo Tate?" Claire asked.

"Show up on Sunday and find out," Holt said.

Claire sighed. "What time?"

"Noon. We'll have lunch aboard and try our luck when they bite in the afternoon."

"Okay, but this is strictly business," Claire said.

"Dress for fishing," Holt said.

"I don't know what that..." Claire said as Holt hung up.

Claire set the phone down and looked at Snowball.

"You like fish," she said. "What do you wear to catch them?"

* * * * *

Claire returned from her morning run to find Rose waiting for her on the front doorstep.

"Do you always do that?" Rose asked as she stood up. "Go running."

"I do," Claire said. "Why are you here?"

"Were you planning to come to the office today?" Rose asked.

"Maybe later. Why?"

"Michele Burke is back in town," Rose said.

Claire looked at Rose.

"Grab a shower, I'll make some coffee and we'll talk," Rose said.

* * * * *

Wearing a robe, her hair still wet, Snowball on her lap, Claire sipped coffee and looked across the kitchen table at Rose.

"Ten years ago today, Michele Burke was a twenty-one year old newlywed and young mother," Rose said. "Her husband was on his second tour in Iraq at the time and she brought her six-month-

69

old son to the beach. She was sitting on a bench with the baby in a stroller when, as she described it, a man wearing a hooded sweatshirt came onto the beach and attacked her. She claims they fought and he knocked her out. When she came to the baby and stroller were gone. Some passersby found her bloody and screaming on the beach. I was still an EMT at the time and responded to the call. We took her to General where she was sedated."

Claire sipped some coffee and stroked Snowball.

"The Smoky Point and county sheriff's departments teamed up to investigate, but Michele was heavily sedated and could barely speak to them," Rose said. "A week later, her husband was killed by a sniper in Iraq while he was waiting to take emergency leave stateside."

"Jesus Christ," Claire said.

"Michele was hospitalized for two years," Claire said. "The following year she showed up at the beach looking for her baby."

"Is that where she is now?" Claire asked.

"I like to take walks on the beach when it's empty," Rose said. "I spotted Michele on a bench and I called Short and asked him to keep an eye on her."

"Give me five minutes to get dressed," Claire said.

*　*　*　*　*

Claire followed Rose to the beach and parked next to Knox's cruiser.

He was leaning against the cruiser keeping an eye on Michele Burke.

"She hasn't moved since I been here," Knox said.

"Wait here," Claire said.

She walked through the opening in the wall and approached the bench.

Michele Burke was wearing a bathrobe and house slippers. She had an open bottle of beer and was smoking a cigarette. Her blonde hair was a matted mess. She looked more fifty than thirty.

"Hello," Claire said. "I'm Claire."

Michele looked at Claire. Her eyes were glazed over and after sipping some beer, she nodded to Claire.

"Mind if I sit?" Claire asked.

Michele shrugged.

Claire sat on the bench.

"Are you waiting for your baby?" Claire asked.

Michele took a hit on the cigarette. "My baby and my husband," Michele said. "He's never seen his son you know. He's in the war you know."

"I'm sorry to hear that," Claire said. "Where is your baby now?"

"Gone."

"Where?"

"Just gone."

"Aren't you cold in just that robe?" Claire asked.

"No matter."

"Where do you live?" Claire asked.

"I don't… I'm not sure."

"That's a nice robe. Mind if I look at it?"

Michele shrugged.

Claire looked inside the collar of Michele's robe.

"Would you wait right here for me," Claire said. "I forgot something."

Michele nodded.

Claire returned to Rose and Knox.

"She's wearing a robe from a place called Shady Acres. Know it?" Claire asked.

Rose shook her head.

"Gimme a minute," Knox said and took out his cell phone.

After thirty seconds, Knox said, "It's a private hospital about an hour west of here."

"What kind of hospital?" Claire asked.

"For mentally unstable people," Short said. "Like a rest home."

"Call them and have them send somebody for her," Claire said. "Tell them she'll be in the squad room."

"Right," Knox said.

While Knox made the call, Claire and Rose went to the bench.

"Michele, I'd like you to go with us now," Claire said.

"Go? Go where? I have to wait for my baby and my husband," Michele said.

"I know, but I think you might be more comfortable if you waited in my office," Claire said. "It's much warmer and I have a nice comfortable sofa you can use."

"I'm hungry," Michele said.

"We'll get you something to eat. What would you like?" Claire asked.

"What day is this?" Michele said.

"Saturday."

"We always have scrambled eggs with sausage patties and toast on Saturday."

"No problem," Claire said.

*   *   *   *   *

Claire sat at her desk while Rose and Michele occupied the sofa. Michele was eating scrambled eggs with sausage and toast from a takeout carton.

"Michele, tell me about that day on the beach," Claire said. "Can you remember?"

"Yes, I remember," Michele said.

72

"Tell me about it," Claire said.

"I like the beach," Michele said. "Even in winter. In the morning it's so peaceful and fresh and I like listening to the waves crash. It's beautiful."

"I know it is. So what happened?"

"I take my baby to the beach on nice days," Michele said. "He's only six months old but he likes the sound of the ocean like I do."

Claire sighed.

"And that day your baby was taken, what happened?" Rose asked.

Michele looked at Rose. "I know you, don't I?"

"Yes," Rose said. "You've been here before."

"Then you know what happened," Michele said. "The man took my baby. The man in the hooded sweatshirt."

"What did he look like?" Claire said.

"Like the man in the hooded sweatshirt," Michele said.

Knox tapped on the door and opened it. "Claire, Shady Acres is here," he said.

"Send them in," Claire said.

Two male nurses from Shady Acres entered Claire's office.

"There you are Michele," one of the nurses said. "We were worried about you."

"I'm eating scrambled eggs while I wait for my baby and husband," Michele said.

The second nurse took Michele's hand. "Now Michele, we both know they're not coming back, don't we?" he said.

"Can I finish my eggs?" Michele asked.

"Yes, but don't take too long."

While Michele finished her breakfast, Claire took one of the nurses to the squad room.

"How long has she been at the Shady Acres?" Claire asked.

"Around two years," the nurse said.

73

"Who runs the place?"

"Doctor Morris Monroe."

Claire turned around when the other male nurse guided Michele into the squad room.

"Thank you for the eggs," Michele said.

*   *   *   *   *

Claire sat on the edge of Rose's desk and looked at Knox, Turley and Rose.

"She's been here before like that?" Claire asked.

"Several times," Knox said.

"Four or five that I know of," Rose said.

"None of you were around ten years ago. Who was?" Claire asked.

"Before Holt?" Knox asked.

"There are hundreds of reports signed Sheriff Patrick C. Shaw," Rose said.

"Rose, pull whatever there is on that incident," Claire said. "Consider yourself on the clock."

Knox and Turley looked at Claire.

"I'm curious," Claire said and went to her office. She closed the door and sat behind her desk. She thought for a moment and then picked up the phone, dialed information and asked for the number to Shady Acres.

When she had the number, Claire called the private hospital and asked for Doctor Monroe.

"Who is calling please?" A female voice asked.

"Sheriff Evergreen of Smoky Point," Claire said. "I'm calling about Michele Burke."

"Oh yes. Please hold."

Claire was on hold for a full three minutes before Monroe came on the line.

"Sheriff Evergreen is it?" he said. "I'm Doctor Monroe, director of Shady Acres."

"I'm calling about one of your patients, Michele Burke," Claire said.

"I know. She's en route."

"I'd like to talk to you about her if you can afford me some time."

"When?"

"Next week. Pick what's good for you."

"Wednesday at ten-thirty."

"Very good. I'll see you then."

After hanging up, Claire returned to the squad room.

"Where's Rose?" she asked Knox.

"Basement looking up old files."

"Tell her to bring whatever she finds to my house," Claire said.

* * * * *

Claire was in the backyard with a mug of coffee when Rose arrived around three in the afternoon.

She was carrying a cardboard box designed for storing files.

"This is everything I could find," Rose said.

"Grab a coffee from the kitchen and sit with me for a minute," Claire said.

Rose entered the kitchen through the sliding glass door and returned with a mug. She sat at the table with Claire.

"Nice view," Rose said.

"They never found her baby or a suspect, did they?" Claire asked.

"Not that I'm aware of," Rose said.

"Where can I find Patrick Shaw?" Claire asked.

"Fairview Cemetery."

"When?"

"Shortly after Holt came aboard," Rose said. "He was shot in the back of the head on the Grand Central Parkway late at night. State police said it was probably a case of road rage. No one was ever arrested."

Claire sipped some coffee and then said, "I'll return the files on Monday. And thank you for today."

"What are you... I mean... hell I don't know."

"It always comes down to details, Rose," Claire said.

*   *   *   *   *

The county sheriff's office and Sheriff Shaw wrote detailed reports of the incident.

It was an unusually warm day for late April and temperatures reached seventy-five degrees by seven-thirty in the morning. Michele Burke left her house with her son and drove to the beach where she walked the stroller along the sand until settling on a bench.

According to Michele's disoriented statement, a man wearing a hooded sweatshirt came out of nowhere and attacked her. She fought to defend her baby, but he overpowered her and when she woke up the stroller and baby were gone.

A pair of joggers stopped when they saw Michele screaming hysterically on the sand. There were no witnesses to the abduction. Michele's cuts and bruises were defensive in nature and it was a punch to the right side of her face that rendered her unconscious.

The joggers saw only Michele's silver Honda in the beach parking lot. Deputies combed the area and went house-to-house searching for a witness but there were none to be found.

State Police checked highways, state roads and side streets without results.

Even the FBI got in on the act since the incident was deemed a kidnapping. However ransom demands were never forthcoming and there were no leads or suspects.

There were crime scene photographs. A few decent shots of footprints showed a trail from the parking lot where the sand began to the bench and then back again. Footprints at the scene of the bench indicated a scuffle and weren't much use as evidence.

The to and from footprints were interesting in that they were prints made by what experts at the FBI called dress shoes size eleven.

Also interesting was a white button found on the bench that was consistent with buttons found on men's dress shirts.

Claire set the files aside for a few minutes and thought.

Who wears dress shoes to the beach?

And a dress shirt for that matter?

Michele Burke had very little in the way of luxury. Her husband was a soldier and at the time of the kidnapping she was a stay-at-home mom with no income other than her husband's Army pay.

The kidnapping wasn't about ransom. That's why demands never came forward, there weren't any.

The kidnapping wasn't planned. Had it been, the kidnapper would have worn appropriate clothing for the beach. Say he targeted Michele after following her and learning her pattern of visiting the beach. A man wearing appropriate attire for a day at the beach would be less likely to draw attention to himself walking onto a beach than a man wearing business attire.

The kidnapping was a crime of passion.

What drives a man to kidnap a baby on the spur of the moment?

*　　*　　*　　*　　*

Claire had just toweled off from a hot bath when her cell phone rang. She walked naked from the bathroom to the bedroom where the phone sat on the nightstand and she scooped it up.

"Sheriff Evergreen, Lieutenant Miller."

"Hello Lieutenant," Claire said as she sat on the bed.

"Well, I went to see Boyd at his headquarters next to their body shop," Miller said. "The man is no dummy. He can quote state and federal law and the Bible for that matter."

"So can a trained parrot," Claire said.

"Yeah, but the difference is Boyd understands what he's quoting," Miller said.

"What are you trying to say, Lieutenant?"

"He's as slick as oil on a waxed floor," Miller said. "He basically told me that the purpose of a motorcycle club is to ride the open road. He said the club makes its spring pilgrimage to visit other clubs and that as long as they break no laws in doing so they will continue to do so. He said they carry no illegal weapons and bring plenty of their own cash to pay their way and that there is nothing anybody can do to prevent their leaving in a few weeks."

"By leaving you mean to here?"

"Unless they changed their route."

"Thanks for the heads-up, Lieutenant."

"Keep in touch."

Claire set the phone aside, tucked her Glock under the other pillow, put on a T-shirt and waited for Snowball to assume her rightful place beside Claire's stomach.

Chapter Ten

AFTER HER MORNING WORKOUT AND run, Claire showered and dressed in jeans, white blouse and casual blazer with black walking shoes.

She drove to Holt's house on the ocean using the GPS because she hadn't memorized the route as yet.

She parked in his driveway in front of the closed garage. There was a note taped to the garage door.

Already on the boat. Matt.

Claire walked down to the ocean and stepped onto the dock where Holt's boat was tied. He wasn't on deck, but when she stepped onto the gangway he popped up from below.

Holt wore khaki-colored cargo pants with a maroon colored polo shirt.

"I should have mentioned to bring a hat," he said.

"I don't own any," Claire said.

"I have some extras," Holt said. "Hey, grab the ropes while I start the engine."

Holt went topside. Claire removed the two ropes holding the boat to the dock. The engine started and slowly the boat moved away from the dock.

"Come on up," Holt called to her.

Claire took the stairs topside where Holt stood behind the wheel and a dashboard of instruments. It was immediately apparent that

Holt knew what he was doing.

"We'll head northeast for about seven miles and drop anchor," he said.

"Mind if I go down?" Claire asked. "It seems more stable down there."

"Go below and open the medicine chest in the bathroom," Holt said. "There are some quick-acting motion sickness pills."

"Thanks."

Claire went below to the bathroom, opened the chest and found a box of chewable motion sickness tablets. She chewed two. They tasted like minty chalk. She ran the water, filled a small glass on the sink and drank it. Then she looked at herself in the mirror. Her face was pale, almost sickly looking.

She did a quick brush of her hair and then went to the deck and took a seat at the table. She avoided looking at the water, but she could still feel the motion of the boat as Holt drove it over the waves.

Slowly the tablets kicked in and her stomach started to settle. And maybe it was her imagination but the waves seemed to calm down as well.

After a few more minutes, the boat stopped, the engine shut down and there was a whirling nose as the anchor dropped.

A few seconds after that, Holt appeared at the table.

"You really don't like boats, do you?" he said.

"I don't like anything that makes me sick to my stomach," Claire said. "Boats, small planes and roller coasters."

"Horses?"

"I don't know. I've never been on a horse," Claire said.

"Well, I'll drop a line and we can talk about what you want to talk about."

Holt went below and returned with a long rod and a tackle box and a large white cooler. He set up at one of the swivel chairs close to the railing and then cast off.

"Feeling better?" he asked Claire.

"Yes, a bit."

"Sit next to me and we'll talk."

Claire took the swivel chair next to Holt.

"You wanted to talk about Boyd and Tate?" Holt said.

"And a few other things," Claire said. "Let's start with Boyd."

"It's like you already know," Holt said. "They show up, get drunk, get into a fight or two and spend the night in the cage. In the morning they pay the fines and for damages and go on their merry way."

"I know all that," Claire said. "Tell me about Boyd. You must have interacted with him."

"I have on several occasions," Holt said. "He doesn't always show up when the Disciples do. Sometimes Tate comes and sometimes both or none."

"What's he like, Boyd?" Claire asked.

"Not what you'd expect," Holt said. "For one thing he's very soft-spoken. For another he's highly intelligent. Pick a topic and he can converse on that topic for hours. Another thing is he never gets into a fight himself. He usually just stays in the background while his boys let off steam. I've never put him in the cage with the others and he always pays the fines and damages in cash."

"And this just goes on year after year?" Claire said.

"It's not 1880 where the marshal tells you to get out of town," Holt said. "Unless someone is actually wanted for something you're not going to be able to do much unless they break the law."

"Are you lecturing me?" Claire asked.

Holt grinned. "Sorry."

"While his boys are in the cage, where does Boyd go?" Claire asked.

"Motel I suppose," Holt said.

"What about…?"

"Hold on, I got a bite," Holt said.

He reeled in a large fish, removed the hook and placed it in the cooler that was filled with ice.

"What was that?" Claire asked,

"Striper. A good one."

"What's a striper?"

"Sea bass."

Claire nodded although she wouldn't know a sea bass from a sea horse.

"You were saying?" Holt asked as he cast out again.

"What about Tate?"

"Same deal as Boyd," Holt said. "Never gets into fights, highly intelligent although not as polished as Boyd."

"You sound like a fan," Claire said.

"Hardly," Holt said. "You know, those two plus decades I was a cop in the City I worked the toughest neighborhoods in The Bronx, Brooklyn and Manhattan and if there is one thing I learned it's this, you can only do what you can do to make a difference."

"I believe that only if you give your best," Claire said.

"Which I did and I'm sure you do," Holt said. "I already told you I retired because my hobby was becoming more important than the job. I wasn't giving it my best so I packed it in. It happens to all of us sooner or later, you included."

"What about...?"

"Hold on," Holt said as he had another bite and reeled in a second striper.

Claire watched him remove the striper from the hook and place it in the cooler.

"Go ahead," Holt said as he checked his spinner and then cast out.

"Michele Burke stopped by yesterday," Claire said. "Or should I say we stopped by the beach and picked her up."

Holt looked at Claire. "A tragic case that one," he said. "It happened

82

before I came on board. When I met Michele Burke it was under similar circumstances. She was on the beach waiting for baby and husband to return."

"Ever look into it?"

"I did actually," Holt said. "The FBI, State Police, County Sheriff all got nowhere with it. I read all the reports and concluded as did Sheriff Shaw that there was little to nothing we could do about it. The last time I saw her was two years ago when she wandered onto the beach and I believe it was Turley who picked her up."

"Had you ever met Shaw?" Claire asked.

"No, never did," Holt said. "I understand he was a fine sheriff and a decent man."

"Do you buy the road rage as the cause of the shooting?" Claire asked.

"The State Police and County Sheriff's office does," Holt said. "I have no information to the contrary."

Claire nodded. "Want to come back as a summer deputy?"

"I do not. But what I do want is lunch. Hold the line while I start the grill."

"Hold the…" Claire said as Holt handed her the pole.

Claire held the pole while Holt went to the grill. There was a sudden jerk on the line and the pole bent nearly in half.

"Hey, hey Matt, something's happening here," she said.

Holt looked over from the grill.

"Set the drag and pull back until the hook is set," he said.

"I don't know what any of that means," Claire said.

Holt returned, took the pole, set the drag and gave it a yank. Fish hooked, he reeled in a third striper.

"I think that's it until after lunch," he said.

"What's on the menu?" Claire asked.

"Baby back ribs, all you can eat."

"Mind if I grab a few more of those sickness pills?"

* * * * *

Besides the smoked ribs there was a Crock-Pot of baked beans and cole slaw and beer from the keg below.

The sky was cloudless and the sun had heated up quite a bit. Holt wore a Stetson cowboy hat and gave Claire an Australian outback hat to shade her face as they ate.

"I feel I owe you a disclosure," Claire said when lunch was consumed and she nursed a beer. "If this is a seduction it won't work. I'm not in the market for a man and if I was, motion sickness and a cooler of smelly fish isn't my ideal date situation."

Holt grinned.

"It's not," he said. "But everybody could use an extra friend or two."

"I agree," Claire said. "Now I'm going to take a few more sickness pills and then could you please get me off this Godforsaken boat."

* * * * *

Holt walked Claire to her car.

"My wife died, Claire," he said. "In my eyes, she can't be replaced. I wouldn't inflict that kind of ghost on another woman. Understand?"

"I do."

Claire opened the car door and then realized she still wore the hat. "Your hat," she said.

"Keep it," Holt said. "It looks good on you."

"Thanks for lunch and the hat," Claire said as she got behind the wheel. "And the sea sickness pills."

Chapter Eleven

ON HER WAY HOME CLAIRE stopped by the office to drop off the carton of reports Rose had brought her.

Turley was on duty at his desk.

"How's it going?" she asked.

"Slow. Short comes on at four," Turley said.

After she set the box behind Rose's door, Claire sat on the edge of Turley's desk.

"The summer deputy's report tomorrow," Claire said. "I want you to handle all training and assignments. Two men ride with Knox per shift until they are trained and ready for Memorial Day. If Rose isn't on assignment she rides with one of them."

Turley nodded.

"Let me ask you something," Claire said. "What's your opinion of Holt as a sheriff?"

"Capable. Very capable."

"As a man?"

"Decent. Maybe as decent as they come," Turley said. "Why?"

"I just want to know what I have to live up to," Claire said.

"Well, for my two cents worth, you've made a hell of an impression on me," Turley said.

"Thanks. See you in the morning."

"Hey, where did you get the hat?"

"A friend."

*   *   *   *   *

Claire had just entered the house when her cell phone rang. It was Mitzi Maxwell calling.

"I'm lonely," Mitzi said. "Feel like some company for dinner."

"Sure. What time?"

"I'll pick you up around seven-thirty. Dress is casual."

"Okay."

Claire set the phone on the nightstand, stripped down to her tank top and took an hour-long nap. She awoke with Snowball tucked into her stomach. When she got out of bed, Snowball woke up briefly, yawned and returned to sleep.

Claire showered and dressed in dark slacks, gray T-shirt and a casual blazer. She chose black shoes with low heels. She locked the Glock in a steel case and tucked it into the closet and removed a hammerless .357 Magnum revolver from a second steel case and placed it and one speed loader into her handbag.

She didn't bother with makeup. She rarely did. Her hair, although damp just sort of fell into place as it dried, but she tucked a brush into the handbag anyway.

After filling Snowball's food and water dish, Claire went outside to wait for Mitzi. She pulled up at exactly seven-thirty.

"Like Italian?" Mitzi asked when Claire entered the car.

"The men or the food?"

Mitzi grinned.

"This place called The Roma is about thirty minutes east on the highway, but it's worth the drive," Mitzi said. "I usually go there when I'm in the dumps."

"Why?" Claire asked.

"In the dumps?"

"Yes."

"Three ex-husbands, no boyfriend and no prospects," Mitzi said. "It doesn't happen often, but every once in a while being man-less sort of smacks me between the eyes."

"I was really down after my first husband left me," Claire said. "He said he couldn't take being married to a cop. The hours, plus he wanted children."

"And you didn't?"

"No. Husband number two said he couldn't take the long hours I was working in homicide," Claire said. "He started sleeping around. I sent him packing. If I'm going to get an STD it won't be second hand from some little office bimbo."

"Aren't we a pair," Mitzi said. "We're here."

The Roma was a bit upscale with etched glass windows and doors and the parking lot was nearly full.

"I made a reservation," Mitzi said.

*   *   *   *   *

As they munched on salad, Mitzi said, "How are you enjoying being sheriff of our small town?"

"Surprised."

"How so?"

"There's a lot more to this town than I thought," Claire said.

"We're no Peyton Place, but Smoky Point has had its moments," Mitzi said.

"How long have you lived here?"

"I left Queens in ninety-two, so it's been a while."

"I met Michele Burke yesterday when she ran off from the Shady Acres hospital and wandered onto the beach," Claire said.

"That poor woman," Mitzi said. "I can't imagine such heartache. Losing her baby and husband a week apart like that. It's enough to drive anyone to a breakdown."

"Were you on the town council at the time?" Claire asked.

"None of us five were back then," Mitzi said. "I'm into my eighth year and Carl is going on six years as town manager."

"Did you know Sheriff Shaw?"

"Know him? Hell, I dated him for a while."

"I read about what happened to him," Claire said. "Tragic."

"To say the least," Mitzi said. "Pat was a fine man. He deserved far better than what he got."

"Holt seems to be a decent man, too," Claire said. "I've met him twice now. He was highly thought of by his deputies."

"And the community," Mitzi said. "Do you know how he told the council he was retiring? He called a meeting of all five and told us he was retiring because he felt he no longer could give the town his best and the people deserved better than that. I'd say it's safe to say Matt Holt is a class act."

"How is the dessert in this place?" Claire asked.

"Heavenly. They have a chocolate cheesecake to die for."

After the main course of chicken parm was finished and the plates were cleared away, they ordered the cheesecake and coffee for dessert.

"Do you think you'll ever get married again?" Mitzi asked.

"No, probably not," Claire said. "Men don't like what I do and I'm not about to stop doing it to become some slob's overweight housewife."

"Even if he were also a cop?"

"Especially if he was a cop," Claire said.

"Me, I'd love to be married again, but I suppose three time losers are not all that bankable as a spouse," Mitzi said.

"I think that would depend upon the man," Claire said. "For now I'm content with Snowball and a job."

"If only it was that easy for all of us," Mitzi said. She sliced into her cheesecake and washed it down with a sip of coffee. "But, there is always cheesecake," she said.

* * * * *

When Claire walked through the front door, Snowball was waiting for her. She scooped up the cat and Snowball purred loudly.

"We don't need no stinking man, do we girl?" Claire said as she rubbed Snowball's ears.

Snowball's purring grew louder.

"Easy for you to say," Claire said. "You've been spayed."

Chapter Twelve

CLAIRE SAT BEHIND HER DESK and looked at the four recent graduates of the training academy.

They were Janelle Pederson, twenty-three years old, Robert Dawson, also twenty-three, Alex Cole, twenty-four and Brett Ricard, twenty-three. Pederson, a woman, was black. Dawson was Hispanic.

Claire sipped coffee as she gave a pep talk and told them her expectations.

"Questions or comments?" she asked.

"I was expecting to spend the summer working as a security guard until I get placed into a permanent position," Pederson said. "I'm grateful for the opportunity and I'm sure we will all do our best not to disappoint you."

"For the next ten days or so consider it paid training," Claire said. "After Memorial Day the fun starts and you will work long shifts and be quite busy. Deputy Turley will be in charge of your scheduling and dispatches. Deputy Knox will oversee your training and be your senior man. Rose is my investigator and will serve as your backup when needed. Questions?"

There were none.

"First day of training lunch is on me. Go," Claire said.

As the four filed out, Claire said, "Hold on a second Janelle."

Pederson stood back and closed the door.

"Yes, Sheriff?" she said.

"Never be a kiss ass, deputy," Claire said. "It won't gain you respect and the ass you're kissing will wind up resenting you for it."

Pederson nodded. "Yes ma'am. I mean Sheriff."

"Claire. Call me Claire."

Pederson smiled. "I mean Claire."

* * * * *

Turley and Rose were at their desks when Claire entered the squad room.

"Knox out with the rookies?" she asked.

"Went out a little while ago," Turley said.

"Claire, got your pistol permit and badge," Rose said.

"I'll take the permit, but get me a flap wallet so I can wear the badge on my belt," Claire said. "I'll be at the town office for a while if you need me."

* * * * *

"Sheriff Evergreen, what can I do for you?" Carl Walker asked as Claire took a seat opposite his desk.

"Nice office," she said.

"It belongs to the town, not me," Walker said. "Now I have a great deal to do this morning, so if you will get to the point I would appreciate it."

"A few things, Carl," Claire said. "May I call you Carl?"

"You may."

"Call me Claire."

"The point?" Walker said. "Claire."

"In a few weeks, less, these idiot motorcycle clubs are going to start rolling in off the ferry causing all sorts of trouble," Claire said.

"I'm aware of the history," Walker said. "Everyone who lives in this town is aware."

"They need to be taught a lesson," Claire said.

"This isn't Dodge City, Sheriff," Walker said.

"Claire."

Walker sighed. "This isn't Dodge City, Claire."

"I know it isn't, Carl. However I need to know the town is behind me when I enforce the law."

"Enforce?"

"Yes, enforce. No more pay the fine and waltz away," Claire said. "If they get drunk, get into fights and destroy property I'm sending them down to county to go before a judge."

"I expect the law to be enforced," Walker said. "To whatever measure is legal, warranted and necessary."

"Thank you, Carl," Claire said. "The other thing is Turley, Knox and Rose all have been around for years. I'd like to give them corporal stripes and a slight raise as a show of appreciation and also as a test of leadership."

"Test?"

"One of them will earn a third stripe before my year is up and that one will make an excellent replacement for me," Claire said. "Wouldn't you agree, Carl?"

"I would, actually, Claire," Walker said. "Town employees typically receive an increase on January second. I can put through your three deputies for a three percent increase effective immediately."

"Can you go three and a half?"

"I can, but I expect results for the money."

"Thank you, Carl," Claire said as she stood up. "Oh, by the way, I met Michele Burke the other day on the beach."

Walker nodded. "Very sad what happened to that woman," he said.

"It is. Well, thank you Carl."

"You're welcome, Claire."

* * * * *

Claire was at her desk with the door open. "Rose, can you come in here for a moment?" she said.

Rose appeared a moment later.

"I need a friend in the county sheriff's office and state police," Claire said. "Who do I call?"

"How high up the food chain?" Rose asked.

"Inspector or at least a captain," Claire said.

"I'll make some calls," Rose said.

Claire glanced at her watch. "Call Short and tell him we're having a meeting at noon. He can break the deputies for lunch then."

Rose nodded and returned to her desk.

Claire thought for a moment and then stood up and went to the squad room.

"I'll be back by noon," she said. "Order three large pizzas with the works, garlic bread and drinks. I'll pick up the tab. Ask for a noon delivery."

"Sure thing, Sheriff," Turley said.

"Call me Claire."

* * * * *

Claire sat on the same bench as she sat with Michele on Saturday. It was a warm morning, around sixty degrees and sunny. A few people were walking their dogs by the water. Some gulls were squawking and fighting over scraps.

The baby was never found alive or dead.

Ransom demands never came forward.

A man wearing dress shoes and probably a dress shirt approached Michele Burk, attacked her and kidnapped her baby.

Wrong word.

You kidnap for ransom.

There were no ransom demands.

He stole the baby.

Claire stood and walked down to the beach. The gulls scattered as she passed them, then they regrouped.

A few small sailboats were gliding across the water. In the distance, a cargo ship made its way slowly out to sea.

She turned and looked back at the bench. From a distance the wall hid the bench from the parking lot and the street. But not from anybody nearby on the beach. Since no witnesses ever came forward, it was safe to assume none were present that morning.

A quick snatch and run after an even quicker beat down and you have the kid.

Question was why?

If you didn't plan on ransom, why snatch the baby?

Claire sighed openly and then returned to her car and drove back to the office.

* * * * *

At her desk, Claire looked at Turley, Rose and Knox.

"Where are the new hires?" she asked.

"Break room eating pizza," Knox said.

"Oh, flap wallet for your badge," Rose said and set the wallet on the desk.

"Thank you," Claire said. "So, here's the deal. Corporal stripes and an immediate three and a half percent raise in pay. Rose, if we don't have stripes available, order some. Questions?"

"For all of us?" Knox asked.

"Yes, Short, for all of you," Claire said. "Now, I would like to join the rookies and have some of the pizza I'm paying for."

*   *   *   *   *

Around four o'clock, Rose tapped on Claire's door and then entered the office. She held a sheet of paper in her hand.

"Got a name for you," she said and set the paper on Claire's desk.

Claire looked at the name. Captain William Cruz of the County Sheriff's Department.

"Thank you," she said.

"I'm clocking out," Rose said. "See you in the morning."

"Wait a second," Claire said. "Do you have extras of the flap wallets?"

"I do."

"Grab one for yourself and wear plain clothes tomorrow," Claire said.

Rose nodded.

"Is it too late to call this Captain Cruz?" Claire asked.

"Probably."

"I'll do it in the morning. Good night, Rose."

"Hey, thanks for the stripes and the raise," Rose said.

"You'll earn it," Claire said.

After Rose left, Claire went to the squad room where Turley was at his desk.

"Short's gone home and will be back around eight with two of the rookies for night duty," Turley said.

"First impressions?" Claire asked.

"Pederson may be the brightest of the bunch, but I don't know if she can be trusted," Turley said.

"Because?"

"You won't hold this against me, right? Because she's a woman and feels she has to prove herself to the men," Turley said. "She'll try extra hard to show the men she belongs and that can and probably will make her careless at some point."

"I can't hold against you what I agree with you on," Claire said. "I'll speak to her the first chance I get."

Turley nodded. "Mind if I ask you a personal question? When you…"

"The chip on my shoulder was the size of a two-by-four," Claire said.

*   *   *   *   *

On her way home, Claire stopped at the only pet store in town and picked up a bag of food for Snowball and a small catnip plant.

Snowball greeted Claire at the door and immediately caught the scent of the minty catnip plant and meowed loudly.

Claire broke off a few leaves and gave them to Snowball and she gobbled them up and then proceeded to lose her mind for a few minutes.

While she soaked in a hot tub, Snowball crashed on the bed.

Not two minutes after she entered the tub her cell phone rang. She checked the number and said, "Captain Dugan, it seems every time you call I'm in the tub. Why is that?"

"Lucky I guess," Dugan said.

"So what's the honor?"

"Homicides are backing up," Dugan said. "The head honcho says he will suspend your suspension if you agree to apologize to the Congressman in writing, to the department and in person to said Congressman."

"Forget it," Claire said.

"Jesus Claire, must you be such a…"

"If you say bitch, captain or no captain, I'll drive to Rhode Island and shoot you in the privates," Claire said.

"Stickler was the word I was going to use," Dugan said.

"I've known you too long to believe that," Claire said.

"Murders in Rhode Island are going unsolved, Claire," Dugan said.

"Hey you know what, there are murders going unsolved right here in Smoky Point," Claire said. "See you in three months at my hearing, captain."

"Claire, wait—" Dugan said as Claire hung up.

Chapter Thirteen

ROSE SAT ON THE SOFA in Claire's office and looked at Claire behind her desk.

Rose wore a light gray pants suit. Her badge was visible on her belt in a flap wallet.

"Somebody has to speak for the dead and the victims that can't speak for themselves," Claire said.

"You're talking about Michele Burke," Rose said.

"And Sheriff Shaw," Claire said.

"Michele Burke happened ten years ago and Shaw at least eight," Rose said.

"I'm aware of the timetable," Claire said. "There's no statute of limitations on either incident. Did anybody make coffee?"

"I did a few minutes ago," Rose said and started to stand up.

"I'll get it," Claire said.

She scooted out of the office and returned a minute later with two mugs of coffee and set them on the desk.

"Thanks," Rose said as she grabbed a mug.

"Who kidnaps a baby?" Claire asked.

"Are we talking profile?"

"For the moment."

"Somebody desperate for money," Rose said. "Should I be taking notes?"

"Yes," Claire said. "And you're correct, somebody desperate for money. Except than no ransom demands ever came forward. Why?"

"Any number of reasons."

"Such as?"

"Maybe the kidnapper made a mistake and thought Michele Burke came from money?" Rose said.

"Possible. But then what did he do with the baby?" Claire said. "Four possibilities as I see it. He dropped the baby off at the nearest hospital, but if that were the case the baby would have been reported to the county sheriff or state police. He kept the baby and that is highly unlikely. In a panic, he killed the baby. Four is he sold the baby on the black market."

"Black market?"

"You are aware that the black market exists?"

"Sure, for guns, cigarettes, alcohol and drugs, but babies?"

Claire sipped some coffee and then said, "A few years back in Idaho… I think it was Idaho, I'd have to check. Anyway, they decided that the leading brand of dishwasher detergent was harmful to the environment and they banned it. People didn't want the cheaper brands that don't work as well and that created a black market for the dish-washing detergent. If there is something people want and they can't get it legally you will have a black market for that something be it dish-washing soap or babies."

Rose scribbled notes on her pad and then looked at Claire.

"What if… what if the intent was to sell the baby on the black market all along?" Rose said.

"My very first thought when I learned there were no ransom demands," Claire said.

"So… do we look in the phone book under black markets?" Rose said.

Claire grinned, sipped some coffee and said, "Do you know what's really great about most criminals?"

"What?"

"They are stupid," Claire said. "Here's what I want you to start with. Make a list of every adoption attorney on Long Island that's been in business at least fifteen years."

"Rose, Claire, Mrs. Adams on line one," Turley called from his desk.

"I'll get it," Rose said and stood and grabbed Claire's phone. "After a few seconds, she said, "Someone will be right over," and hung up.

Rose looked at Claire. "Her son is on the roof again," she said.

"Why?"

"He didn't get the latest video game he wanted."

"What? How old is her son?"

"Thirty-nine."

"Get started on things," Claire said. "I'll take the call."

* * * * *

Claire arrived at the two-story home of Mrs. Adams and her son and parked in the driveway. The home had two front gables and a man was seated on one of them.

Claire parked and walked to the front porch where a woman around sixty-five was seated in a rocking chair. There was a second rocking chair with a small table between the two. A pitcher of lemonade and two glasses rested on the table.

"Are you Mrs. Adams? Is that your son on the roof?" Claire asked as she went up to the porch.

"I am and he is," Mrs. Adams said. "Who are you?"

Claire moved her blazer to show her badge.

"A lady sheriff, huh. Good for you."

"Why is he on the roof?" Claire asked.

"Every time he wants some new piece of junk for his computer and I don't have the money he goes out on the roof and threatens to throw himself off."

"What is he like forty?" Claire asked.

"In two months."

"Why doesn't he have a job?"

"He's a genius," Mrs. Adams said. "A helpless, hopeless genius."

"What's his name, the genius?"

"Ronny, short for Ronald. Would you like a glass of lemonade? He isn't going nowhere."

"Sure, why not?"

Mrs. Adams filled the second glass with lemonade as Claire took a seat in the rocking chair.

"How long has this been going on, Mrs. Adams?" Claire asked.

"Since my husband died some twenty years ago."

"That long, huh," Claire said.

"I get $1,500 a month from social security and another $600 in a widow's pension from my husband," Mrs. Adams said. "I don't always have the extra money for his games."

"Mrs. Adams, how do I get up on the roof?" Claire asked.

"You want to go up on the roof?"

"Yes."

"Take the stairs to the second floor and the first bedroom on the left. Open the window and step out."

"Be right back."

Claire entered the house, went to the second floor and into the bedroom on the left. She opened the window and poked her head out.

"Ronald Adams," she said.

"Who are you? Why are you in my bedroom?" Ronald asked.

"I'm Sheriff Claire Evergreen."

"You're a lady," Ronald said.

"I am," Claire said. "Now are you coming in or am I coming out?"

"What happened to the man sheriff?" Ronald asked.

"He retired. He's probably out fishing. In or out?"

"I'm going to jump," Ronald said.

"Knock yourself out," Claire said.

"What… how do you mean?"

"You're what, twelve feet high. You won't even break an ankle."

"I don't care. I'm jumping."

"Oh for…" Claire said and stepped out onto a gable.

"Hey… hey… you can't be out here," Ronald said.

"Why not? You're out here."

"I live here."

Claire looked down at the crowd of neighbors that had gathered.

"I know you have problems Ronald, but this is not the answer," Claire said. "Your mother is an old woman. You're going to give her a heart attack doing this."

"But I'm the only one in my circle without the new edition of Worlds at War."

"Too bad. Get a job and buy it yourself."

"A job. I never had a job before."

"Do you know how to clean?"

"Clean? You mean like around the house?"

"Exactly."

"Sure. I do it all the time."

"Then you have a job," Claire said. "Come down with me and we'll discuss it with your mother."

* * * * *

Claire entered the squad room with Ronald Adams.

Rose and Turley were at their desks.

"I see he didn't jump," Rose said.

"Ron, go have a seat on the sofa in my office," Claire said.

"That's where?" Ronald asked.

Claire pointed. "Right in there."

"Okay," Ronald said and opened Claire's door and stepped inside.

"And close the door," Claire said.

He closed the door.

"I noticed that we have a budget of $12,000 for cleaning expenses and never use it," Claire said.

"That's because we take turns cleaning ourselves," Turley said.

"Well, from now on Ron will do the cleaning," Claire said. "Six nights a week from six to eight in the evening. He's quite good at it and we might as well spend the money or the town will stop allocating it."

"At least he won't be on the roof anymore," Turley said. "Unless it's ours."

"Rose, can you make him some kind of official ID he can hang around his neck?" Claire asked. "I'm going to give him a tour and explain to him his duties."

*　*　*　*　*

"What have you got so far?" Claire asked.

Rose, seated on the sofa, looked at her notes.

"Six adoption attorneys on Long Island that have been around longer than ten years," Rose said. "Two that were active at that time have since retired. All have excellent ratings with the Bar Association."

"What does an adoption attorney do?" Claire asked. "Specifically. Find out."

Rose made a note on her pad.

"The two that retired, are they still alive?" Rose asked.

"I don't know," Rose said.

"When you find out what an adoption attorney does, find out if those two are still alive," Claire said.

Rose nodded and stood up and returned to her desk.

Claire picked up Rose's sheet of paper with Captain Cruz's number on it and picked up the phone.

After six or seven transfers and a long pause on hold, Cruz came on the phone. "This is Captain William Cruz," he said.

"Sheriff Claire Evergreen from Smoky Point," Claire said.

"Holt's replacement?"

"That's correct," Claire said.

"What can I do for you, Sheriff Evergreen?"

"Give me an hour of your time?" Claire said.

"When?"

"I could swing by now," Claire said. "Had lunch?"

"Actually, no."

"Let's make it a late lunch then," Claire said. "I'm starved."

"How soon can you get here?"

"Thirty, thirty-five minutes."

"See you then," Cruz said.

Claire hung up and went to the squad room.

"I'll be at the county sheriff's office," she told Rose and Turley.

*   *   *   *   *

"I have 150 deputies to guard the jail and patrol the towns without police or sheriff departments," Cruz said. "That covers a population of over one million. The state police help out where they can but they usually have just four men on patrol on a shift to cover the entire island."

They were in a family-style diner a few blocks from the county sheriff's office. Cruz stood only about five foot eight, but he was as wide as a barn door. His brown hair was short in a buzz cut. His eyes were dark, almost black.

"I know what that's like," Claire said.

"You were with the state police?"

"Rhode Island. Homicide."

"What the hell are you doing in Smoky Point?" Cruz asked.

"I was suspended for one year for tazing a drunken Congressman after a drunk stop," Claire said.

"That was you. I read about that," Cruz said. "Good for you for not backing down."

"Thank you," Claire said.

"So what can I do for you?" Cruz asked. "Specifically."

"A few things, actually," Claire said. "Are you familiar with a kidnapping that happened in Smoky Point ten years ago?

"Ten years ago I was Sheriff of Westchester County," Cruz said.

"A baby was snatched from his stroller right off the beach around seven-thirty in the morning. The mother was badly beaten," Claire said. "The County Sheriff's Department, State Police, FBI and Smoky Point all came up empty."

"I'm sorry to hear that, Sheriff Evergreen, but as you…"

"Call me Claire."

"Alright. As you know, Claire, Eighty percent of crimes go unsolved," Cruz said. "It's the nature of things I suppose."

"When did you come over?"

"Eight years ago."

"Sheriff Shaw?"

"Now that one I'm familiar with," Cruz said. "It was one of the first major crimes I handled on the Island."

"That was never solved," Claire said.

"No."

"I read all the reports," Claire said. "I don't buy road rage."

"We found his car on the shoulder of the road," Cruz said. "He had been shot at near point blank range. Two fishing rods in cases were found on the back seat. He was either getting an early start on a fishing trip or returning late from one."

"Was he armed?"

"We found a snub-nose .38 Special revolver in an ankle holster on his right ankle," Cruz said. "It hadn't been drawn."

"There was no mention of skid marks on the road in any of the reports," Claire said.

"Because there weren't any," Cruz said.

"The ballistics report said Shaw was shot with a .40 caliber bullet," Claire said.

"One of the most common rounds on the market today," Cruz said.

"Do you know what I think?" Claire said. "I think it sounds like an execution. What do you think?"

Cruz looked at Claire for a moment. "It was an execution, but that doesn't mean it also wasn't a case of road rage."

"So Shaw gets into it with another driver on a dark highway and pulls off to the shoulder and the other driver stops, gets out and shoots Shaw, a highly trained law enforcement officer in the face, and then the other driver gets back into his car and simply drives away," Claire said.

"That's the conclusion my department and the state police investigators came to based upon the evidence at the scene," Cruz said. "Shaw's background was looked into from every possible angle and the man was clean. A pro execution happens for a reason. We couldn't find even one. The shooter was probably off the Island by the time the driver who stopped called 911. It's the way it goes sometimes."

"Did you find a cooler?" Claire asked.

"A what?"

"A cooler. Know what a cooler is?"

"I know what a... is there some... say what you mean, Sheriff."

"Call me Claire."

"Claire then."

"I didn't know anything about fishing until recently," Claire said. "A man goes fishing he brings his tackle box, his rods and a cooler. Maybe two coolers. One for food and drinks and the other to keep his catch fresh. You said there wasn't a cooler in his car, so where was it? Another way of saying that is where did it go?"

Cruz stared at Claire.

"That's guesswork," he said. "There is no evidence to suggest there ever was a cooler in the car."

"That's what's bugging me," Claire said. "Think about it a while, it will start to bug you too."

Cruz shook his head and allowed his stern face to smile. "I have too much to worry about in the here and now to worry about the unsolvable then," he said.

"What's good for dessert in this place?" Claire asked.

*   *   *   *   *

"One is alive and one isn't," Rose said when Claire entered the squad room.

"Where's Turley?" Claire asked.

"Off duty. Short will be here in a bit with two of the rookies."

Claire sat on the edge of Rose's desk.

"An adoption attorney weeds through all the red tape required by social services in order to adopt a child," Rose said. "The procedure could take years. Without one, navigating the paperwork would be impossible."

"An entire career built around laws nobody can understand," Claire said. "Like a tax accountant. Make the laws complicated enough and you create a need for someone to translate them. What happened to the damn cooler?"

"The... what cooler? What are you talking about?" Rose said.

"I think Michele's baby wound up on the black market," Claire said.

"I'm having a hard time following you," Rose said.

"Go home, Rose," Claire said. "I'll watch the store until Short comes on duty. Tomorrow is another day."

"What do you want me to do tomorrow?"

"Background checks on all those lawyers."

Rose nodded. "Good night, Claire."

"Good night, Rose."

Claire went into her office and sat behind her desk.

"Something stinks and it isn't the fish," she said aloud.

A few minutes later, Knox, Pederson and Dawson came on duty.

Knox knocked on Claire's door and opened it. "We're set for tonight, Claire, if you want to take off."

"Come in and sit for a minute," Claire said.

Knox closed the door and sat on the sofa.

"What's up?" he said.

"Keep an eye on Pederson," Claire said. "She's smart. She aced the academy, but I don't want her to think she has to prove herself to the men. Understand?"

"I do," Knox said.

"Ever go fishing?"

"Sometimes with a few buddies. Why?"

"Ever not bring a cooler?"

"Most times two," Knox said. "One for the catch and one for the beer."

Claire nodded. "I think I'll go home now," she said.

Chapter Fourteen

CLAIRE PARKED IN THE GUEST parking lot of the Shady Acres hospital. Before she exited her car she used her cell phone to call the office.

Turley answered the phone.

"Smoky Point Sheriff's Department, Deputy James Turley speaking," he said.

"It's Claire."

"Hi Claire," Turley said.

"I'm at the Shady Acres hospital," Claire said. "I'm not sure how long I'll be."

"I'll see you when you get here," Turley said.

*   *   *   *   *

Doctor Morris Monroe was around sixty years old with white, thinning hair, a neatly trimmed white beard and blue eyes behind stylish glasses.

"I'm not entirely sure as to the nature of your visit, Sheriff Evergreen," he said.

"Call me Claire."

They were in Monroe's large, well-furnished office, he behind his desk, Claire in a leather chair opposite it.

"Alright, Claire," Monroe said. "Perhaps you can explain to me the interest in an event that happened ten years ago, long before you assumed your duties in Smoky Point."

"You checked up on me," Claire said.

"Just a few phone calls," Monroe said. "I always like to know my visitors."

"I'd like to speak with Michele," Claire said.

"Whatever for?"

"I'm interested in what happened to her."

"Good God, Sheriff, please tell me you're not reopening a decade-old kidnapping case," Monroe said.

"Claire. Call me Claire."

"The woman has suffered enough, Claire," Monroe said. "Wouldn't you agree?"

"I do, but I'd still like to see her for a few minutes," Claire said. "And the case was never officially closed."

"But there is nothing to gain except to cause her undue harm," Monroe said.

"There is nothing to lose either," Claire said. "And she remembers the exact date and time it happened, doctor. Otherwise she wouldn't escape on that day and return to the beach where it happened. And she had the wherewithal to purchase a beer and cigarettes, so sometimes somebody is home."

Monroe sighed. "Michele is in the garden."

* * * * *

The Shady Acres hospital was constructed in a horseshoe configuration with a one-acre garden in the center. Budding flowers lined the perimeter and a large frog pond with benches around it was a focal point.

Michele was on a bench at the pond.

Monroe led Claire to Michele.

"Hello Michele," Monroe said in a pleasant voice.

Michele looked up at Monroe.

"Hello," she said.

"Michele, this is Sheriff Evergreen," Monroe said.

Michele looked at Claire.

"Scrambled eggs," Michele said.

"Yes, scrambled eggs," Claire said. "Do you mind if I sit?"

"I don't mind."

Claire sat next to Michele.

"Would it be alright if I asked you a few questions?" Claire said.

Michele looked at Claire. "I don't mind," she said.

"Okay, good," Claire said. "The man who attacked you and took your baby, you said he wore a hooded sweatshirt."

Michele nodded.

"A button from a dress shirt was found on the bench," Claire said. "Did you see if he wore a dress shirt under the hooded sweatshirt?"

"Gold," Michele said.

"What was gold?" Claire asked.

"It was gold," Michele said. "I remember now. Sometimes I forget, but I remember now. It was gold."

"What was gold, Michele?" Claire asked.

Michele tapped her right wrist. "Gold."

"He wore a gold chain?" Claire said.

Michele tapped her right wrist. "Gold, gold."

"A watch?" Claire said. "He wore a gold watch?"

Michele nodded. "Watch."

"On his right wrist?"

Michele nodded.

"Good. Very good," Claire said. "Can you…"

"I'm very tired now," Michele said.

"Sheriff, that's enough for today," Monroe said.

"Alright, Michele, we'll talk again soon," Claire said.

*   *   *   *   *

Turley and Rose looked up from their desks when Claire entered the squad room.

"Rose pull all reports on Michele Burke and bring them into my office," Claire said.

"I thought I already did that," Rose said.

"Do it again," Claire said. "We have some reading to do."

"Okay," Rose said.

Claire went into her office and sat behind her desk. She looked at her yellow pad of notes and flipped pages.

Turley buzzed her phone.

"Sheriff Cruz on line one," he said.

She snatched up the phone.

"This is Claire," she said.

"You and your damn cooler," Cruz said.

"Thought about it, huh?"

"I must have asked fifty of my men, a dozen relatives and most of my friends," Cruz said. "Every one of them brings at least one cooler."

"So maybe Shaw had one, too?" Claire said.

"Maybe."

"Can you do me a favor?" Claire asked. "Can you pull reports on Michele Burke and see if there is any mention of the word gold or gold watch?"

"Gold watch?"

"Or just the word gold."

"What happened to the cooler thing?" Cruz said.

"I'll get back to you on that," Claire said.

Cruz sighed and said, "I'll call you back."

"Thanks."

Claire hung up as Rose entered the office with a stack of reports.

"Grab half and see if there is any mention of the word gold or gold watch," Claire said.

Rose set half the stack on the desk and sat on the sofa with the other half.

They read for thirty minutes and when Claire set her files aside, she said, "No mention of gold or gold watch."

"Same," Rose said. "Do you mind filling me in now?"

"I spoke with Michele today," Claire said. "She remembered that her attacker wore a gold watch."

"It's not in any reports," Rose said.

"I know," Claire said. She stood up and went around to the front of the desk. "Stand up a minute."

Rose stood.

"Punch me in the face," Claire said.

"What?"

"Punch me in the face."

"Why?"

"Just do it."

"Claire, I don't want to punch you in the face," Rose said. "I watched you bring down Dwayne, I'd hate to think what…"

"Make believe then," Claire said.

Rose made a fist and slowly swung at Claire, missing by about a foot.

"Happy?" Rose said.

"You're right handed," Claire said. "You made a fist with your right hand."

"I am and I did," Rose said.

"What side did you hit me on?" Claire asked.

Rose looked at Claire. "The left side of your face."

"What side was Michele struck on?"

"By all reports the right side."

"To hit someone on the right side of their face if you are facing them you'd have to use your left hand," Claire said.

Rose looked at Claire. "Correct."

"Sit. Take notes," Claire said.

Rose sat on the sofa while Claire sat on the edge of her desk.

"Our kidnapper used his left hand to strike Michele Burke," Claire said. "There were no primary bruises on the right side of her face indicating he more than likely is left-handed. He wore dress shoes and the button found on the bench came from a dress shirt, probably white. He wore a gold watch on his right wrist. What wrist do you wear your watch on?"

Rose held up her left wrist.

"Me too," Claire said. "Because we're right-handed."

"Claire, Sheriff Cruz on line one," Turley shouted from his desk.

Claire scooped up the phone.

"This is Claire," she said.

"The word gold and watch is not mentioned in any reports," Cruz said.

"Good. Thanks. I'll call you back," Claire said.

"Wait a…" Cruz said as Claire hung up.

"No gold watch or the word gold in any reports," Claire said.

"Is this how you usually work in homicide?" Rose asked.

"Pretty much," Claire said. "Was Shaw married?"

"Divorced."

"Kids?"

"Two."

"Are they still around?"

"I don't know."

"Find out."

Rose nodded and stood up and returned to the squad room.

Claire sat behind her desk, picked up the phone and called Cruz.

"I'm beginning to think you're a crazy woman," he said.

"The man who attacked Michele Burke and kidnapped her baby wore dress shoes, a gold watch on his right wrist, struck her with his left fist and wore a dress shirt under a hooded sweatshirt," Claire said. "What does that tell you?"

"It tells me you're friggin' nuts if you think you're going to solve a decade old crime based upon that," Cruz said.

"I'll call you back about the cooler," Claire said.

"Don't hang up…" Cruz said as Claire hung up.

Claire went to the squad room where Rose was searching her computer.

"Shaw's ex-wife lives in Valley Stream," Rose said. "That's about two hours west of here. First name is Heidi. Age listed as fifty-nine. Want the phone number and address?"

"Who's named Heidi and yes, write it down for me," Claire said.

Rose scribbled on her pad and ripped off the sheet of paper and gave it to Claire.

"If you need me, call me on my cell," Claire said. She started for the exit door, paused and turned around. "How do I get to Valley Stream?"

Chapter Fifteen

THE HOUSE WAS SMALL, ALMOST what Claire considered a 'starter home' for a young, newly married couple.

Valley Stream shared a border with the Borough of Queens and had a decent population of close to 40,000. From what Claire observed as she drove along side streets was that the town was upper middle-class.

The garage door was open and a green Ford was parked inside.

Claire parked in front of the garage and walked to the front door. She rang the bell, waited a full minute and rang it again.

Heidi Shaw was half in the bag when she opened the door. She was medium height with graying hair and blue eyes. Years of hard drinking had ruined her looks, but Claire could see the pretty woman that Heidi had been in youth.

"Who are you?" Heidi asked, slightly slurred.

"Claire Evergreen, sheriff of Smoky Point," Claire said and moved her blazer to show her badge.

"A woman sheriff, how progressive," Heidi said.

"I'd like a few minutes of your time," Claire said.

"Come in," Heidi said. "I'm having cocktails."

*   *   *   *   *

The backyard was small, maybe 300 square feet. A wood fence

provided privacy from neighboring houses. The lawn hadn't been mowed and the spring grass was six inches high.

Heidi and Claire sat at a small patio table.

"Wanna drink?" Heidi asked. "I'm having highballs."

"I'm on duty," Claire said.

Heidi laughed. "On duty," she said. "So whaddaya wanna talk about?"

"Your ex-husband."

"Old Pat," Heidi said. "What about him?"

"Did he like to go fishing?" Claire asked.

"Fishing? You came all this way to ask about fishing?"

"He was shot and killed on the side of the Grand Central Parkway between midnight and one in the morning near the town of Bay Shore," Claire said. "He lived near Smoky Point, so I'm asking myself if he was on his way for some early morning fishing. His rods were found in his car."

"If it walks like a duck and quacks like a duck, whaddaya you think?" Heidi said. "I'm gonna have another highball."

There was a pitcher of highballs on the table and Heidi filled her glass.

She took a sip and said, "Old Pat never missed an alimony payment, I'll give him that. He was reliable, Old Pat. Know why we got divorced?"

"No."

"I couldn't stand being married to a cop," Heidi said. "Pat could have been so much more, but he loved police work. Even after he retired from the City he had to go and be a sheriff. This place was our first home. Even after we moved we kept it and our son lived in it. Now I live here all alone."

"When he'd go fishing, did he ever bring a cooler?" Claire asked.

"A cooler?"

"Yes, a cooler. To put the fish in," Claire said.

"Most time he'd bring two," Heidi said. "One for beer and one for the fish. They all do that these fishing nut jobs."

"Before he was killed did you see or talk to him?" Claire asked.

"Maybe? Who remembers? It was more than eight years ago. Ask that broad he was banging at the time, that what's her name Mitzi something or another."

Claire nodded.

"Wanna drink?" Heidi asked.

"I have to be going now," Claire said.

*   *   *   *   *

"You have a nice office," Claire said. "Way better than mine."

"Sheriff Evergreen, are you...?" Cruz said.

"Call me Claire."

"Again with that," Cruz said. "Alright, Claire, you told my dispatcher you had something to discuss with me, so discuss."

"Don't you find it interesting that Michele Burke's attacker was a left-handed, gold watch wearing man in dress shoes wearing a hoodie on a beach?" Claire said.

Cruz sighed. "What's so interesting about it? The incident happened ten years ago. The man could be dead by now for all we know."

"Only the good die young," Claire said.

"That explains it," Cruz said.

"What?"

"Why my mother-in-law is still around."

Claire grinned.

"Okay, why is it interesting?" Cruz asked.

"I don't think the kidnapping of Michele Burke's baby was planned," Claire said. "I'm not saying our kidnapper wasn't in the market for a baby, he probably was, just not Michele's baby *per se*. I think he spotted her alone on the beach, had the sweatshirt in the car and it was a crime of impulse."

Cruz looked at Claire. "Say it was a spur of the moment decision to kidnap the baby, so what? It happened a decade ago and there isn't one shred of evidence to point to a suspect. Unless you want to do a line up with every left-handed male on the Island who may or may not have owned dress shoes, a gold watch and a hoodie ten years ago?"

"Shaw's ex-wife said he regularly went fishing and always brought a cooler, sometimes two," Claire said.

"Sheriff Evergreen, the..."

"Claire."

Cruz sighed. "Claire then. The inside of your head is like a ping pong match."

"So you'll lend the resources of your department to assist me with this?" Claire said.

"This, what?" Cruz said. "There is no this. There isn't even a that."

"I have to get back to the office," Claire said. "Thanks for your help and support."

After Claire left his office, Cruz shook his head. "What the fuck just happened?" he said aloud.

* * * * *

Claire sat on the edge of Rose's desk and said, "Shaw regularly went fishing and always brought a cooler and sometimes two."

"She told you that, the ex?" Rose asked.

Claire nodded.

"Why didn't you just call and save four hours driving?"

"I can't see a person's eyes on the phone," Claire said. "How are you doing?"

"I'm doing background checks on all of the adoption attorneys on the Island."

"And?"

"Ask me tomorrow."

"I will," Claire said. "Go home and I'll see you in the morning."

Claire entered her office and sat behind her desk, thinking for many minutes. She pulled out her cell phone, scrolled for Mitzi Maxwell's number and pressed the call button.

Mitzi answered on the third ring. "Mitzi Maxwell," she said.

"It's Claire."

"Well hello, Claire," Mitzi said. "I was thinking of giving you a call."

"I was wondering if you had a few minutes to spare?" Claire said.

"Sure. When and where?"

"How about we meet for a drink?" Claire said. "On me."

"I never turn down free booze," Mitzi said. "I'm showing a condo. How about thirty minutes at the China Pavilion on Twenty-seven East."

"Meet you there," Claire said.

Knox and two of the summer deputies were in the squad room when Claire checked out.

"Good night, Claire," Knox said.

"Good night, Short," Claire said. She paused and turned around. "Ever go fishing?"

"I went a few times with Holt on his boat," Knox said. "I'm not real big on it otherwise. Why?"

"Bring a cooler?"

"Sure. Full of ice and beer."

"Thanks."

* * * * *

"How did it go?" Claire asked.

"What?" Mitzi said.

"Your condo."

"Oh. Rented for the next fourteen weeks at two grand a week," Mitzi said. "My commission is fifteen percent. Not bad for a few hours work."

"Not bad at all," Claire said.

"So what's this about?" Mitzi asked.

"My nose for details won't leave me alone," Claire said. "It's a homicide thing."

"What details?" Mitzi said.

The waiter arrived with their drinks. Screwdrivers.

Mitzi lifted her glass. "Cheers," she said and sipped. "So what details are bugging you that you think I can help with?"

"You dated Shaw."

"I did, yes."

"Did he ever take you fishing?"

"Fishing? Let me think. Twice as I remember. No, three times," Mitzi said. "He had this beat up old boat he kept at the marina and he took me out on that. Now that I think about it, he fished and I watched. So what's bugging you?"

"When he took you fishing, did he bring a cooler?" Claire asked.

"A cooler?" Mitzi said.

"Maybe one for cold drinks and the other for the catch?"

Mitzi sipped her drink and nodded. "Yes, yes he did have coolers. One for cold drinks and the other was full of ice for the catch. I'm still not getting this though."

"Shaw was killed execution style on a deserted highway between midnight and one in the morning," Claire said. "In his car were his fishing rods, but no coolers and tackle box. I spoke with his ex-wife and she told me he always had coolers when he went fishing for his catch and drinks."

"So... wait... are you saying that whoever killed Shaw took his coolers and tackle box?" Mitzi said. "That doesn't make sense. Maybe he didn't have a cooler that night?"

"That's what I thought at first," Claire said. "But Shaw was either coming back from a late night fishing trip or getting an early start on some morning fishing and either way he..."

"Would need at least one cooler for his catch," Mitzi said. "Yes, that makes sense."

"So what's rattling around in my mind is where was he going fishing and what happened to the cooler or coolers?" Claire said.

"Oh dear," Mitzi said. "I'm afraid I have no answers for you, Claire. I doubt that anybody does."

Claire took a small sip of her drink. "I know and it's going to bug the hell out of me," she said.

"Maybe you should discuss this with another trained professional like Holt?" Mitzi suggested.

Claire took another small sip of her drink. "I think I will," she said.

Mitzi polished off her drink and set the glass down. "Well, sweetie, I have a dinner date with a warm body at eight, so..."

"Go ahead," Claire said. "I'm going to sit here and nurse my drink."

After Mitzi left, Claire sat and muddled for a minute. Then she pulled out her cell phone, scrolled and called Matt Holt.

His voice mailbox answered.

"Matt, Claire Evergreen. I have a question so call back when you have a chance," Claire said and then hung up.

*   *   *   *   *

Snowball was cradled against Claire's stomach, giving herself an evening grooming when Claire's cell phone rang.

Claire stretched her right arm over Snowball and answered the call.

"Claire, Matt Holt."

"Matt, are you tied up tomorrow morning?" Claire asked.

"Let me check my social calendar," Holt said. "Nope, not a thing."

"Can we meet for breakfast?" Claire asked. "I'd like to run a few things by you for input."

"Eight thirty at the family diner on Twenty-seven okay?"

"Yes, thank you," Claire said.

"See you then."

Claire set the phone on the nightstand and looked at Snowball. She had her left leg high in the air and was grooming her stomach fur.

"Well, that's pretty undignified," Claire said and turned off the bedside lamp.

Chapter Sixteen

CLAIRE ORDERED PANCAKES WITH A side of bacon and coffee. Holt went with the house omelet, sausage and coffee.

"So what's bugging you, kid?" Holt asked.

"What makes you say that?" Claire asked as she used her fork to slice into the pancakes.

"You wouldn't have called to run some things by me otherwise," Holt said.

"It's a couple of things that don't really matter anymore, but my homicide detective nose for details won't let them rest," Claire said.

Holt sliced into his omelet. "I've been there. Every cop has. Go ahead and fill my ear while I fill my stomach," he said.

"Ex-sheriff Pat Shaw was found shot to death execution style on the Grand Central Parkway between midnight and one in the morning," Claire said. "Two fishing rods were found in the car. Nothing was missing from his body. Wallet, credit cards, cash were intact. Even the revolver in an ankle holster wasn't disturbed. What wasn't found in the car was a cooler."

"A cooler?" Holt said.

"For drinks and for your catch," Claire said. "Like the cooler full of ice on your boat that day. Shaw didn't have a cooler. By all accounts he was a big fisherman. If he was on his way back from night fishing there should have been a cooler with his catch in it and probably a second one with food and drinks. If he was getting an early start on morning fishing, same thing. But there were no coolers. Why? I have to ask myself why an experienced fisherman like Shaw didn't have a cooler that night."

"I have no idea," Holt said. "It could be any number of reasons. Thing is, the case is eight years old and counting."

"I know that," Claire said. "What's perplexing to me is that there is no mention of a cooler in any report written by the county sheriff or state police."

"Why would there be?" Holt asked. "Why mention something in a report that didn't exist at the time the report was written?"

"It's something that a good homicide detective should have picked up on," Claire said. "Or at least sensed."

"Maybe the investigating officers don't fish, who knows?" Holt said. "What I do know is you're not going to solve an unsolved homicide with a cooler that probably never existed in the first place, especially after eight years."

Claire sighed. "I know you're right of course, but my brain won't let me leave it alone," she said.

"Tell your brain to take a vacation," Holt said. "I'm doing an engine test on Saturday. Two hours west and back, want to tag along?"

"I don't know. Maybe. I'll give you a call," Claire said.

"Okay."

"Where do you suppose he was going to or coming from?" Claire asked.

"He was traveling west, right?" Holt said. "Could be anywhere. Bay Shore maybe, into Fire Island. Great fishing there early in the morning. Who knows?"

"Yeah, who knows?" Claire said.

"You're not going to figure it out, Claire," Holt said. "It is what it is, an old unsolved case. Let it go and worry about the here and now. That's all a cop can do anyway."

"You're right, I know," Claire said. "And that's what's bugging me."

After breakfast, Holt and Claire walked to their cars.

"Call me about Saturday," Holt said. "I could use the company."

* * * * *

Turley and Rose were at their desks when Claire entered the squad room. Rose was in plain clothes, wearing a black skirt, white blouse and flat black shoes.

"Morning Claire," Turley said.

"Morning," Claire said.

Rose stood up from her desk and followed Claire into her office.

"I've been conducting background checks on these lawyers," Rose said. "A few parking tickets, one or two for speeding and that's about it. Financially they are all sound."

"Get ahold of the Bar Association and check for complaints," Claire said. "Maybe somebody isn't what they appear to be."

"Okay," Rose said.

"Rose, what do you know about Bay Shore and Fire Island?" Claire asked.

"Not much," Rose said. "They hold a bunch of fishing tournaments every year."

"See if Shaw ever competed."

"Okay," Rose said and returned to the squad room.

Claire sat behind her desk and tried to clear her head. Her phone buzzed and she picked it up.

"Sheriff Cruz on line one," Turley said.

She picked up the phone and said, "This is Claire."

"Morning, Claire," Cruz said. "Thanks to you I had a sleepless night."

"This isn't going to be perverted, is it?" Claire said.

"What? Jesus," Cruz said. "I kept thinking about that damn cooler thing. The more I thought about it the more it makes sense. Shaw should have had a cooler with him, possibly two, yet he didn't. So I did some poking around this morning."

"And?"

"Google the Fire Island Master's Fishing Tournament," Cruz said. "You can thank me later," he said and hung up.

"Thank you..." Claire said and stood up. She went to the squad room to Rose's desk.

"Google the what's its, the Fire Island Master's Tournament," Claire said.

"Sure. Why?"

"I'm not sure. But Sheriff Cruz feels I should thank him," Claire said.

Rose Googled the site and the web page brought up a dozen or more links.

"And?" Rose said.

Claire looked at the links and pointed to *Past Winners*. "Try that," she said.

Rose clicked on the link and it brought up a complete list of previous winners of the tournament by *First, Second* and *Third Place* finishes.

"Scroll," Claire said.

Rose scrolled down the list until Claire said, "Stop."

"Sheriff Patrick Shaw of Smoky Point wins Fire Island Bass Fishing Tournament," Claire read. "Keep going."

Rose scrolled through twenty years' worth of tournaments. Shaw won two, placed second three times and third twice.

"There's a link for photos," Rose said.

"Check it."

Rose scrolled through photo albums and found dozens of Shaw.

"That one," Claire said. "Can you enlarge it?"

Rose cut and pasted the photograph of Shaw and then opened and enlarged it.

"For second place finish Shaw received a ribbon, five hundred dollars and a custom-made cooler," Rose said. "Inscribed with the words *Fire Island Master's Tournament.*"

"Check the other second place finishes," Claire said.

"Another cooler and a mug," Rose said when she finished scrolling.

"Hold that thought," Claire said.

She went to her office and called Cruz.

"See it?" Cruz said when he answered the call.

"Don't be smug," Claire said. "It was my idea."

"I anticipated your next move and pulled the evidence file from the home Shaw was renting in Smoky Point at the time of his death," Cruz said. "Want me to read it to you?"

"Fax it to me," Claire said. "Wait."

Claire set the phone down and poked her head into the squad room. "Rose, do we have a fax machine?"

"We do," Rose said. "The number is…"

Claire returned to her desk.

"Fax it," she said.

"What's the number?" Cruz asked.

"Rose, what's the…?" Claire said as Rose handed her a slip of paper.

Claire read the number to Cruz.

"Call me back after you've read it," Cruz said.

Claire hung up and looked at Rose.

"I'll get it," Rose said.

Claire flopped into her chair behind the desk. After a minute she stood and went to the squad room where Turley was behind his desk.

"Where's Rose?" she asked.

"Closet," Turley said.

Claire turned and walked to the closet door next to the bathrooms and as she reached for the door, it opened.

"A bit anxious are we?" Rose said.

"How many pages?" Claire asked.

"Five."

They went to Claire's office and sat on the sofa to read. The county sheriff's department and state police had done a careful inventory of Shaw's home. Everything from his clothes to kitchen appliances to his shoes and socks, including all his trophies and ribbons won in fishing tournaments.

Highlighted was his gun safe in the basement that had to be drilled open. It contained two shotguns, one a pistol grip and one Remington 700 series hunting rifle, one .40 caliber Glock pistol and one .357 revolver and ammunition for each, including ammunition for the .32 revolver Shaw had on him when he was murdered.

In the garage were seven fishing rods, two tackle boxes, a freezer full of deer meat and fish, one machine for making homemade flies, a work bench and assorted tools.

When they reached the last page, Claire said, "Read it again."

After they read the pages a second time, Claire went to her desk and called Cruz.

"Let me guess, you figured out what's missing," Cruz said.

"No coolers in the car and none in the house," Claire said.

"It's new information," Cruz said. "I don't know what you can do with it, but it's new."

"No, it's overlooked information," Claire said.

"And eight years old," Cruz said.

"Right."

"Talk to you later," Cruz said.

Claire hung up and looked at Rose.

"For now keep this to yourself," she said.

Rose nodded.

"How are you coming with the attorneys?"

"Nearly complete."

"We'll review it when you're done," Claire said.

* * * * *

Knox tapped on Claire's door and then opened it. "Got a minute?" he asked.

"Sure," Claire said.

Knox entered, closed the door and sat on the sofa.

"The summer crew shows potential," he said. "I'd like to divide them up into day, mid and night shift."

"One on the day shift with Turley, one with you on the mid and two on the overnight," Claire said.

"About how I see it," Knox said.

"Work out a schedule with Turley," Claire said.

"Sure."

Knox stood and Claire said, "Hold up a second."

"Sure."

"I underestimated you, Short," Claire said. "I don't know if it will do any good, but if you want, I'll write a letter of reference for you to the state police."

Knox grinned. "I'd like that, Claire," he said.

* * * * *

"Mitzi, it's Claire. I hate to keep pestering you with this, but if I could ask one more time about Shaw's coolers," Claire said.

"Make it quick, I'm showing a rental," Mitzi said.

"The coolers that you did see, can you remember anything distinctive about them?"

"Distinctive like what?" Mitzi said.

"Colors, logos, wording?" Claire said.

"Oh boy, I'd have to think on that one," Mitzi said. "It was a long time ago."

"Sure, I understand," Claire said. "Call me back."

"Okay, kiddo," Mitzi said.

Claire hung up the phone, left her desk and went to the squad room.

"I'm just about done with the background checks," Rose said.

"Grab what you got and let's go," Claire said. She looked at Turley. "Jim, call on my cell phone if you need me."

*   *   *   *   *

"Again with the beach," Rose said.

They were on Michele's bench. The temperature was pushing seventy and there wasn't a cloud in the sky. A few people were sitting on blankets and a few in wet suits were riding waves and body surfing.

"You read all the reports and by all accounts Shaw was a serious fisherman," Claire said.

"He was, yes," Rose said.

"There is no way he would have thrown out two coolers won in tournaments," Claire said. "Nor gone fishing without at least one of them in his car."

"He wouldn't, no," Rose said.

"I don't think Shaw was on that road that night to go fishing," Claire said. "I think he was there to meet somebody and that somebody killed him."

"Jeez, Claire, that's quite a leap of faith," Rose said.

Claire's cell phone rang and she checked the number.

"Hi Mitzi," she said when she answered the call.

"White body with a red top and handle," Mitzi said. "Inscribed with some tournament logo I can't remember. That's the best I can do."

"Thanks, Mitzi," Claire said.

"Sure, kiddo," Mitzi said.

Claire replaced the phone into the pocket of her blazer.

"Mitzi identified one of Shaw's coolers from the tournament," she said.

"From more than eight years ago," Rose said.

"So what do you got that's interesting?" Claire asked.

"The only remotely interesting thing about any of these attorneys is that one of them spent ninety days in a rehab clinic for cocaine addiction," Rose said.

"When?"

Rose flipped pages in her notes.

"Ten years this May," Rose said.

"And he's an adoption attorney?" Claire asked.

"Was," Rose said. "It looks like three years ago he switched to divorce."

"Other than being a coke head, anything else?"

"Clean record. No arrests. It appears he checked himself in voluntary without police involvement."

Claire sighed. "Let's sit on all this and give our minds a few days to clear of things," she said.

"Which things?" Rose asked. "The cooler or the kidnapping?"

"Both."

"Why don't you head home and take the weekend off," Claire said. "We'll get a fresh start on Monday."

"You're the boss," Rose said and stood up. "Claire, you can only do what you can do, you know."

"I know."

Alone on the bench, Claire pulled out her cell phone, scrolled and hit the number for Holt.

"Matt, it's Claire," she said.

"Hey," Holt said.

"Still want some company when you test your boat?"

"I leave at ten," Holt said.

"Should I bring anything?"

"Just yourself and your hat."

"See you at ten."

Chapter Seventeen

AFTER HER MORNING WORKOUT, CLAIRE showered and then dressed in a teal colored warm-up suit with a white tank top underneath. She put the .357 revolver and switchblade knife, badge and cell phone into her purse.

In the bathroom, she took a motion sickness pill from the pack she picked up on the way home last night.

Snowball was grooming herself on the sofa when Claire left around nine in the morning. Her sunglasses and Australian hat were in the car and she put both on before starting the engine.

*   *   *   *   *

"Ahoy," Claire said as she stepped onto the gangway of Holt's boat.

Holt came up from below.

"Hey, come aboard," he said and extended his hand.

Claire took Holt's hand and stepped down onto the deck.

He looked at her jogging shoes. "I should have told you not to wear those," he said. "Poor traction. Go below and pick out a pair of deck shoes in the closet."

"Okay, be right back."

Claire went below and in the main living space there was a closet opposite the table. She opened the door and found six pairs of men's and women's deck shoes. She switched out her jogging shoes for a pair of deck shoes that fit her and left her shoes beside the table.

Before she returned topside, Claire caught a whiff of something cooking and she entered the small galley. A Crock-Pot of baked beans was on the counter. A coffee machine was brewing coffee. On the galley floor six coolers were stacked against the wall.

Claire went topside where Holt was at the helm.

"Grab the ropes," he said.

Claire pulled in both ropes while Holt started the engine. A moment later the boat pulled away from the dock.

"Fix us a couple of coffees and come up," Holt said.

Claire returned to the galley and grabbed two large mugs. She filled them with fresh coffee and then went topside and to the helm.

She handed a mug to Holt.

"Thanks. And there are plenty of motion sickness pills if you need one."

"Took one before I left home."

"Good."

"So what are you testing for?"

"Reliability mostly," Holt said. "I had the engine overhauled and I need to make sure it's reliable on a long run if I'm to take guests charter fishing."

Claire sipped from her mug.

"Hold on," Holt said.

"If it's not?"

"I call the Coast Guard for a tow."

He opened the engine and the boat lurched forward.

"So how far are we going?" Claire asked.

"We'll be traveling at about twenty-five knots for at least two hours, so that's about seventy land miles or so," Holt said.

"How much is a knot?"

"About one and a half miles an hour."

"Would you mind if I went down to the table?" Claire asked.

"Go ahead."

Claire took her mug down to the table and sat with her back to the ocean. The motion sickness pill had kicked in a while ago, but the higher speed of the boat made her uncomfortable.

She sipped from her mug and tried to clear her mind. A few moments later, Holt joined her at the table.

"Who's driving the boat?" she asked.

"Auto pilot for a few minutes," Holt said. "We're in open waters with nothing in front of us and I can see everything from here I need to see."

"Matt, I don't think Shaw was killed in a random act of road rage," Claire said.

"Jesus, Claire, don't you ever give up?" Holt said.

"He won several red and white coolers in fishing tournaments. There are photos of them. The county sheriff and state police inventoried his home and there isn't one cooler on the list and it's highly detailed. He was on his way to or from fishing and there wasn't a cooler in the car," Claire said. "Shaw kept his trophies and ribbons so where are the damn coolers?"

Holt sighed. "Maybe he was doing catch and release that night?"

"I thought of that," Claire said. "Have you ever gone night fishing without at least a Thermos of coffee, sandwiches and snacks in a cooler?"

Holt sighed again. "No I have not."

"Hell, you have six coolers below right now," Claire said.

"Jesus, Claire, whatever happened eight years ago is not going to be solved by looking for a missing cooler, if one even existed," Holt said. "What have you got for motive? Who are your suspects? Was the shooting random as is believed or was Shaw killed by somebody with a grudge against him? All of that was already looked at by trained professionals and they came up empty except for a road rage shooting."

"There were no skid marks on the road," Claire said.

"What?"

"County Sheriff Cruz was on-scene and he remembers there were no skid marks," Claire said. "Two guys fueled by testosterone get into it on the highway. Shaw's car is found on the shoulder. What did he do, roll to a gentle stop? It figures he and the other driver hit the brakes hard. Where are the skid marks?"

"God, your brain never stops, does it?" Holt said.

"Why do you think I have two failed marriages?" Claire said.

Holt sipped from his mug, shook his head and said, "Okay, I admit it looks a bit different from your angle. But—and there is a very large but here—what have you got that solves or proves anything?"

"You just said it, a different angle," Claire said.

Holt grinned. "Welcome aboard the SS Claire," he said.

"Hey, what are those over there?" Claire said and pointed.

"Dolphins," Holt said. "Come on up for a better look."

Holt led Claire to the helm where he slowed the boat to a crawl and allowed it to drift closer to the dolphins.

"What are they doing?" Claire asked.

"Feeding," Holt said. "Let's see if I can grab their attention."

Holt opened up the engine and created a large wake. Claire watched as several of them and then all of the dolphins swam beside the boat.

"They like to ride the wake," Holt said.

"I'll say," Claire said. "What kind are they?"

"Bottlenose," Holt said. "It wasn't so long ago the sound was so polluted they stopped coming here to feed."

"What do you call a group like that?" Claire asked.

"A pod," Holt said. "Let's leave them alone so they can finish feeding."

He slowed the boat and turned slightly south toward the coastline. The dolphins lost interest and swam away.

"Pick a spot you want to stop and I'll get lunch going," Holt said.

* * * * *

"Where are we?" Claire asked.

"Near Sound Beach," Holt said.

"In miles?"

"Maybe sixty east of Smoky Point."

Holt was at the grill where he was cooking burgers.

"Almost done if you could grab the beans from below," he said. "And a bottle of cold beer from a cooler. The keg is just about empty."

Claire went below and carried the Crock-Pot up to the table.

"One more flip and that's it," Holt said and turned the burgers.

A minute later, he carried burgers and toasted buns to the table.

"The secret to a great burger is the raw diced peppers mixed in," Holt said. "They roast and release juices as the burger cooks. I made you two."

"I could eat them. I missed breakfast."

"The secret to the beans is slow cooking with two ounces of bourbon," Holt said.

Claire dished out the beans. "Smells wonderful," she said.

Holt took a bite of his burger and washed it down with a sip of beer. "I've been thinking about your theory," he said.

"My theory?"

"The cooler," Holt said. "Had I been investigating on scene, I probably would have picked up on the fact there wasn't one. I don't know what if anything there is to do about it now, but there it is."

"Thank you for that," Claire said.

"So when do you think you might be reinstated?" Holt asked.

"My review is in two months, but I don't expect to return for the full year."

"That's a valuable waste of resources," Holt said.

"I won't apologize," Claire said. "Which is what it would take to satisfy the Congressman."

"Well, things being what they are, welcome to Smoky Point," Holt said.

He and Claire clinked beer bottles and sipped.

"Welcome to Smoky Point," Claire said.

*　*　*　*　*

As he guided the boat to the dock, Claire tossed the ropes over the posts on each end. They snagged and the boat jutted to a stop.

Holt turned off the engine and joined Claire on deck.

"Got everything?" he asked.

Claire held up her handbag.

Holt walked her to her car and said, "You're a hell of a cop, Claire. But you can only do what you can do."

"Seems I've heard that one before," Claire said.

"Call me if you want to bounce something off me," Holt said. "Or call me just because."

"I will."

*　*　*　*　*

Claire sat in a chair in her tiny backyard with Snowball on her lap. She sipped coffee from a mug and listened to the waves crashing on the beach.

"That's the ocean," Claire said as she scratched Snowball's ears.

Snowball purred loudly on Claire's lap.

"Maybe I should have listened to my first husband when he said I needed to enjoy the little things in life," Claire said. "Or was that my second husband? I'm not sure. They both were kind of self-righteous assholes."

Snowball rolled over and rubbed her ears against Claire's stomach.

"Well hell, I've had you longer that I had either of them," Claire said. "And neither of them ever rubbed my tummy."

After husband number two packed his bags, Claire decided the apartment was too empty so she went to the animal adoption center and looked around for a cat. She spotted a six-month-old bundle of fur and fell in love with her on the spot. She paid the fee and filled out the adoption papers with a promissory note that the kitten would have a vet checkup and shots within one week.

That was six years ago.

Claire sipped some coffee and listened to the waves.

"So let's go have a bath, a bite to eat and hit the sack," Claire said.

Claire stood, held Snowball in one hand, the mug in the other and went inside through the kitchen sliding door.

*   *   *   *   *

She was sound asleep and then, like the shutter on a camera, Claire's eyes snapped open.

"Adoption papers," she said. "Of course."

Chapter Eighteen

TURLEY AND ROSE WERE IN the squad room when Claire walked in just before nine in the morning.

"Morning, Claire," Turley said. "Two of the recruits are on duty in a cruiser. Short and another recruit will be on at six. Rose is backup."

"Thanks, Jim," Claire said as she walked to her office.

Rose was in uniform.

Claire paused and turned around.

"Jim, can you manage without Rose for a few hours?"

"Sure, Claire," Turley said. "I can always call Short at home in a pinch."

Claire looked at Rose. "Let's go."

"Where?"

*   *   *   *   *

"Who's this?" Cruz asked.

"Rose Bailey, my investigator," Claire said.

"Your investigator?" Cruz said. "How does Smoky Point afford an investigator?"

"She works cheap," Claire said.

"Is this about the coolers? I have several meetings this morning I have to…"

"No," Claire said. "I need a friendly judge."

"For coolers?"

"No," Claire said

"Then why?"

"Because Social Services isn't going to let us examine their records without a court order," Claire said.

"Would you mind telling me just what the hell you're talking about?" Cruz said.

"Don't look at me, I'm never really sure," Rose said.

"It's a really long shot, I know, but it's worth a look," Claire said. "And in order to look I need authorization from a judge."

"What in hell are you talking about?" Cruz asked.

"Either coolers or kidnappers, pick one," Rose said.

Cruz and Claire looked at Rose.

"Hey, I'm just along for the ride," Rose said.

"I'm talking about Michele Burke," Claire said.

"I was wondering," Rose said. "I thought it might but I wasn't sure."

"What about Michele Burke?" Cruz asked.

"Somebody has to speak for her," Claire said.

"So speak," Cruz said. "Why do you need a judge for that, you seem to speak just fine without one."

"Like I said, it's a long shot but worth a look," Claire said. "If I could have a look at people waiting to adopt ten to fifteen years ago and who their attorneys were it might shed some light on who may have been desperate enough to kidnap a baby if they kept getting rejected."

Cruz stared at Claire.

"She amazes, doesn't she?" Rose said.

"I have to admit, it's worth a look," Cruz said. "It probably should have been looked at ten years ago and a judge will probably think we're all crazy, but I know one I can call."

"Thanks, Bill," Claire said.

"Bill, is it?" Cruz said.

"And you can call me Claire."

"I already call you Claire," Cruz said.

"See, we're equals," Claire said.

"Find a place to wait while I make some calls," Cruz said. "Claire," he added.

*   *   *   *   *

"When did you think of that?" Rose asked.

They were in a coffee shop a few blocks from the Sheriff's Department.

Claire sipped her coffee. "Last night after I fell asleep when I was rubbing my cat's tummy."

"I'd love to see what you'd come up with if you had a dog," Rose said.

"I know this is way out there, but it should have been looked at ten years ago," Claire said. "Desperation leads a man down many a dark path, Rose."

"Is that Shakespeare?" Rose asked.

"Fortune cookie from this great Chinese restaurant in Providence."

Rose grinned and sipped from her mug.

"Cruz is a good guy and a good sheriff," Claire said. "He cares and it shows. If he would have been around ten years ago, we might not be sitting here wondering what happened to Michele Burke's baby."

"Are we off the cooler thing then?" Rose asked.

"Get used to juggling more than one thing at a time," Claire said.

Claire's cell phone rang and she snatched it from the table.

"This is Claire," she said.

"Judge Jack Pope," Cruz said. "His office is in the county courthouse.

He's in his chambers. He said he'll give you fifteen minutes."

"When?"

"Now."

"Thanks Bill."

"You're welcome," Cruz said. "Claire."

*　*　*　*　*

Judge Jack Pope was sixty years old and had snowy white, perfectly cut hair, bright blue eyes and hawk-like features. His suit jacket was slung over the back of his chair. He wore a paisley tie with a crisp white shirt.

Claire and Rose sat in leather chairs opposite his rustic wood desk. In fact, the entire office was rustic and resembled the reading room in an old library.

"Who is who?" Pope asked.

"I'm Sheriff Claire Evergreen of Smoky Point," Claire said. "This is Rose Bailey, my deputy and lead investigator."

"Sheriff Cruz told me that you are investigating a ten-year-old kidnapping case and that what you want to do has some merit," Pope said. "He said that you want to examine Social Services records going back fifteen years or more with the idea that someone waiting for a child might be desperate enough to kidnap one."

"That's correct, your honor," Claire said.

"Why wasn't this done ten years ago?" Pope asked.

"I can't speak for ten years ago, your honor," Claire said. "But someone needs to speak for the missing child and his mother and there is no statute of limitations on a kidnapping."

"This happened in Smoky Point, didn't it?" Pope said.

"It did, but that's not why I want to do this," Claire said. "I'm new to Smoky Point and if Michele Burke, the baby's mother, hadn't escaped from her hospital and wandered onto the beach looking for her baby and husband who was killed in Iraq, I probably wouldn't be aware the situation ever happened. But I spoke with her and saw the pain still in her eyes and I feel that enough wasn't done to speak for her."

Pope looked at Rose. "She's good, isn't she?" he said.

"You don't know the half of it, your honor," Rose said.

"Sheriff Evergreen, I'm…" Pope said.

"Call me Claire, your honor," Claire said.

Pope raised an eyebrow and looked at Rose.

"It's a quirk," Rose said.

"Alright, Claire," Pope said. "I'll grant your request and issue a search warrant."

"Thank you, your honor," Claire said.

"But I expect you to keep me in the loop every step of the way," Pope said.

"I will, your honor," Claire said.

"Call me Jack," Pope said.

"Really?" Claire said.

"No," Pope said.

*   *   *   *   *

"I can't believe we got a search warrant," Rose said.

They were seated on a bench in the courthouse garden.

Claire pulled out her cell phone, scrolled for the number and called Cruz.

"Bill, it's Claire," she said.

"Again with the Bill," Cruz said.

"We got it, we got a search warrant," Claire said.

"Pope is a decent judge and a good guy," Cruz said. "Do you want some manpower help?"

"I'll let you know if I do," Claire said. "And thank you."

* * * * *

"Claire, a Lieutenant Miller called for you," Turley said when Claire and Rose entered the squad room.

"Thanks," Claire said. "Rose, see if you can find out who runs the show over at Social Services."

Rose went to her desk.

Claire went to her office, closed the door and sat at her desk. She picked up her phone and called Miller.

"Lieutenant Miller," he said when he answered the call.

"It's Claire. You called?"

"I did."

"About?"

"Thought you'd like to know the Disciples are mobilizing early," Miller said. "I don't think they're going to wait for Memorial Day this year."

"Any particular reason?"

"My sources close to the club tell me it's because the weather is so nice they want to get an early start on their road trip."

"What were your sources smoking at the time?"

"It could be true," Miller said.

"Yeah, and I could be Snow White," Claire said. "If you know their departure date, call me with a head's up."

"That I can do," Miller said. "And stay away from poison apples."

Claire hung up and went to the squad room.

"Claire, I located the director over at social services," Rose said.

"Call and make an appointment for the both of us," Claire said.

She walked over to Turley.

"What time do they knock off for today?"

"Six."

Claire looked at her watch.

"Call them in," Claire said. "I think I'll take a ride-along."

*   *   *   *   *

Pederson drove the cruiser while Cole rode shotgun in the passenger seat. Claire sat behind them and looked out the window.

"Anyplace in particular you want us to go, Sheriff?" Pederson asked.

"I'm not here and call me Claire."

"Yes ma'am. I mean, Claire."

"You're on patrol, so just drive around," Claire said.

Pederson took them down Main Street and through the center of town. She turned and was headed toward the beach when Turley contacted the car on the radio.

"Dispatch to car one," Turley said.

Cole picked up the radio. "Car one to dispatch, go ahead."

"There's a disturbance on the beach," Turley said. "A woman called it in. Two men fighting."

"We got it," Cole said.

"Should I hit the wailer?" Pederson asked.

"Hit the lights, but not the wailer," Claire said.

"Right," Pederson said.

Cole hit the lights and Pederson sped the five blocks to the beach. She parked beside a van and opened her door.

Cole opened his door and he and Pederson walked to the wall. Two men in their early twenties wearing black wet suits were beating each other's brains out on the sand. Two women around the same age were screaming at them to stop.

Pederson and Cole hopped over the wall.

Cole looked back at Claire who was now at the wall.

"Are you coming?" he asked.

"It's your call," Claire said.

Claire watched as Cole and Pederson rushed to the two men fighting. They were pummeling each other as they rolled around on the sand while the two women yelled at them to stop.

"Police. Stop," Pederson shouted.

The men ignored Pederson and continued fighting.

"That's enough, break it up," Cole said.

The two men rolled around and continued punching, kicking and biting each other.

Claire came up beside Pederson. "Problem?"

"They won't stop fighting," Pederson said.

"I see that," Claire said.

"What should we do, Claire?" Pederson asked.

Claire removed her pepper spray from her belt and gave each of the men a healthy dose right in the face.

Instantly, they stopped fighting.

"There," Claire said. "When they stop vomiting on each other, cuff them and transport them to the station."

"Jeez," Cole said.

Claire looked at the two women. "Do you have a car?"

One of them nodded. "A van."

"Good. You can drive me to the station," Claire said.

* * * * *

Claire sipped coffee from her mug as she sat on the edge of Rose's desk and watched as Cole and Pederson booked the two men at Turley's desk.

The two women sat quietly in chairs at Knox's desk.

The faces of the two men looked like raw hamburger.

"I can't see shit," one of them said.

"Serves you right, asshole pervert," the other man said.

"I told you and I'll tell you again," the first man said. "You were already in the water and all I was doing was helping her into her wet suit."

"By squeezing her ass?" the second man said.

"I was squeezing the wet suit," the second man said. "Not her ass."

Claire and Rose looked at the two women.

One of them shrugged. "It's true," she said. "I couldn't get into my wet suit."

"Well her ass was inside the wet suit at the time you were squeezing it," the first man shouted.

"Both of you shut up," Turley said.

The two men looked at Turley.

"You're being charged with fighting in public, public endangerment, assault and… resisting…" Turley said.

"What public?" the first man asked. "There was no public."

"Shut up," Turley said. "And resisting arrest."

"What resisting arrest?" the second man asked.

"We told you to stop," Pederson said. "You didn't."

"Cole, Pederson, take them for prints and issue them a desk appearance ticket," Turley said.

"What's that, desk appearance ticket?" the first man asked.

"You go before a judge and he'll issue you a fine," Turley said.

"A fine? For what?" the second man said.

"For being stupid," Turley said.

"Let's go," Cole said.

After Cole and Pederson took the two men to the back room for prints, the two women stood up.

"What about us?" one of them asked.

"Those two are your boyfriends?" Claire asked.

They nodded.

"Upgrade," Claire said.

*   *   *   *   *

Rose tapped on Claire's office door, opened it and stepped inside.

"Our rookies have a lot to learn," Claire said.

"They do and they will," Rose said. "We have an appointment with social services at eleven tomorrow morning."

"Do you know where it is?" Claire asked.

"I do."

"Then you can drive," Claire said. "Right now it's quitting time."

*   *   *   *   *

Claire shaved her legs while soaking in a hot tub. Snowball watched from her spot on the closed toilet lid.

She nicked a spot by her right ankle and tiny droplets of blood rose to the surface.

Claire sighed and looked at Snowball. "One of the great things about being a woman," she said.

Snowball meowed.

"Oh, be quiet before I shave your belly," Claire said.

After she drained the tub, Claire slipped into panties and a long T-shirt and got into bed. Snowball assumed her rightful position next to Claire's stomach.

About to click off the lamp, her cell phone rang. She checked the number and answered the call.

"Matt, is something wrong?" Claire asked.

"No, why?" Holt said.

"It's after eleven. That usually means bad news."

"I'm doing some night fishing in the Sound," Holt said. "Lost track of time I guess."

"So what are you calling about?" Claire asked.

"I'm taking another run this Saturday. Thought maybe you'd like to tag along. We could go for dinner afterward."

"Are you asking me for a date?" Claire said.

Holt was silent for several seconds.

"Was the question too difficult?" Claire asked.

"No, no, it's just I didn't think of it as a date."

"Well is it or isn't it?"

"I guess it is."

"Ask me again on Friday," Claire said. "If I'm not tied up with work I'll say yes."

"Umm... okay, sure," Holt said. "I guess."

"Don't be so clumsy," Claire said. "I won't bite."

"Alright then. I'll call you Friday."

"Night," Claire said and hung up.

She turned off the lamp and settled in with Snowball.

"I don't bite, do I, girl?" Claire said and closed her eyes.

Chapter Nineteen

ABIGAIL PAIGE SAT BEHIND HER desk and waited for the Social Services attorney to finish reading the warrant.

Paige was in her early sixties and had the stern look of an Army barracks sergeant, which, at one time in her life she actually was.

Paige looked at Claire and Rose with a careful, scrutinizing eye as the lawyer read.

Finished, the lawyer folded the warrant and stuck it into his suit jacket pocket. "It's in order," he said. "But what I don't understand is why you are looking now ten years after the fact."

"Because apparently ten years ago nobody looked," Claire said. "There is no statute of limitations on kidnapping, so what the hell, why not look?"

The lawyer nodded.

"Abigail, I'll be in my office if you need me," he said.

After the lawyer left, Abigail said, "What records do you need and please be specific. I haven't got all day."

"All applications for adoptions going back fifteen years to nine years ago," Claire said. "And records of those approved and what children were adopted and those rejected and why. And if it isn't on the applications, who were their attorneys."

"Attorney information should be on all applications," Abigail said. "Good."

"It will take quite some time and only photo copies will be allowed to leave this office," Abigail said.

"How long?" Claire asked.

"Probably the rest of the day."

"I'll be back first thing in the morning," Claire said.

*   *   *   *   *

Claire bit into a medium done bacon burger and washed it down with a sip of Coke.

Rose opted for a chicken sandwich and iced tea.

They were at a family style diner near the Social Services building.

"What are the odds somebody trying to adopt that was turned down kidnapped Michele Burke's baby?" Rose asked.

"It isn't about odds," Claire said. "It isn't about hunches or guesses, gut feelings, reading tea leaves or women's intuition. It's about details and meticulous investigative work. That's what solves crimes."

"I'm learning a great deal from you, Claire," Rose said. "By the time you decide to leave I may even know what I'm doing. Sometimes."

"I'm counting on that," Claire said.

"That's not what I mean," Rose said. "I know you have a homicide job waiting for you in another eleven months, but I'm hoping you might change your mind and decide to stay."

"Rose, do you any idea how difficult it is to make homicide investigator with the state police?" Claire asked.

"No, I don't, but I can imagine," Rose said.

"It's my life's work," Claire said.

"Don't blow your stack at me, but if it truly is what you say you would apologize to that Congressman and go back to work," Rose said.

Claire looked at Rose.

"I said it's my life's work," Claire said. "I didn't say it's my life."

Rose took a bite of her sandwich. "A lot can happen in eleven months."

"One thing at a time," Claire said. "Tomorrow we look at records from Social Services."

Rose nodded. "I didn't mean to upset you."

"You didn't," Claire said. "Order dessert. Lunch is on me."

*　*　*　*　*

"Claire, there's a Captain Dugan from Rhode Island in your office," Turley said when Claire and Rose entered the squad room.

Claire went to her office, opened the door and found Dugan seated on the sofa with a mug of coffee.

"What the hell are you doing here?" Claire said.

Dugan stood up. "Nice to see you too, Claire," he said.

"Oh don't give me that," Claire said as she walked to her desk. "I'm glad to see you. I'm just surprised to see you."

"We need to talk," Dugan said.

Claire sighed. "Come on, I'll buy you a cup of coffee."

*　*　*　*　*

Dugan sipped coffee and smiled at Claire. "Nice little town," he said.

They were in a coffee shop walking distance from the station.

"Don't patronize," Claire said. "It doesn't become you. Try coming to the point of your little trip south. Did you take the ferry by the way?"

"Flew into Macarthur Airport and rented a car," Dugan said.

"You flew? If the department paid to fly you here you must have something important to say," Claire said.

"I do," Dugan said. "And it's straight from the boss."

"Leave Bruce Springsteen out of this," Claire said.

Dugan grinned and sipped some more coffee.

"Don't sit there grinning like a fool, tell me what you came to say."

"You have to sit out until your hearing in July, but, and this is a very large but, if you apologize to the Congressman at the hearing, the boss will reinstate you on the spot with a promotion to lieutenant," Dugan said.

Claire sat back in her chair and looked at Dugan. "I apologize to a drunken sexist and I go from stripes to bars," she said. "Just like that, huh?"

"No, not just like that, Claire," Dugan said. "From me to the colonel and all the way up the food chain to Providence. Even the Congressman acknowledges your value to the department."

"Then let the Congressman apologize," Claire said. "I'd be happy to accept it and we can all get back to work."

"Jesus Christ, Claire. I put my neck out for this," Dugan said.

"I didn't ask for nor do I want your neck," Claire said. "And I won't compromise my principals to satisfy the Congressman's sexist ego."

"Can't you just for once see the bigger picture?" Dugan said.

"I see it, all of it and it stinks," Claire said. "Would I have been suspended and asked to publicly apologize if I were a man?"

"I can't answer that," Dugan said.

"Can't or won't."

"Maybe it is a little of what you say, but it's politics and sometimes politics stinks," Dugan said. "And sometimes you have to play the game to get what you want. In your case, lieutenant's bars."

Claire stared at Dugan.

"Make me happy, Claire," he said. "At least think it over."

Claire nodded. "Okay, I'll give it some thought."

* * * * *

Al Lamanda

Rose tapped on Claire's office door, opened it, and stepped inside.

"Are you okay?" Rose asked. A folder was tucked under her arm.

"Close the door," Claire said.

Rose closed the door and stood in front of it.

"If I apologize to the Congressman, I can return to work with a promotion to lieutenant," Claire said.

"And you said?" Rose asked.

"It's not going to happen," Claire said.

"That's a big dog to turn down," Rose said. "That ring might not come around a second time."

"I know," Claire said. "And let's forget about it for now."

"So anyway, I was thinking about something," Rose said. "Going back to Shaw and the night he was killed."

"Sit. Tell me," Claire said.

"We know Shaw had no coolers with him in the car and no food or drinks," Rose said. "I remembered the detailed list the detectives made of his house and car and I took another look at it." She set the folder on Claire's desk and then sat in a chair.

"You found something. What?"

"Turn to the second page where I highlighted in yellow."

Claire opened the file and flipped to the second page. Rose had highlighted in yellow the contents of Shaw's car and the clothes he wore that night.

Khaki colored chino pants, dark blue polo shirt, black socks and black loafers with tassels.

"I don't know anything about fishing, but that doesn't sound like what a man would wear for a night of it," Rose said.

"No, it doesn't," Claire said.

"I'm really starting to agree with you, Claire, that Shaw wasn't going fishing that night," Rose said. "He was on that road for another reason."

"I know he was," Claire said. "And he was killed for it."

"So what do we do?" Rose asked.

"We keep looking for that reason," Claire said. "Until we find it."

* * * * *

Claire wore a silk robe over shorts and tank top as she carried a mug of coffee and her cell phone to the table in the backyard. Snowball followed her and as Claire sat, she jumped onto her lap.

She scrolled through numbers and pressed the number for Holt.

After three rings, he said, "This is Matt."

"It's Claire."

"Hi Claire."

"If your offer for Saturday is still on the table, I'd like to go."

"It is and I'm glad."

"One thing," Claire said. "I'm not so easy, in fact, damn near impossible to seduce, so if you're thinking your twig and berries might get watered forget it."

"Jeez, Claire. Twig and berries?" Holt said.

"I'm just making myself clear," Claire said. "Clear?"

"Crystal."

"Good. What time?"

"Noon okay?"

"Fine. It's going to be fairly warm if you want to bring a bathing suit and grab some sun. Do you like steak?"

"Who doesn't?"

"Good."

"Okay then."

"Goodnight, Claire."

"Matt, I can be seduced," Claire said. "You just have to know how to do it."

"Is this a quiz?"

"With a prize if you guess the right answer."

Chapter Twenty

ABIGAIL PAIGE SET A LARGE cardboard box designed for holding files on her desk "That's it, that's everything you asked for," she said.

"Thank you, Abigail," Claire said. "Your help is much appreciated and if I need additional information I will let you know."

"I trust that whatever you find will not be made public," Abigail said. "We have a reputation and public image to uphold."

"Unless someone employed at Social Services has committed a felony, I see no reason it should come up," Claire said.

"Certainly no one here has committed a felony or any other type of crime," Abigail said.

Claire picked up the box.

"I'll be going now," she said.

* * * * *

Claire carried the box into the squad room and into her office. Rose stood from her desk and followed her.

Claire set the box on her desk.

"Abigail's worried about her department's reputation," Claire said.

"Tisk, tisk," Rose said.

"We need a place where we can work together," Claire said.

"The break room is rarely used," Rose said. "Give me a few minutes to tidy it up."

Rose left the office and Claire followed her out to the squad room to Turley's desk.

"Who's on day duty?" she asked.

"Dawson and Ricard," Turley said. "Cole rides with Short tonight and Pederson has the day off."

"Where's a good place for take-out lunch?" Claire asked.

"Depends on what you're in the mood for."

"Pizza with everything, garlic rolls, soft drinks."

"Pat's Original on Twenty-seven."

"Order for the three of us for around twelve-thirty. My treat."

"You got it, Claire."

Claire returned to her office and carried the box to the break room. Rose was wiping down the table with a damp cloth. A fresh pot was brewing in the coffee machine. Claire set the box on the table and said, "Be right back."

She went back to her office for two legal pads, pens and her coffee mug.

"Grab A, I'll take B and we'll work our way through the alphabet." Claire said. "Check for people on the adoption waiting list that go back ten or more years from the time of the kidnapping and note anyone that's not on the list the following year. If they didn't adopt, put their names on a separate list."

Rose opened the box and looked inside. "This is a lot of names."

"What's the population of Long Island?"

"Seven plus million if you include Queens and Brooklyn."

"It stands to reason there would be a lot of names," Claire said. She filled her mug and then Rose's mug with coffee and took a chair at the table. "Let's go to work," she said.

"Let's," Rose said.

*   *   *   *   *

Claire and Rose were just starting the files for E and F when Turley carried two large pizza boxes and a two-liter bottle of Coke into the break room.

"I'll pay the delivery boy and be right back," Claire said.

She went to her office to dig forty dollars from her bag, paid the delivery man and returned to the break room.

Turley was placing slices onto paper plates. Rose was filling paper cups with soda.

Just as Claire bit into a slice, the phone in the squad room rang.

"I'll get it," Turley said.

He left the break room and returned a minute.

"Claire, Mitzi Maxwell on line one for you," Turley said.

Holding a slice of pizza, Claire went to her office. She picked up her phone and said, "Hi Mitzi, what's up?"

"Can you make a two o'clock meeting at the town hall this afternoon," Mitzi asked. "It's about Memorial Day weekend."

"Sure."

"Thanks, hon. See you at two."

Claire hung up and returned to the break room.

"Rose, can you continue without me for a while?" she asked. "There's a two o'clock meeting at the town hall about Memorial Day I have to attend."

"No problem," Rose said.

"Probably the same as last year and the year before," Turley said. "Walker makes a speech at a podium in front of the town hall, we stand around looking regal in full uniform, and he cuts a ceremonial ribbon and officially declares the beaches and park open."

"I don't have a uniform," Claire said.

"I can order one and have it by Monday," Turley said. "What size are you?"

Claire looked at Turley.

"I'll take care of it," Rose said.

"What did I say?" Turley asked.

"Never mind, Jim," Rose said.

"What did I say?" Turley said again.

"Phone's ringing," Rose said.

After Turley left the break room, Claire looked at Rose. "Eight. Size eight," she said.

Rose looked at her watch. "I'll keep working," she said.

"And I will be back," Claire said.

She went for her bag and stopped in the bathroom to wash the pizza grease off her hands and brush her teeth. Her hair was going to do what it wanted to do so there was little point in brushing it.

On the way out she stopped at Turley's desk.

"What did I say?" he asked.

"Nothing and keep right on not saying it," Claire said. "I'll be back after the meeting."

* * * * *

The town hall was so stuffy, the meeting so boring, it was all Claire could do to stay awake. They met at a conference table in a separate room. Besides the five members of the council, the manager of the amusement park and the head lifeguard for the beach were present.

The meeting lasted ninety minutes. Claire drank several cups of coffee with little to no affect. Walker's secretary took minutes of the meeting.

Finally it ended.

Claire caught Walker and Mitzi aside.

"Could you spare five minutes in your office, Carl?" she asked.

* * * * *

"Okay Sheriff, what's on your mind?" Walker asked from behind his desk.

"I realize Patrick Shaw has been dead eight plus years now, but something doesn't add up about his murder," Claire said.

"Sheriff Evergreen, please tell me you're not…" Walker said.

"Just hear me out, Carl," Claire said. "Shaw was a big time fisherman. He won trophies and ribbons and at one event several coolers with tournament logos on them. The night he was murdered there were no coolers in his car. What experienced fisherman doesn't bring at least one cooler for his catch and a second for food and drinks?"

Walker and Mitzi exchanged glances.

"Go on," Walker said.

"The county sheriff and state police inventoried Shaw's home and they found not one cooler," Claire said. "Shaw was dressed in chino's, a polo shirt and black loafers with tassels. Does that sound like a man on his way to go fishing to you?"

"I have to admit it does not," Walker said. "However, I don't see what you can do about it now eight years after the fact."

"Honestly, I don't know," Claire said. "But if I could make a case to the state police and county sheriff to reopen the investigation maybe they can do something about it. I feel we owe it to Shaw and Smoky Point to take a second look. He was, after all, your sheriff."

"Alright, say you could, what do you want from us?" Walker said. "I wasn't mayor then and Mitzi wasn't on the board."

"But you did live here and you must have known Shaw," Claire said. "Interacted with him at least."

"He gave me a parking ticket once," Walker said. "That's about it."

Mitzi looked at Claire. "I already told you everything I know," she said.

"We are going to get very busy in another week," Walker said. "I'm not telling you not to keep checking into this, but it isn't your priority at the moment. Our summer is short. After that you have plenty of time to make your case. Agreed?"

Claire nodded. "Agreed, Carl."

"Come on, sweetie, I'll walk with you," Mitzi said.

* * * * *

"Carl means what he said about not making it a priority," Mitzi said.

They were on the bench in the park in front of the town hall building.

"I know," Claire said. "But the man was your sheriff for eight years. I think his death deserves a second look. That's all I'm saying."

"I agree with you. Carl agrees with you," Mitzi said. "I think all Carl was saying is not to make it your priority during season. Okay?"

"I'm aware of that and I won't," Claire said.

Mitzi smiled. "Good. Well, I have several rentals to show. I'll see you later."

* * * * *

"How are you doing?" Claire asked Rose when she walked into the break room.

"Just finished K," Rose said. "Seven names that were on waiting lists for ten or more years that dropped off around the time Shaw was killed. Five because they were in their fifties and got tired of waiting and two because the women got pregnant."

"We'll check each dropout after we've finished the list," Claire said.

"I need to stand, stretch and get some air," Rose said.

"Go ahead," Claire said. "I need to make a call."

*   *   *   *   *

"Bill, it's Claire," Claire said when Cruz answered his phone.

"Hello, Claire," Cruz said. "How are you doing with Social Services?"

"Got everything we need so far," Claire said. "Bill, I think you should reach out to the state police and reopen the Shaw murder."

"I'm fine too, Claire," Cruz said. "Glad to see you haven't lost your ability to focus."

"Come on, Bill. Hear me out," Claire said.

"You have thirty seconds to make a case," Cruz said.

"By all accounts Shaw was an experienced, award-winning fisherman," Claire said. "The night he died in his car he had no coolers for his catch or food and he was dressed in chinos, a polo shirt and black, tasseled loafers. Who dresses like that to go fishing?"

Claire counted to ten and then Cruz said, "Nobody."

"Is my thirty seconds up?" Claire asked.

"Don't be a… oh, fuck," Cruz said.

"You see it, too, don't you?"

"Christ sake," Cruz said.

"So maybe you can call the state boys and run it by them?" Claire said. "Maybe put a task force together and take a second look. Maybe."

"Enough with the maybe," Cruz said. "I'll call you back later."

"Thanks, Billy," Claire said.

"Billy? What happened to…?" Cruz said as Claire hit disconnect.

Grinning, Claire returned to the break room. Rose was still outside getting air. Claire picked up the file marked L and opened it.

*   *   *   *   *

Ronald Adams opened the break room door and was startled to see Claire and Rose at the table.

"It's alright, Ron, come in," Claire said.

"I didn't know anybody was in here," Ronald said.

Claire glanced at her watch. "We didn't know it was this late, Ron," she said. "Rose and I were just about to leave."

"Thank God," Rose said.

"Rose, what's today?"

"Friday."

"Go home and don't think about any of this until Monday," Claire said.

Rose stood and stretched her back. "I'll help you carry all this to your office."

*   *   *   *   *

Claire sipped coffee from her mug and looked at the list of names she and Rose compiled from the Social Services records. They had gotten to the letter N before Ronald came in to clean.

Seventeen names so far. Seventeen couples waiting to adopt over a fifteen-year period that, for various reasons had dropped off the list at the time the Burke baby was kidnapped.

Four, according to reasons given, because the mothers gave birth to their own natural child.

Eight, according to reasons given, decided that after ten to fifteen years on various waiting lists they were too old to adopt. Three because a spouse had died. Two because they moved out of state prior to the kidnapping.

Claire closed the files and placed the legal pads in her desk drawer. She sighed and sipped from her mug.

"Let's call it good and go home," she said aloud just as her cell phone rang.

She checked the number and answered, "Hello, Bill, how are you?"

"Claire?"

"It is."

"You sound so… polite."

"Oh, I'm sorry," Claire said. "Let's try again. What do you want shorty? There, is that better?"

"Shorty?"

"I'm sure you called for a reason," Claire said.

"Can you make a ten o'clock meeting at my office on Monday to discuss Shaw's murder with a state police homicide detective?" Cruz asked.

"Will there be donuts?"

"Donuts?"

"We're cops, Bill."

"If you want donuts you'll have to bring…" Cruz said.

"I'll see you at ten on Monday," Claire said. "And thank you, Billy."

"Billy again," Cruz said and hung up.

Claire placed her phone in her bag, stood and put on her blazer and went to the squad room.

Pederson was at Turley's desk.

"How's it going, Janelle?" Claire asked.

"Fine, Claire," Pederson said. "I have dispatch for the weekend. Deputy Knox and Dawson have night shift on patrol."

"Who's on backup?"

"Cole and if needed, Ricard."

"I'll be on cell phone tomorrow," Claire said. "But if needed, call me in on Sunday."

"I will. Thanks, Claire and good night," Pederson said.

"Oh, by the way, do you know a place I can get really good donuts?" Claire asked.

Chapter Twenty-one

WEARING A TEAL WARM-UP SUIT over a white tank top, Claire stepped onto Holt's dock carrying an oversized handbag that held shorts and a towel. She wore dark sunglasses and the Australian hat Holt gave her on the first trip.

"Ahoy," she said as she took the gangway onto the deck.

Holt popped up from below.

"Bring a bathing suit?" he asked.

"Don't own one," Claire said. "Brought shorts."

"Bring your appetite?"

"Skipped breakfast after a one hour workout," Claire said. "I'm starved."

"Good. Grab the ropes and I'll bring us out and then get started on lunch."

*   *   *   *   *

Claire sat barefoot at the table. Under the shade of a large umbrella, she watched the dock fade from view as Holt took them into the Sound. It was a windless, sunny afternoon with temperatures in the low seventies.

She heard the engine noise grow louder and as the boat speed increased, Holt turned the boat slightly east. After ten minutes or so, the speed slowed and then the boat stopped. There was the noise of the anchor being lowered and then the engine went quiet.

A few moments later, Holt appeared at the table.

"I'll start up the grill," he said. "The ribs are going to take a good hour. We can work on our tan while they cook."

Holt went below and when he returned, he had changed into a bathing suit and a T-shirt. He carried a platter of ribs and set them on the grill.

"Be right back," Claire said.

She switched out the pants for shorts, but left the jacket on and returned topside.

Two chaise lounge chairs were set up in the sun.

"There's sun block number forty-five there on the table," Holt said. "Sun's not that hot, but it's cloudless and you'll burn."

Claire removed the warm-up jacket and grabbed the sun block. She rubbed her legs, arms and face and then turned to Holt. "Can you do my upper back and neck?"

"Grab a chair, I'll be right over."

Claire took a lounge chair and Holt took the sun block and rubbed it into the back of her neck, upper back and shoulders.

Holt removed his T-shirt and gave his chest, arms and legs a healthy dose of sun block and handed the tube to Claire. "Can you return the favor?"

She took the tube while Holt sat and squeezed some onto his back. He was barn door wide and felt like he was carved out of wood. And while his close-cropped hair had little gray, his chest hair was almost entirely gray. "Okay," she said when finished.

Holt reclined his chair and put on sunglasses.

Claire reclined hers and kept her hat and sunglasses on.

"Odd but I'm not seasick and I forgot to take one of those pills," Claire said.

"We boaters refer to that as getting your sea legs," Holt said.

There were a few more moments of silence.

"So let me ask you a question," Claire said. "Is this an outing between two friends or an official date between a man and a woman?"

"I'm not sure I know what the difference is," Holt said.

"An outing between friends is generally platonic," Claire said. "A date involves a lot of hand-holding, kissing, sweat, grunts and physical contact."

"I had a dog once and I used to hold his paw and he'd give me kisses and I'd hug him a lot, does that mean I dated my dog?"

"Don't be a jackass," Claire said. "Those ribs smell wonderful."

"And they need to be turned."

Holt went to the grill, turned the ribs and returned to his lounge chair.

"So where were we?" he asked.

"You were being a jackass," Claire said.

"Right," Holt said. "Truth is, I don't know."

"When you figure it out let me know," Claire said.

"You'll be the first."

Moments of silence passed and then Claire said, "Shaw wasn't going fishing the night he was murdered."

"For God's sake Claire," Holt said.

"Shaw would not have gone fishing without at least one cooler," Claire said. "None were found in the car or his house."

"Claire, I…"

"He was dressed in chinos, a polo shirt and wore black, tasseled loafers," Claire said. "Not exactly fishing attire, is it?"

Holt sat up. "No, it isn't," he said. "We went over this already."

"I don't know anything about fishing, but I'm a quick learner," Claire said. "Maybe it's possible Shaw forgot his coolers or maybe they broke and he hadn't replaced them before he was killed, but, as a fisherman, would you go fishing without your tackle box?"

"No I would not," Holt said.

"I doubt Shaw would either."

"And who have you discussed this with?"

"Cruz over at county," Claire said. "He set up a meeting with the state police homicide division."

"It means they missed it eight years ago," Holt said.

"Seems that way."

"Well shit," Holt said.

"Did I ruin the mood?" Claire said. "I'm sorry."

"I need to turn the ribs," Holt said. "And then move us a bit. We're starting to drift."

*   *   *   *   *

"These are delicious," Claire said as she bit into a rib. "What's the sauce?"

"My own," Holt said. "Molasses, honey, a pinch of salt and garlic powder and a few ounces of bourbon."

"I cook when I can, but I'm not good at it and I don't really enjoy it much," Claire said.

"My wife was a great cook," Holt said. "I learned a lot from her."

"Neither of my husbands could make toast without burning the toaster," Claire said.

"I've been thinking about Shaw," Holt said. "All of what you say not only makes sense but it's damn fine police work. The thing is there is no motive or suspect and after eight years the trail is stone cold."

"I know," Claire said. "Want to help me warm it up a bit?"

"My days of fighting crime are over, Claire," Holt said.

"I could really use an extra trained eye," Claire said.

"You have the state police and county sheriff involved," Holt said.

"They can do a hell of a lot more than I can. Let them run with it."

Claire looked across the table at Holt.

"You know I'm right, Claire," Holt said.

"Can I have another rack of ribs?" Claire said.

* * * * *

Claire watched from her lounge chair as Holt pulled back on his rod and then reeled in a large striper.

The muscles in his back, shoulders and arms went tight as he brought the fish out of the water and placed it in a large cooler.

"Claire, why don't you give it a try?" he said. "I have a rod all set up for you."

She sat up in the chair. "Alright," she said.

Claire took the chair next to Holt. There was a long rod in a white sleeve in front of the chair.

"What do I do?" she asked.

* * * * *

After an hour or so of casting and reeling in, Claire caught one tiny fish to Holt's six large ones. Of the six, he kept two in the cooler.

"I smell like fish," Claire said. "I think I'm done."

"Want to do another round of tanning?" Holt said.

"I'm afraid you'll have to do my back again."

"No problem."

She stood with her back to Holt and he squeezed lotion onto her upper back and massaged it in. His hands were strong and felt really good as they rubbed her skin.

Claire felt a sensation in… *no… no… no, you will not fall for this old blockhead and his strong hands.*

Not happening.

Not now.

Not ever.

"Your neck is a bit tight," he said as he gently massaged it.

"Too many pull-ups this morning," Claire said.

"You have a knot," Holt said and went to work on it.

His fingers pressed into the knot and after a sharp pain in her neck, the knot began to loosen and the stiffness faded.

Not happening.

Not now.

Not ever.

She felt his hands move from the knot to the base of her neck and to her shoulders. His thick fingers pressed into her shoulder muscles and massaged away the weariness.

"Good?" Holt said.

"God yes," Claire said.

"Know what I'm in the mood for?" Holt asked.

Don't answer, don't answer. It's a loaded question. "What?" Claire said.

"Some fresh coffee. Would you like a cup?"

"Yes, I would."

"Be right back."

Holt went below and Claire stood there for a moment, and then took a lounge chair to wait. She put on her hat and sunglasses and reclined and five minutes later, Holt returned with two large mugs of coffee.

Claire sat up and took a mug.

Holt sat. "So I've been thinking," he said.

Claire sipped. It was good. "About?"

"Shaw, what else?"

"And?"

"Are you up for a little blackmail?"

Claire looked at Holt. "That depends upon the ransom."

"I'll take a look at everything you have on Shaw and render an opinion and suggestions in exchange for a real dinner date," Holt said.

"A dinner date and what?"

"And dinner," Holt said. "Maybe take a drive into the City to this Italian place I know on Broadway."

"When?"

"I was thinking next Saturday. Traffic going into the…"

"When will you look at what I've got?" Claire asked.

Holt stared at her.

"Let me rephrase that," Claire said. "Can you look at what I have on Shaw's murder possibly tomorrow?"

"Where?"

"Come by the station around noon."

"I can do that."

"Good."

"I think it might be time to head back," Holt said.

"I think I agree."

*   *   *   *   *

At her car, Holt said, "I had a nice time, thank you. I'll swing by your office around noon."

"See you then," Claire said.

Claire took Twenty-seven East to town and as she passed the office, she pulled into the parking lot next to Mitzi's car.

As Claire took the steps into the office, she bumped into Mitzi on the way out.

"There you are," Mitzi said. "I stopped by the house and you weren't there, so I thought I'd see if you were working. Looks like you got some sun."

"A few hours this afternoon," Claire said. "So what's up?"

"I'm having a small dinner gathering tomorrow night," Mitzi said. "The town council and a few local business people. We do it every year before Memorial Day. It's my turn to host."

"What time?"

"Seven."

"I'll be there."

"Everybody brings one thing," Mitzi said. "You can bring more, but at least one. I'll be doing the meats, so maybe a dessert."

"Okay."

"Deputy Pederson is a lovely girl," Mitzi said. "See you tomorrow."

Mitzi walked down to the sidewalk and paused to turn around. "I left a Post-it note on your desk," she said. "About tomorrow."

Claire nodded. "Night, Mitzi."

She went into the squad room where Pederson was behind Turley's desk.

"Claire, you just missed…" Pederson said.

"She caught me on the way in," Claire said. "How's it going tonight?"

"Slow," Pederson said. "Honestly, I can't wait for Memorial Day."

"Tell you the truth, me neither," Claire said. "Be right back."

She went to her office and sat behind her desk for a minute. The stacks of files and box were as she left them on Friday. Stuck to her phone was a yellow Post-it note.

Claire, house party tomorrow night at 7. Call me later.

She tossed the note into the trash can and returned to the squad room.

"I'll stop in tomorrow to catch up on paper work," Claire said.

Pederson nodded. "Good night, Claire."

* * * * *

Before stepping into a hot bath, Claire inspected herself in the full-length mirror behind the bathroom door. Her face, neck, shoulders and arms had gotten quite a bit of color. The outline of her tank top was traced along her skin by the contrast of pale white and tanned.

She looked at Snowball on the lid of the toilet.

"What?" Claire asked. "Don't look at me like that or I'll toss you in the tub with me. All he did was rub my neck."

Snowball meowed.

Claire got into the tub.

Snowball meowed again.

"I do have a gun, little lady," Claire said. "Scold me at your own peril."

Chapter-Twenty-two

BEHIND HER DESK, CLAIRE READ the stack of folders on Patrick Shaw. Earlier, before she arrived at the station around eleven, Knox and Cole brought in an OUI and the man blew a 2.4 and was now passed out in the cage.

Knox tapped on her door, opened it and carried in two mugs of coffee.

"I'm going back on patrol in a few minutes," he said and set one mug on the desk. "I told Pederson to call me when he wakes up so I can print him and have him sent to county."

"Is he a resident?" Claire asked.

"Brooklyn of all places."

"He drove all this way drunk?"

"From what I could gather before he passed out, he got drunk here and was headed back," Knox said. "We found him asleep on the shoulder of Twenty-seven West."

"The shoulder on Twenty-seven isn't wide enough to park a car safely," Claire said.

"No, he was physically asleep on the shoulder," Knox said. "He drove off the shoulder into a ditch, got out, walked a few feet and fell asleep on the shoulder."

Claire looked at Knox.

"It's true," he said. "We had the car towed to county impound."

"Let me ask you something, of the four temps, who is being the cream?" Claire asked.

"Well, all four have a decent grasp of patrol duty," Knox said. "Pederson is the only one so far who seems to shine behind the desk on dispatch. If I was to pick one at the end of the summer to stay on full time it would be her."

"Thanks, Short," Claire said.

"Well, if you're around I'll see you later," Knox said.

"Leave the door open," Claire said.

Knox nodded and left.

Claire scanned several files and reports and looked up when Holt appeared in the open doorway.

He wore loose-fit jeans, a gray polo shirt and black walking shoes. He held a paper bag in his left hand.

"I didn't bring flowers or chocolate, but I can't resist a good coffee roll when I read investigative reports," he said.

"Pull up a chair while I grab us some fresh coffee," Claire said.

*   *   *   *   *

Claire ate a coffee roll while Holt sat on the sofa and read reports. Some reports he read twice and set those aside.

After nearly forty-five minutes, Holt closed the last file and looked at Claire.

"Do you want my opinion or suggestion first?" he asked.

"Opinion."

"You're absolutely right that they missed it eight years ago when Shaw was murdered on the highway," Holt said. "He wasn't going to or on the way back from fishing. He wasn't pushed off or skidded off the side of the road, he stopped and parked. Keys were in the ignition with the engine off. I asked myself, would I turn off the engine if I stopped to have a road rage confrontation with a stranger? No coolers, no bait, not even a late night cup of coffee. His revolver was untouched in the ankle holster and all his credit cards and money were intact. Shaw wasn't there by accident as originally believed, he was there to meet somebody in a specific place at a specific time and that somebody killed him. And in my opinion it came as a surprise to him."

Claire sipped from her mug. "Suggestions?"

"You said you were meeting with state homicide, correct?"

Claire sipped and nodded.

"Give them everything you have and let them do with it as they wish," Holt said. "You have a tiny department with an even smaller budget and no resources for this kind of investigation. The state police have the resources and manpower to reopen it if they deem it necessary. My suggestion is to convince them to do just that and then leave it alone."

Claire sipped from her mug and looked at Holt.

"Do you disagree?" he asked.

"No."

"What time should I pick you up?"

"Are we going to the City?"

"I'd like to."

"Takes a couple of hours, right?"

"Two, a bit more sometimes."

"Four o'clock okay?"

"Perfect."

Holt stood up and set the stack of reports on the desk.

"Thank you," Claire said.

"Welcome. See you at four," Holt said. "Anything changes give me a call."

He paused in the doorway. "You know, Claire, sometimes the obvious is so obvious it's invisible," Holt said.

Claire nodded.

After Holt left, Claire packed away all the reports and went to the squad room.

"Leaving, Claire?" Pederson asked.

"I have to go home and bake cookies," Claire said.

*   *   *   *   *

Claire baked three dozen chocolate chip cookies, two dozen oatmeal raisin and a platter of brownies. She wore a charcoal gray pants suit with three-inch heels that bumped her up to about six foot one.

Makeup was minimal, just a bit around the eyes and cheeks.

Mitzi had a twelve-room home on the ocean about a mile west of the home Claire rented. It was a lavish home full of fine furnishings and artwork. Mitzi owned a tiny white dog that, immediately upon spotting Claire, began to hump her leg.

Claire shooed the dog away, but he returned again and again. No matter whom she talked to or where she went in the house, the tiny dog found her and tried to hump her leg.

Enough.

Claire found Mitzi talking to Carl Walker on the deck.

"Mitzi, your dog won't stop humping my leg," Claire said.

Mitzi laughed. "I'll go lock him in his crate," she said.

Alone with Walker, Claire said, "I owe you the disclosure, Carl. I'm talking to state homicide about my findings about Shaw and turning it over to them."

"They have the resources to deal with it," Walker said. "Let them."

"About how I see it," Claire said.

Mitzi returned to the balcony. "Carl, it's time for your announcement."

Claire followed Walker to the living room where the thirty or so guests had gathered in a circle.

Walker's first announcement was about the ribbon cutting ceremony that was scheduled for ten in the morning on Memorial Day. His second announcement concerned the Memorial Day fireworks show that usually took place at nine-fifteen in the evening.

"Thanks in part to a less harsh winter this year, we have extra money in the general fund and I have allocated enough to extend the fireworks display to a full thirty minutes this year," Walker said.

Claire ate a chocolate chip cookie while she listened to Walker speak.

"And for those who haven't met our new sheriff, I would like to introduce Sheriff Claire Evergreen," Walker said.

Said just as she was brushing cookie crumbs off her shirt.

A bit later, Claire said her goodnights and walked to her car.

Walker followed her.

"Claire," he said as she reached her car.

"Yes, Carl."

"I'm not unsympathetic to what you're trying to do for Patrick Shaw," he said. "In fact, I have high regard and respect for what you've been able to determine after eight years."

"Thank you, Carl."

"Good night," Walker said. "Claire," he added.

*　　*　　*　　*　　*

Claire soaked in a hot tub and placed a washcloth over her eyes as she rested her head against the rim.

Sometimes the obvious is so obvious it's invisible.

Claire removed the washcloth.

"And sometimes it isn't," she said.

Chapter Twenty-three

CLAIRE CARRIED A LARGE BOX into Cruz's office and set it on his desk. He was alone and looked at the box.

"Is that…?" he said.

"One dozen still warm assorted donuts from The Donut Hut," Claire said. "I'm told they are the best on the Island."

"We really should wait for Lieutenant Kellerman," Cruz said. "He'll be here in a few minutes."

"Where can I get us some fresh coffee?" Claire asked as she set her briefcase on a chair.

There was a light knock on the door, it opened and Lieutenant Michael Kellerman walked in. He was around forty-five, Black, around six foot four inches tall and whippet thin. He wore a dark blue suit with a paisley tie and had round eyeglasses. His hair was speckled with gray.

"I smell donuts," he said.

"From The Donut Hut," Cruz said. "Sheriff Evergreen brought them. I'll get us some coffee."

After Cruz left his office, Kellerman looked at Claire. "I'm homicide investigator Lieutenant Kellerman. Cruz tells me you're a hell of an investigator Sheriff Evergreen."

"Call me Claire," she said.

Kellerman nodded.

Cruz returned with a tray holding a coffee pot, three mugs and cream.

Let's move everything to the conference table," he said.

* * * * *

After about an hour, Kellerman finished reading Claire's reports and the notes Cruz made specific to the topic of Shaw's murder and he closed the last file. Of the dozen donuts, six were left and he reached inside the box for a double chocolate.

"My gut isn't going to like me very much later on today," he said as he took a bite.

Cruz helped himself to another donut, a Boston cream. "What does your gut say about Claire's theory?" he asked.

"Eight years ago I was a junior grade investigator in Westchester County," Kellerman said. "Even then I would have had my suspicions as to why more wasn't done on this case. After the fact, it's obvious Patrick Shaw wasn't murdered in a road-rage incident as first believed. However, at that time, with no witnesses or motive I can certainly understand why it was labeled as such and they moved on. It's easier to focus energy on cases that can be solved rather than on those that can't."

"Are you saying Shaw's murder goes by the wayside?" Claire asked.

"I didn't say that Sheriff Evergreen," Kellerman said.

"Claire."

"Claire," Kellerman said. "I said I understand why it was shelved."

"Are you interested in dusting it off, removing it from the shelf and having a go?" Claire asked. "If not I'm afraid I'm going to have to charge you three bucks apiece for the donuts."

Kellerman and Cruz stared at Claire.

"It occurred to me that sometimes the obvious is so obvious that it's missed," Claire said. "I think that's what happened with the coolers and Shaw's clothing. Blink twice if you disagree."

"She's…" Kellerman said as he looked at Cruz.

"Yes, she is," Cruz said. "She's also done more with an eight year old case working alone on no budget than the state and county combined."

"Thank you for that, Billy," Claire said.

Kellerman looked at Cruz. "Billy?"

"We're pals," Cruz shrugged.

"So how about it, Mike, are you having any?" Claire said.

"Mike?" Kellerman said.

"Just go with it," Cruz said.

"I suppose it wouldn't hurt to take a second look considering the new developments brought to light by Sheriff… by Claire," Kellerman said.

"Thank you," Claire said.

"Fair warning though. Don't expect a miracle," Kellerman said.

"I don't," Claire said. "Miracles are for church. Anybody want another donut?"

"I'll settle for copies of all your reports," Kellerman said.

*   *   *   *   *

At her car, Cruz said, "He's a good man and a first rate investigator. If anybody can get results it's Kellerman."

"Thank you, Sheriff Cruz," Claire said.

"What happened to Billy?" Cruz said.

"I thought I'd toss you a bone," Claire said.

"What about your kidnapping?" Cruz asked.

"Running down the lists to see where that leads," Claire said.

"If I can help, call."

"Thanks," Claire said as she opened her car door. "Billy," she added.

*   *   *   *   *

Turley was at his desk when Claire entered the squad room.

"Cole and Pederson are on patrol and Rose is working on something in the break room," he said. "Short and Dawson cover the night shift. Oh, your uniform is in your office."

"Thank you," Claire said.

She went to the break room where Rose, in civilian clothing, was up to her eyeballs in paperwork.

"I picked up your uniform this morning," Rose said.

"Short told me," Claire said. "I'm going to try it on and then I'll be right with you."

Claire went to her office where the uniform was hanging on a hanger on a coat hook and carried it to the bathroom. She changed and returned to the break room.

"How does it look?" Claire asked.

"Spin."

Claire spun once.

"It's too tight in the boobs," Rose said. "I'll exchange it."

"I don't have enough boobs to worry about it being too anything," Claire said.

"Go ask Jim," Rose said.

Claire went to the squad room.

"What do you think?" she asked Knox.

"Jeez, Claire," Turley said.

"What? Never mind. Forget it," Claire said.

She returned to the bathroom and changed, took the uniform to her office, grabbed her coffee mug and went back to the break room.

"Exchange it," Claire said. "So where are we?"

"P."

"Give me Q," Claire said.

*   *   *   *   *

"It's one-thirty," Claire said to Rose. "Let's grab some lunch. I'll treat."

They walked to the Family Style Diner a few blocks from the office and ordered BLTs with fries and iced tea.

"How many names do we have so far?" Claire asked.

"Thirty-one."

"Let's go all the way to Z," Claire said. "And then you take tomorrow off."

"What will I do with that extra time?" Rose said.

*   *   *   *   *

"That's it, that's the last name," Rose said.

"What's the total?" Claire asked.

"Forty-nine."

Claire glanced at the clock on the wall. "It's nine thirty-seven, go home Rose."

Rose stood and stretched. "My back is killing me."

"Go home and soak in a hot tub," Claire said.

"I think I'll do just that."

"And Rose, thank you."

"I'll grab the uniform shirt on the way out," Rose said.

After Rose left, Claire made a pot of fresh coffee and while it brewed she went to the squad room. Cole was on dispatch at Turley's desk.

"Alex, how's it going?" Claire asked.

"Slow and steady," Cole said. "Deputy Knox and Dawson are on patrol. They called in a little while ago for dinner break. Oh, and the kid who cleans said to tell you he didn't want to bother you in the break room, that he'll get it tomorrow."

Claire nodded. "I just put on some coffee," she said.

"I could use some."

Cole followed Claire to the break room where he filled a mug. "Can I give you a hand with any of this?" he asked.

"No, but thanks."

"I'll be at the desk."

Claire filled her mug and took a chair. She scanned her legal pad of notes.

"Forty-nine names," she said aloud. "Ninety-eight people. Let's see what we got."

*　*　*　*　*

Knox walked into the break room and said, "Claire, it's after one in the morning, what are you still doing here?"

"Spinning my wheels, Short," Claire said. "Looking for answers in all the wrong places."

"Need help?"

"I need sleep. Grab some of this and help me carry it to my office."

*　*　*　*　*

Claire had many sleepless nights when working a homicide and things didn't click. It usually came down to Holt's point of the obvious being too obvious to see that cost her sleep.

Forty-nine names, ninety-eight people that waited years and in some cases a decade and a half for an adoption and then dropped off the waiting list.

Why?

Age was a factor. If you were thirty-five when you applied for an adoption and still waiting fifteen years later, would you still want a child at age fifty?

Health. If your health took a serious turn for the worse while waiting for an adoption, you might think twice.

Finances. A lost job, a tanked 401, bad investments, all good reasons to remove yourself from the list.

Relocation. If you moved away due to a job transfer or personal reasons, why stay on the list?

Death. The loss of a spouse would be a game changer.

Pregnancy. You make a kid of your own and there is no need to adopt one.

Divorce. Why adopt a child when you're going separate ways?

Miscellaneous. Yeah, that's the one.

Like going fishing at night wearing tasseled loafers without bait and a cooler.

Miscellaneous.

Claire rolled over in bed and Snowball moved to accommodate the turn. Claire hugged the cat and as Snowball purred, Claire slowly closed her eyes.

Chapter Twenty-four

AT HER DESK, CLAIRE WEEDED through the mountain of paperwork and started to whittle it down into separate piles.

Four deaths.

Seven relocations.

Nine for health reasons.

Six for financial reasons.

Another six due to advancing age.

Four had a child of their own.

Thirteen miscellaneous.

Claire went to the break room for a mug of coffee and when she returned to her office, Rose was entering the squad room.

"I thought you were taking today off," Claire said.

"I got bored," Rose said. "I figured you might need some help."

At his desk, Turley said, "Claire, Lieutenant Miller on line one."

"I'll get it in the office," Claire said.

She returned to her desk with Rose behind her and picked up the phone.

"This is Claire," she said.

"Lieutenant Miller here. I got a heads up for you, Claire," Miller said. "Memorial Day Weekend kicks off this Friday and so do the Disciples."

"Headed my way?"

"My sources tell me one dozen of the biker bad boys will be on the noon ferry," Miller said. "I don't have names, but the number seems reliable."

"Let the pilgrimage begin," Claire said.

"Hey, who knows, maybe they will show some common sense this year and head west off the ferry," Miller said.

"I wouldn't count on it," Claire said.

"Neither would I," Miller said.

"Thanks," Claire said.

"Welcome."

Claire hung up and looked at Rose.

"The biker assholes?" Rose said.

"Will be here early Friday evening," Claire said.

"Lovely," Rose said. She looked at the stacks of files on the desk. "So, what do we got?"

*　　*　　*　　*　　*

"Jesus, Claire, have I got a headache," Rose said.

"I know the feeling," Claire said.

"Where do we go from here?"

"The tedious task of checking each name that dropped off the waiting list right before or just after Shaw was murdered."

"Even the couples that had babies of their own?"

"All of them."

"That could take weeks."

"Michele Burke has waited ten years for answers. What's another few weeks?"

Rose nodded. "Who do you want to start with?"

"Take the dead and health reasons lists," Claire said. "And note their attorneys."

Rose grabbed the stacks and went to her desk.

Claire picked up her phone and dialed Holt's cell phone. He answered on the third ring.

"Claire?" Holt said. "Hold on, let me kill the engine."

Claire heard the engine go silent and then Holt said, "I'm getting a little practice in. So what's up?"

"Can I get a rain check on Saturday?" Claire said. "The disciples are coming down on Friday and I don't think I should be away until they leave."

"Those idiots never learn," Holt said.

"So you understand then?"

"I do."

"Make it the weekend after."

"Sure. The Saturday after."

"Thanks, Matt."

"Watch yourself," Holt said. "They may be idiots but that doesn't mean they aren't dangerous."

"Consider me watched."

* * * * *

"Do you really think anybody on all these lists had anything to do with Michele Burke's baby being kidnapped?" Rose asked.

She and Claire were in the break room, eating Chinese takeout from a restaurant up the street.

Claire was working on a carton of noodles and paused to look at Rose. "No, I don't and before you blow your stack at me the time we are spending to check every detail we can think of is owed to Michele Burke and her son."

"I know," Rose said. "Thing is, if we fail to produce anything what then?"

"We don't quit until we've exhausted every possible explanation and even then we don't quit," Claire said. "There is no other way to solve unsolvable crimes."

"This could take years," Rose said.

"That's what not quitting means."

"You don't have years," Rose said. "Not here anyway. Remember?"

"Rose, it's not that I…" Claire said.

"It's alright, Claire," Rose said. "You have your entire career to think about."

"What's left of it," Claire said. "Want an egg roll?"

* * * * *

At her desk, Claire read through the names of couples that removed themselves from waiting lists because the mother got pregnant and had a baby of their own.

Four couples.

One of them had twin girls.

One had a girl.

Two had boys.

Claire read the names and the names of their lawyers. Her ears started to buzz as she scanned names and stopped at the name John Donald Alford, attorney for Ben and Melissa Harper.

"Rose, John Donald Alford rings a bell," Claire said loudly to Rose. "Why?"

"Let me check my notes," Rose said from her desk.

Claire read the bio information on Ben and Melissa Harper. At the time of the kidnapping, Ben was thirty-eight years old, Melissa a year younger. They were married eleven years and childless. They were on the waiting list for nine years. Their criteria were very specific. A young, male child of either Irish or English descent. No minority children as they planned not to tell the child he was adopted.

Rose appeared in the doorway with her notepad.

"John Donald Alford is the attorney who checked into rehab for cocaine addiction," she said.

Claire looked at Rose.

"I think he switched to divorces," Rose said.

Claire looked at the list on her desk. Her vision narrowed so that all she saw was the name Alford. Her hearing blocked all noise. Slowly, she looked up at Rose.

"Find out everything you can about John Donald Alford," Claire said.

"Sure," Rose said. "Why?"

"He's our man," Claire said.

*   *   *   *   *

Claire sipped coffee from a to-go cup and watched the tide roll in from Michele Burke's bench.

Rose sat next to her with her legal pad.

"John Donald Alford is forty-seven years old and currently a practicing divorce attorney to the rich and famous in the Hamptons," Rose said. "Graduated NYU with a degree in law. From Queens. After he passed the bar exam he took a job with a small firm in Forest Hills that specialized in adoption. After three years he moved to Long Island and hung out his own shingle. Ten years ago he checked into the Wellness Center for treatment of Alcohol and Drugs. After ninety days he checked out and resumed practicing law in divorce."

"Find out how much it cost to go through rehab at this place," Claire said.

Rose jotted a note on her pad.

"Find out where he lives, how he lives, anything about his finances, friends, women, what kind of car he drives and anything else you can think of," Claire said.

"We have NCIS, Claire, not the FBI data bank," Rose said.

"Try the teletype communications data bank," Claire said.

"Who uses teletype anymore?" Rose said. "I never even heard of it."

"I think it's called Tele-communications now," Claire said. "It's old school. Most don't know it even exists."

Rose made a note.

"Go home, grab a hot bath and I'll see you in the morning," Claire said. "Don't think about anything until the morning."

"We took my car to the beach," Rose said.

"I'll walk back," Claire said. "I could use the air to clear my head."

"Do you really think this Alford character had something to do with the Burke kidnapping?"

"I don't think," Claire said. "It's simply a matter of following the evidence. The evidence does the thinking for you."

Rose nodded and stood up. "Good night, Claire," she said.

"Night, Rose."

After Rose left, Claire watched the sun touch the horizon and glow a bright orange.

She removed her cell phone and called Holt.

"Matt, it's Claire," she said when he answered the phone.

"Hey, Claire. I'm on my boat watching the sun set," Holt said.

"I'm watching it too," Claire said. "At the beach."

"So what's up I can help you with?"

"Do you know anybody locally at the FBI?"

"FBI? Not anymore. I can make some calls for you if you'd like."

"That's alright," Claire said. "I'll manage."

"I don't think the FBI would be all that interested in coolers and loafers, Claire," Holt said.

"It's not about that," Claire said. "This is about the Burke kidnapping."

Holt sighed. "You need a social life, Claire," he said.

"This has nothing to…"

"And so do I," Holt said. "I've been thinking, and at the risk of scaring you away, I really want to see you again and before next weekend."

"Matt, I…"

"Dinner tomorrow night," Holt said. "You'll be tied up all weekend, I get that, but you can spare a few hours tomorrow night. You have to eat anyway so you might as well have some company."

"Seven thirty," Claire said. "Pick me up at home."

"Dress casual and bring your appetite," Holt said. "And I'll make some calls about the FBI in the morning."

"Thanks," Claire said.

She hung up and watched the sun touch the horizon and cast a glowing orange tint in the water.

Once the sun was down and the sky was gray, Claire stood up and walked back to the station.

Pederson had the desk. Short and Cole were talking to her as they drank cups of coffee.

"Hey, Claire," Knox said. "We were just discussing assignments for the Memorial Day Weekend."

"And what did you come up with?" Claire asked.

"Rotate the rookies on the day shift, me and one of them on nights, Jim at the desk and Rose as a backup if needed," Knox said.

"Exactly what I would do," Claire said.

Pleased, Knox grinned.

Claire went to her office and closed the door.

She sat behind her desk and thought about what was nagging at her and she couldn't place a finger on it.

John Donald Alford?

In reality he was guilty of nothing except cocaine addiction and even then he checked himself into a rehab clinic of his own free will without police involvement so that's points for him.

So maybe it was nothing more than coincidence that he represented the Harper's who waited on adoption lists for a decade and then suddenly dropped off when Melissa Harper gave birth to a son.

A decade of waiting to adopt a baby and miraculously you give birth to your own.

At the same time your attorney checks into rehab.

A white baby that could pass for Irish or English so they could raise the child as their own without telling him he was adopted.

Michele Burke was as white Irish as they come.

All of it circumstantial and none of it passed the smell test.

But there was something else. Something that was festering, that would grow and take root in the back of her mind and not leave her alone.

She could feel it coming.

Whatever it was.

Knox tapped on her open door.

"Claire, we're headed out," he said.

"You know what, Short, me too," Claire said.

* * * * *

From her perch on Claire's stomach, Snowball pushed Claire's hand to scratch her ears.

"He's going to want to have sex," Claire said.

Snowball turned her ears to allow Claire to scratch them.

"Because that's how men are I'm afraid," Claire said. "Sex, food and football and after that it's pretty much nothing. Well, maybe fishing."

Snowball pressed her left ear into Claire's fingers.

"All that sweating and grunting and then stupid pillow talk," Claire said. "A pulled hamstring. Who has time for that?"

Snowball rolled over and Claire scratched under her chin and Snowball meowed.

"Easy for you to say, you don't have to shave your legs," Claire said.

Chapter Twenty-five

AFTER HER MORNING WORKOUT, CLAIRE was so lost in thought she ran an extra twenty minutes without realizing it. Only when she started to notice unfamiliar surroundings did she look at her watch.

The preoccupation continued and when she was halfway to the office, Claire had to turn around when she remembered she forgot to fill Snowball's food and water bowls. While she was filling the food bowl, she noticed she had on one blue shoe and one black. She switched out the blue and left for work a second time.

When Claire finally arrived at the office, Turley was at his desk in the squad room and Rose was on the phone.

Claire filled a mug with coffee, went to her office, removed her jacket and sat at her desk.

She picked up the phone and punched in a number.

When Cruz came on the line, Claire said, "I need a contact with the local FBI, who do you know?"

"I'm good, thanks for asking," Cruz said.

Claire sighed. "I don't have time for… yes, you're right of course. How are you, Bill?"

"I'm fine, Claire, how are you?"

The difference between being a state cop and a small-town sheriff, Claire was learning, was as a state cop you demanded and as a small-town sheriff you begged.

"I'm good, Bill, thank you."

"So what can I do for you?" Cruz said.

"You said if I needed you I could call."

"I did say that, yes," Cruz said. "Seems like only yesterday."

"I need a contact with the local FBI," Claire said.

"The kidnapping?"

"Yes."

"Let me give Kellerman a call," Cruz said. "I don't interact with them much."

"Thanks, Bill," Claire said.

After she hung up, Claire grabbed her mug and went out to the squad room.

"$25,000, that's what it cost to go to rehab at the Wellness Center if you don't have insurance coverage willing to foot the bill," Rose said.

"And did he?" Claire asked.

"Have insurance?" Rose said. "Probably through his firm, but who knows if they covered it."

"Keep on it," Claire said. She touched up her mug and returned to her desk.

She signed on to her laptop and started a search of the Harpers. Apparently they fell off the earth ten years ago. Arrest records were clean on both. A birth certificate was registered to a baby boy born at Long Island General dated a few months before the Burke kidnapping.

Ben Harper's real name is Sebastian and that's what they named the boy.

Sebastian Jr.

She backed out and did a full-scale people search on Sebastian Harper Sr.

It brought up more than 200.

"Who names their kid Sebastian?" Claire said aloud.

Her phone buzzed and she picked it up.

"A Lieutenant Kellerman on line one," Turley said.

Claire picked up her phone. "Lieutenant Kellerman, you got my distress call from Sheriff Cruz," she said.

"Only a few minutes ago, Sheriff Evergreen," Kellerman said.

"Claire. Call me Claire."

"Claire then and yes, he called me," Kellerman said. "He said you want a contact at the FBI. Shaw's murder doesn't qualify for…"

"This isn't about Shaw, Mike," Claire said. "I'm looking into an old kidnapping that happened here in Smoky Point ten years ago."

"Ten years… what are you talking about? What kidnapping?"

"Look, I know it sounds crazy, but the FBI never closes the file on an unsolved kidnapping and I have a potential lead that could mean something important," Claire said.

"I have worked with a few agents locally," Kellerman said. "I'll make a few calls on your behalf."

"Thanks, Mike," Claire said. "About Shaw?"

"I one hundred percent agree with you that Shaw was murdered for reasons that had nothing to do with a chance encounter of road rage," Kellerman said. "However, unless some new evidence or clue comes to light to point to a motive or suspect, there's not a whole hell of a lot I can do about it."

"But you'll keep it active?"

"I will."

"Thanks Mike."

"You're welcome… Claire."

Claire hung up just as Rose walked in with her notepad.

"Alford was married for five years prior to his rehab stint," she said. "It appears according to dates that his wife filed for divorce when he was in his second month at the clinic. She remarried five years ago. Alford is still single. I can't quite get a handle on his finances, but his practice is just a few blocks from his home in the Hamptons. "

"So he's making money," Claire said.

"If you go by his address, yes."

"Hang with it for a while longer," Claire said.

The phone buzzed and Claire scooped it up.

"Claire, the FBI is on line one," Turley said.

"Thank you," Claire said and hit the button for line one.

"This is Sheriff Claire Evergreen," Claire said.

"Special Agent Wang with the FBI. Lieutenant Kellerman with the state police asked me to give you a call. He said you might possibly have some new information on an old kidnapping case. Is that correct?"

"Yes. Do you know where Smoky Point is?"

"Sure. I take my kids there quite often in the summer."

"Can you meet me on the beach and I'll give you everything I have," Claire said.

"Have on whom?"

"Most people would say that incorrectly and use the word who instead of whom," Claire said.

"What? Sheriff Evergreen, what are you talking about?"

"A ten year old kidnapping," Claire said. "What are you talking about?"

"Apparently the same thing although I'm not quite sure now."

"Meet me on the beach," Claire said. "I'll fill you in and give you what I have then."

"Kellerman said you were damn good but a bit eccentric," Wang said.

"Well, no more donuts for him," Claire said. "I'm in plain clothes and I'll be on a bench."

"How will I know you?" Wang asked.

"I'll be the only stunningly gorgeous brunette sitting alone on a bench with a briefcase," Claire said.

"Sheriff Evergreen, my time is valuable," Wang said.

"I'll buy you a coffee as compensation," Claire said. "And call me Claire."

"One hour," Wang said.

Claire hung up, gathered all material and stuffed it into her briefcase and went to the squad room.

"Rose, make extra copies of everything you have on the Burke kidnapping," Claire said. "I'm meeting with the FBI in one hour."

* * * * *

Wearing her sunglass and Australian sun hat, Claire waited on Michele's bench. Behind her she heard a car arrive in the lot and shut down. A door opened and a few moments later Special Agent Wang appeared on the sand.

He was around five-foot-eight or nine, dressed in a sloppy suit with brown shoes. His hair was shaggy and an unlit cigar was pressed between his lips. He reminded Claire of Lieutenant Colombo from the old TV show.

Wang paused in front of Claire and flashed his ID.

"Sheriff Evergreen?" he asked.

"Call me Claire and I brought you a coffee," Claire said and opened the paper bag beside her on the bench.

Wang sat next to Claire.

"Have a first name, Special Agent Wang?" Claire asked.

"Arthur, but most call me Artie."

Claire handed Wang a coffee. "Here you go, Artie," she said.

"Thanks. So what information about what kidnapping case are we talking about Sheriff Evergreen?" Wang asked.

"Claire," she said.

"Claire then."

"How long have you been on the Island?" Claire asked.

"Going on seven years. You?"

"This is my fifth week," Claire said.

"Five whole weeks, huh?" Wang said.

"And fourteen years with the Rhode Island State Police, six in homicide," Claire said. "What do you want to do next, arm wrestle?"

"Something tells me that wouldn't be a good idea," Wang said. "So what do you got you want to show me?"

"Read the initial FBI and state police reports," Claire said as she opened her briefcase.

*   *   *   *   *

Wang closed the last file, sipped some coffee and looked at Claire.

"Initial reaction?" Claire said.

"A great deal was missed in the beginning stages that made it impossible to locate a suspect especially given that ransom demands were never forthcoming," Wang said. "Dress shoes and a button from a dress shirt indicates the kidnapper was probably a professional man and the kidnapping a spur of the moment impulse crime."

"Colombo couldn't have said it better," Claire said.

"What?"

"Now read my findings," Claire said.

*   *   *   *   *

Claire returned from the deli with two fresh cups of coffee and found Wang on the last page of her reports with his cigar lit.

He closed the file, took a coffee and blew a cloud of smoke. "The cigar bother you?" he asked.

Claire shook her head. "I've been known to smoke one or two on occasion."

"A cigar? Really?"

"My reports?"

"I'm not a believer in coincidence or chance," Wang said. "Are you?"

"No, Artie, I'm not," Claire said.

"So when a childless couple on a waiting list for ten years suddenly has a child of their own and then vanishes while their adoption attorney checks into rehab to the tune of twenty-five thousand, I find it rather difficult to shrug it off and say coincidence. Don't you?"

"I called you, didn't I?" Claire said.

"You did, yes."

Wang puffed on his cigar and took a sip of coffee.

"The Harpers are desperate for a child," Wang said. "Their attorney John Alford is desperate for cash and in need of rehab. Alford cuts a deal with the Harpers. Cash for a baby. Alford is driving around in dire need of a fix, rehab, cash and a baby. He spots Michele Burke out for an early morning walk on the beach with her infant son. The opportunity presents itself and Alford goes for it. Is this about how you see it?"

Claire sipped coffee and nodded.

Wang blew a large, dark smoke ring. "I'm going to look at the Harpers," he said. "Inside and out. And them I'm going to call you."

Claire dug out her notepad and pen and wrote her cell number on a page and tore it out.

"Call me on my cell," she said.

"You should get some business cards, Sheriff Evergreen," Wang said.

"Claire. Call me Claire," she said. "And I haven't had the time."

* * * * *

Mitzi was talking with Rose and Turley when Claire entered the squad room. Seated on the edge of Turley's desk, Mitzi stood and smiled at Claire.

"There you are," she said. "I have an urgent request from our esteemed mayor and town manager."

Claire rested the urge to roll her eyes.

"He would like you to say a few words tomorrow at his kick off the summer speech," Mitzi said.

"I don't do speeches," Claire said.

"Just say a few words," Mitzi said. "Introduce yourself as our new sheriff, introduce your staff, wish everybody a safe summer and that's it."

Claire sighed.

"Good girl," Mitzi said. "Well, gotta go. See you tomorrow at the ribbon cutting."

After Mitzi left, Claire looked at Turley.

"He doesn't really cut a ribbon?" she said. "Does he?"

*   *   *   *   *

"How did it go with the FBI?" Rose asked as she followed Claire into her office.

"Special Agent Wang is going to have a look and get back to me," Claire said.

She sat behind her desk.

"He reminds me of the old Lieutenant Colombo TV show," Claire said.

"Wang is Chinese, isn't it? Colombo was Italian," Rose said.

"If they ever do Colombo in China, this is the guy," Claire said.

Rose took a seat on the sofa and looked at Claire.

"What?" Claire asked.

"I remembered something," Rose said. "It's probably nothing, but it's something I hadn't thought about since Shaw was killed."

"And that something is?" Claire asked.

"Shaw took the entire staff and the entire town council and employees at the town office to dinner the last day he was sheriff," Rose said. "I know because someone took ill during dinner and my EMT unit responded. One of the town council members was a diabetic and needed insulin. While we were administrating to the diabetic, I happened to see Shaw pay the bill at the register with hundred dollar bills. He peeled them off a roll as thick as my fist. We wound up transporting the diabetic to the hospital and I guess I sort of dismissed the entire thing until Mitzi reminded me of it a little while ago."

"Mitzi, how? She wasn't there, was she?"

Rose shook her head. "While she was sitting on my desk she picked up a rubber band and was playing with it. You know how people stretch them out and roll them around, like that. Shaw had a rubber band wrapped around his roll of money like you see in old gangster movies."

Claire stared at Rose.

"I think Shaw might have been dirty," Rose said.

"Dirty enough to get killed over?"

"The check that night had to be a thousand dollars," Rose said. "It didn't make a dent in his roll."

"This stays between us for now," Claire said.

Rose nodded.

"See if you can dig around quietly in Shaw's finances," Claire said. "Outstanding credit card bills, major purchases, things that may have been overlooked because he was one of their own."

Rose stood and left the office.

"Close the door," Claire said.

She picked up her phone and dialed in the number for Kellerman. He answered on the third ring.

"Mike, it's Claire."

"Wang call you?"

"Yes, but that's not what I'm calling about," Claire said. "Tell me what you think about this."

Claire recanted Rose's story about Shaw paying the dinner bill from a roll of hundred dollar bills to Kellerman.

"She described the roll as big as her fist," Claire ended the story with.

"Shaw was on a City pension when he took the job of sheriff at Smoky Point," Kellerman said.

"Half pay at best," Claire said. "That's why he worked another eight years. The only way he'd have a roll of hundreds like that is if he carried around his life savings."

Kellerman sighed.

"Everything points to it, Mike," Claire said.

"Have you talked to Cruz? He had an active part in the investigation eight years ago," Kellerman said.

"A small part," Claire said. "State took charge of the investigation because of the location. He knows mistakes were made. Given the chance, he'd like to correct them."

"What do you suggest?" Kellerman asked.

"Let me call Cruz and get back to you," Claire said.

Kellerman sighed again. "Okay," he said.

Claire hung up and called Cruz.

"I could have sworn I already talked to you this morning," Cruz said when he came on the line.

"Bill, just listen," Claire said and told him about Rose's encounter with Shaw the night of his retirement.

"Our theory Shaw was dirty just got a bit dirtier," Cruz said.

"I think the three of us should meet and toss around some ideas," Claire said.

"By three you mean Kellerman?" Cruz said.

"I do," Claire said.

"When?"

"Monday," Claire said. "I have to cut a ribbon tomorrow."

"What?"

"Call me back after you talk to Mike and set up a place and time," Claire said.

"Why do I…?" Cruz said.

"Thanks, Bill," Claire said and hung up.

She sat for a few minutes and let her thoughts freefall and go round and round until her head was spinning and she had to put a stop to it. She stood and went to the squad room.

Rose was standing beside Turley's desk and they were talking.

"Rose, put everything away and take the rest of the day off," Claire said.

Turley looked at Claire.

"Is something wrong, Claire?" he asked.

"Call me on my cell phone if you need me," Claire said. "Otherwise I have to go home and shave my legs."

"What?" Turley said.

Chapter Twenty-six

WHEN HOLT'S TRUCK PULLED INTO the driveway, Claire opened the front door and stepped out wearing a yellow sundress with a thin white sweater and white Keds on her feet. She carried a white summer pocketbook to hold her backup piece and cell phone. Makeup was light, just a touch.

Holt left the truck and went around to open the door for Claire.

"You look wonderful," he said.

"If you were hoping for glamorous this is the best I got," Claire said.

She hopped up into the seat as Holt went back around and got behind the wheel.

"You don't take compliments well, do you?" he said.

"No."

Holt started the truck and backed out of the driveway. "On The Waterfront," he said.

"I've seen it," Claire said. "Brando was fantastic."

"Not the movie, it's a restaurant about forty-five minutes west of here," Holt said. "It's where we're going."

Claire nodded. "Listen, I have to be honest. If you're hoping to wet your wick tonight, it's not happening."

"Good God, Claire," Holt said.

"So what kind of restaurant is this place?"

"Italian."

"Maybe holding hands, but that's about it," Claire said.

Holt shook his head and grinned. "Would you like separate tables," he said.

"Don't be an asshole," Claire said.

*　*　*　*　*

On The Waterfront stood twelve feet off the ground on hurricane stilts so that in the event of a hurricane the high waves would pass under it without causing too much damage.

It faced the beach and the immediate area was well-lit by lanterns.

Holt watched Claire toy with her food as she twirled and twirled linguini.

"Want to talk about it?" Holt said.

Claire looked up.

"I'm sorry, Matt. I guess I'm not very good company tonight."

"Get it off your chest, whatever it is," Holt said.

"It's Shaw," Claire said.

"I figured."

"He was dirty, Matt," Claire said. "I think that's why he was murdered."

"I admit it might look that way, but…"

"The night he retired Shaw took a bunch of people to dinner. He was seen with a roll of hundred dollar bills as thick as my fist. Where does a small town sheriff get that kind of flash money, Matt? Legally I mean?"

"There are a lot of explanations, Claire and they don't have to be illegal," Holt said. "It could be from his pension or he saved it up just for that night. It could even be cash he won from a fishing tournament."

"This was fuck you money," Claire said. "Rolled and wrapped in rubber bands like a wise guy in an old gangster movie."

Holt nodded. "I admit it's damaging on the surface," he said. "But it was eight years ago and Shaw isn't around to question. What are you going to do about it?"

"I've talked to the county sheriff and a homicide detective at state," Claire said. "We're going to meet on it, but where it goes from there is most likely nowhere."

Holt shook his head, looked at Claire and said. "I told myself I wouldn't get involved in this, but if you want my help just ask."

"It wouldn't hurt for another set of eyes to take a look," Claire said. "When?"

"How about after dinner?"

"I think I've just been sucker punched," Holt said.

"Look, I know you'd rather be wick dipping, but the way to my heart isn't with diamonds," Claire said. "Just ask my first two husbands."

"Could we at least order dessert first?" Holt said.

*　*　*　*　*

"I'll make some coffee and change," Claire said. "Get started. I won't be long."

Holt looked at Snowball who was on the coffee table.

"Your cat is giving me the evil eye," he said.

"She won't bite," Claire said. "Unless you touch me."

Holt sighed and looked at the stack of reports on the coffee table. He picked one up and looked at Snowball as she followed his movements.

"Nice kitty," Holt said and started to read.

Claire returned fifteen minutes later wearing jeans, a tank top and white socks.

"Coffee will be ready in a minute," she said.

Turning a page, Holt said, "A little cream, no sugar."

Claire went to the kitchen and returned a few minutes later with two mugs and set them on the coffee table next to Snowball.

Holt turned the last page, closed the file and set it on the table and picked up a mug. "Shaw was dirty no doubt," he said and sipped. "You make good coffee."

"Thanks. So Shaw's dirty, I already know that," Claire said. "What don't I know?"

"Unless someone comes forward and confesses to an eight year old murder he's clearly gotten away with, knowing is all you're going to get," Holt said. "Missing coolers, dressed improperly for some night fishing and flashing a roll of cash to pay for dinner at this point leads nowhere without a suspect or motive and you have neither."

Claire sipped some coffee. "What are you saying?"

"The obvious, Claire," Holt said. "Something you know but are hesitant to say, that Shaw's murder was a pro job by a pro hit man."

Claire sipped some coffee.

So did Holt.

"And you're not going to find who did it or why," Holt said. "Not at this point."

Claire sipped again.

"That's the way it goes sometimes, Claire," Holt said. "Maybe if you were around eight years ago and went after this with the tenacity I'm learning is in you there might be a different outcome, but you're trying to kick a field goal after the game is long ago lost."

Claire stared at Holt.

"That's just my professional opinion," Holt said.

Claire sipped and looked at Holt over the rim of her cup.

Holt looked at Claire and softly bit his lower lip.

Many silent moments passed.

"Blood has rushed to a certain appendage of yours, hasn't it?" Claire said.

"I don't deny that," Holt said.

"It wants a little attention, doesn't it?"

"I don't deny that either."

"I think before we do something stupid that I'll regret tomorrow that it's time to say goodnight," Claire said.

"I think you may be right," Holt said.

Claire walked Holt to the front door where he paused for a moment.

"Do you think I'm too old for you, Claire?" he asked.

Claire shook her head. "I just need some time to work out my preoccupations," she said.

Holt nodded. "Night," he said.

*   *   *   *   *

Snowball, from her perch on Claire's stomach, yawned.

"It's not that I'm against close contact with a man you see," Claire said. "It's just that men are very time consuming and right now I don't have any to spare."

Snowball yawned again.

"They are also very much like babies in that they need constant attention and cry when they don't get it," Claire said. "And sometimes they even spit up."

Snowball closed her eyes.

"Yes, you're right," Claire said. "Let's sleep on it."

Chapter Twenty-seven

CLAIRE AND HER ENTIRE STAFF stood behind the entire town council and they in turn stood behind Carl Walker.

About a hundred people were gathered on the fringe and waited for Walker's speech to open the beach for the season.

A lifeguard was on duty at each of the four towers.

Walker had actually brought two movie stanchions and tied a blue ribbon to them. His speech lasted ten minutes and then he introduced Claire and she spoke for two minutes. Then Walker cut the ribbon with scissors and declared the beach open for the summer.

The crowd moved forward to the sand to spread blankets and towels. Walker and the town council walked to the parking lot. Claire sent her staff to work and took a seat on Michele's bench.

Mitzi returned to the beach and sat next to Claire.

"He really did bring a ribbon," Claire said.

"What's bothering you, hon?" Mitzi asked. "It's not the ribbon that's for sure."

Claire sighed softly and said, "It's Patrick Shaw."

"Oh hon, not that again," Mitzi said.

"Mitzi, I have good reason to believe that Shaw was murdered by a pro hit man," Claire said.

"What? Why?"

"Because he was dirty and it caught up with him," Claire said.

"Dirty? In Smoky Point? Maybe you're mistaken?"

"It's no mistake," Claire said.

"Oh boy," Mitzi said. "Have you told this to Carl?"

"Not yet. I'm waiting for him to return to his office."

"I think you'd better."

"I think you're right."

"Want me to tag along for moral support?"

"Not necessary but thanks."

Mitzi stood up from the bench. "His bark is worse than his bite, you know," she said.

Claire smiled. "I'll keep than in mind."

*   *   *   *   *

Claire could see the anger mounting in Carl Walker's face as she explained the Patrick Shaw situation to him in his office.

"Sheriff Evergreen, I warned you about becoming too involved in something that has nothing to do with your present day duties," he said. "I won't have you neglecting your responsibilities to play Magnum PI on something that happened eight years ago."

"I'm not neglecting my responsibilities," Claire said. "I'm investigating a murder as part of my duties to this town and a previous sheriff."

"I can have you removed from office," Walker said.

"Yes you can," Claire said. "But you can't tell me what to do."

Walker inhaled and the sighed loudly. "Do you really believe Shaw was dirty and murdered because of it?" he asked.

"I do, Carl."

"Can you do whatever it is you're doing quietly so it doesn't impact our tourist season?" Walker asked.

"I never said otherwise."

Walker nodded. "Go back to work," he said. "Claire."

"Thank you," Claire said. "Carl."

*   *   *   *   *

"Claire, Lieutenant Kellerman from the state police called while you were out," Turley said when Claire returned to the squad room.

"Thanks," Claire said. "Where's Rose?"

"She took a walk to the store," Turley said. "We're out of coffee."

Claire nodded, went to her office and called Kellerman.

"Free for lunch?" he asked. "Cruz is buying."

"I am. Can I bring my assistant?"

"We'll pick you up at one."

"Okay," Claire said and hung up.

She went out to the squad room as Rose walked in with a can of coffee.

"Rose, we're going to lunch at one," Claire said. "The four of us."

"Who are the other two?" Rose asked.

*   *   *   *   *

"The question isn't if Shaw was dirty, we believe he was," Kellerman said. "The question is without knowing what he was into, who his associates were and why he was killed, what can we do about it at this point other than speculate."

They were at the Family Diner on Route Twenty-seven in a booth by a window.

"Shaw lived well within his means and what he left his ex-wife and children was all legal and accounted for," Cruz said.

"Legal and accounted for?" Claire said. "What does that even mean?"

"It means we have nothing to go on and nowhere to go to even if we did," Kellerman said.

Claire looked at Rose.

Rose cleared her throat. "I know what I saw the night of Shaw's party," she said. "He must have had $10,000 in hundred dollar bills wrapped in rubber bands. When he left office, his salary was $37,000 a year. I've been asking myself where does Shaw get that kind of flash money on that salary with an ex-wife to support and pay his own bills at the same time."

"We don't doubt what you saw, Deputy," Kellerman said. "But right now is after the fact and we have nowhere to go on this."

"Who's top dog on this island?" Claire said.

"Top dog how?" Kellerman asked.

"The biggest scumbag criminal you two assholes can't touch," Claire said.

"Abby Kleinfield, head of the Jewish mafia," Cruz said.

"Abby as in...?" Claire asked.

"Abner," Cruz said.

"Where can I find him?" Claire asked.

"Find him to do what with?" Cruz asked.

"Talk," Claire said. "If he's top dog around here he has an ear to the ground. Maybe he heard something about Shaw we don't know but need to."

"Why would Kleinfield talk to us unless there was something in it for him?" Cruz asked.

"Don't know unless you ask," Claire said.

"She's not serious, is she?" Kellerman said.

"I think she is, yes," Cruz said.

Kellerman looked at Rose. "What do you think Deputy?"

"I think you're going to give in and see it Claire's way because she's right and because you're over-matched and because you're good cops," Rose said. "But mostly because you're over-matched."

"Damn," Kellerman said.

"Anybody want dessert?" Rose asked.

*   *   *   *   *

"Everything you can find on Kleinfield, Rose and print it out," Claire said when they returned to the squad room.

Claire looked at the coffee pot.

"How old is this?" she said.

"Fifteen minutes," Turley said.

Claire filled her mug and went to her office. She sat at her desk, thought for a few minutes and then used her phone to call Holt.

His voice mailbox answered the call.

"Matt, it's Claire. Call me on my cell phone. Thanks," Claire said and hung up.

She sipped coffee and thought for a while until Rose came in with a folder of reports.

"Abner Kleinfield is one nasty character," Rose said.

Claire opened the folder and started to read. Abner Kleinfield was seventy-two years old and born on Manhattan's lower East side in a Jewish neighborhood. He went bad at a very early age. By age eleven he was running numbers for neighborhood bookies. At fourteen he was helping Italian wise guys with airport hijackings. He was taken under the wing on the Italian mob and quickly rose to power, forming his own Jewish mafia by age twenty. By age thirty, Kleinfield was the most powerful Jewish mobster in the tri-state area. He formed alliances with the Italian and Irish mobs and was very successful in business. Thirty-two years ago, Kleinfield moved his entire family to Long Island and settled in the town of North Fork on a peninsula where he invested in a winery.

Suspected of every crime in the book including murder, drug smuggling, illegal gun dealing and so on, Kleinfield never served a day in prison. It was long suspected but never proven that if police got too close to him, Kleinfield paid an associate six figures to confess to the crime and another six figures upon completion of the prison term.

Married forty-seven years, Kleinfield had three sons and one daughter and eleven grandchildren to date. His youngest son died twelve years ago when struck by a motorcycle on Route Twenty-seven. He was just twenty at the time. His wife Sarah died one year ago from cancer.

Claire closed the file and went to the squad room and sat on the edge of Rose's desk. "Get a phone number for Kleinfield," she said.

"It's unlisted," Rose said.

"We're the police, Rose," Claire said.

"Right."

Claire returned to her office to find her cell phone ringing. She checked the number, hit talk and said, "Hi, Matt."

"I'm glad you called," Holt said. "About last night."

"Can we talk about that later," Claire said. "I need to ask you a question."

"Ask."

"What do you know about a Jewish mobster named Abby Kleinfield?"

"Is this a… are you putting me on, Claire?"

"No. What do you know about him?"

"He's the prince of fucking darkness, that's what I know," Holt said. "When I was a city cop, he ran all Jewish organized crime in Brooklyn and Queens. Hell, the whole city. Why?"

"I'd like to talk to him, that's why."

"Talk to… she's gone flipping nuts," Holt said. "Even if he agreed to see you, what do you want to talk to him about?"

"Patrick Shaw," Claire said.

"Oh, for the love of God," Holt said. "What makes you think he knows anything about Patrick Shaw?"

"He's top dog on the Island," Claire said. "Top dogs tend to hear everything even if it doesn't concern them."

"Hearing and telling are two different things, Claire," Holt said. "If he agreed to see you in the first place."

"It can't hurt to ask, Matt," Claire said.

"Jesus God why am I so turned on by you?" Holt said.

"What's that… you mean last night?"

"I mean right now," Holt said.

"Can we please talk about that some other time," Claire said. "What can you tell me about Kleinfield I can't read in a report?"

"I've worked vice and every type of special task force there is in the City," Holt said. "Kleinfield is always the smartest guy in the room. That is what you need to know about Abby Kleinfield."

"I'll keep that in mind," Claire said.

"Now can we talk about us?" Holt asked.

"Don't be a horn dog," Claire said. "Let the suspense build."

"Let the suspense build?" Holt said.

"See, we agree," Claire said. "I'll talk to you later."

Claire hung up just as Rose walked in with a slip of paper. "Got it from the phone company," she said.

Claire took the slip of paper and used her hard line to call the number.

It rang three times before a man answered the phone.

"Kleinfield residence," he said.

"This is Sheriff Claire Evergreen from Smoky Point calling," Claire said. "I'd like to speak with Abner Kleinfield please."

"Sheriff who?"

"Sheriff Claire Evergreen from Smoky Point."

"And you wish to speak with my father?"

"I do."

"What about?"

"I'm investigating an eight year old murder of Sheriff Patrick Shaw," Claire said.

"That's what you want to talk to him about?"

"Yes. I thought I was clear on the point."

"You're crazy. My father is…"

"I'll come down there and ring the doorbell until somebody answers and agrees to let me in," Claire said. "I'll ring the damn bell all night if I have to so you might as well go ask daddy if we can have a chat."

"Hold."

Claire held the phone for a full five minutes before he returned.

"My father said he can give you fifteen minutes."

"When?"

"How long will it take you to get here?"

"I'm not sure. Hour maybe."

"One hour. Don't be late, Sheriff Evergreen."

Chapter Twenty-eight

THE KLEINFIELD HOME WAS NOTHING like Claire expected. Five bedrooms, two floors, small front yard, two-car garage and the ocean in the backyard off the peninsula. The garage door was closed and two SUVs were parked in front of it.

Claire parked behind them.

As she walked to the front door, it opened and a man stepped out.

"Sheriff Evergreen," he said.

"And you are?"

"David, the oldest son."

He was around Claire's age, tall and well put together, dressed in a nice blue suit.

"Step in," David said. "Remove the gun belt."

Claire followed David into the foyer and removed her gun belt.

"Put it on the coat hook."

She hung it on a coat hook.

"I'm going to wand you," David said.

"Go ahead," Claire said.

David removed an electronic wand from a hook beside Claire's gun belt and ran it up and down her body.

"You're clean," David said. "Follow me."

Claire followed him to the living room. "My father is in the backyard," he said and opened a set of double doors.

The backyard was about a quarter acre of lush lawn and budding spring flowers that ended at a high chain link fence. Beyond the fence was the ocean.

Abby Kleinfield was seated at a patio table facing the ocean.

"Pop. Sheriff Evergreen is here," David said.

Kleinfield turned slightly and looked at Claire.

"Bring us something to drink," he said. "What would you like Sheriff Evergreen?"

"Coffee," Claire said.

"Bring us some, David. Make it fresh."

David nodded and returned to the house.

"Well, Sheriff Evergreen, you wanted to talk to me, sit and talk," Kleinfield said.

Claire went to the table and sat opposite him. Her first impression was that Kleinfield was nothing like she expected. He was a small man, maybe around five-foot-six inches tall. He wasn't fat but he had a small paunch. His hair was as white as snow and worn longish while his eyebrows were jet black. He wore a white shirt open at the collar and a gold crucifix dangled from a gold chain around his neck.

"May I ask you a personal question?" Claire said.

"You're wondering why a Jewish man is wearing a Catholic cross," Kleinfield said. "I saw you looking at it."

"Yes."

"My wife was Catholic," Kleinfield said. "She refused to marry me unless I converted."

"Thank you for answering that," Claire said.

"No problem. Actually, I rather enjoy being Catholic," Kleinfield said. "They have this forgiveness program where if you confess your sins before you die you get to go to heaven. Are you familiar with that?"

"Yes," Claire said.

David returned with a silver tray that held a large glass coffee pot, cups, cream and sugar. He set the tray down and filled the cups.

"Do you like cookies?" Kleinfield asked Claire.

"Sure."

"David, bring us a plate of the almond cookies," Kleinfield said.

David nodded and returned to the house.

Kleinfield looked at Claire. "You're too pretty to be a sheriff," he said.

"Looks do not a sheriff make," Claire said.

"Are you married?"

"Was. Twice."

"My son David needs a wife."

"I'm not good wife material," Claire said.

David returned with a plate of cookies and set them on the table, then returned to the house.

"So what is this about an eight year old murder that you think I have information about?" Kleinfield asked. "What was his name again?"

"Shaw. Sheriff Patrick Shaw."

"I know of no such person."

"He was the sheriff of Smoky Point and retired eight years ago," Claire said. "He was found murdered on the highway shortly after he retired. It was believed it was a case of road rage at the time."

"I have no knowledge of such an incident," Kleinfield said.

"I believe that Sheriff Patrick Shaw was engaged in illegal activity and was killed because of it," Claire said.

"I have no knowledge of any activity Sheriff Shaw was engaged in," Kleinfield said. "I'm a retired investor living on a modest pension."

Claire picked up a cookie and took a bite. "This is really good," she said.

"Take some home with you Sheriff Evergreen," Kleinfield said.

"Call me Claire."

"That's a lovely name. You have great birthing hips by the way."

"Do you plan to not answer any of my questions?" Claire asked.

"But I am answering them, Claire. You just don't like my answers."

Claire ate the rest of her cookie.

"If you don't like your situation, change your tactics," Kleinfield said. "Claire."

Claire took a sip of coffee to wash the cookie down. "Will you help me with my problem, Mr. Kleinfield?"

"Call me Abner, and what problem do you have, Claire?"

"I can't sleep nights," Claire said. "At heart, I'm a homicide detective and when a case goes unsolved I can't sleep. Help me sleep, Abner."

"What would you like me to do, Claire?" Kleinfield asked.

"Help me out. Ask some questions. Maybe you could find out what Shaw was into that got him killed."

"You do realize that I'm a retired investor living on a pension," Kleinfield said.

"Throw me a bone, Abner," Claire said. "What could it hurt?"

"What's the reciprocation?"

"Have any speeding tickets you need fixed?" Claire asked.

Kleinfield grinned.

"I like you, Claire," he said. "Tell you what I'm going to do. I have many friends, retired investors living on a pension like me. I'm going to ask them if they ever heard of such an incident and then my son David will call you."

"Thank you, Abner," Claire said.

"You're welcome, Claire."

On the way out, David handed Claire her holster and a baggie full of almond cookies.

*   *   *   *   *

Pederson was on dispatch duty when Claire entered the squad room.

"How's it going?" Claire asked.

"Full swing, Claire," Pederson said. "Is that a bag of cookies?"

"Yes. A mobster gave them to me," Claire said. "I'll leave them in the break room."

Pederson looked at Claire. "I won't ask," she said and motioned with her eyes.

Claire looked past Pederson at Holt, who was seated at Rose's desk. She walked to the desk.

"Matt, what are you doing here?" she asked.

Holt stood. "Worrying," he said.

"Come in the office," Claire said.

Holt followed her into the office.

"Is that a bag of cookies?" he said.

"Almond. Try one. They're delicious. Kleinfield gave them to me," Claire said. "I think his son baked them, I'm not sure."

"Kleinfield? Abby Kleinfield gave you a bag of cookies?" Holt said.

Claire nodded. "Did you know he's a retired investor living on a pension?"

Holt sank into the sofa. "For God's sake, Claire."

"I should put them in the break room," Claire said.

"You saw Kleinfield?" Holt asked.

"I'm hungry and all I've had since lunch is a cookie," Claire said. "Want to have dinner with me?"

* * * * *

"You're making new friends in low places, Claire," Holt said.

"Eat your noodles," Claire said.

They were in a Chinese restaurant on Route Twenty-seven.

"Seriously, Kleinfield is…" Holt said.

"I know what he is," Claire said. "We have carbon copies of him in Rhode Island. I've had to use a worm to catch a slug before, Matt, it doesn't mean I like, approve or respect the worm."

"Why would Kleinfield agree to help you?" Holt asked.

"I asked him to," Claire said.

"You asked him to. Claire, men like Kleinfield don't do anything unless it benefits them directly," Holt said.

"And that makes him different from all other men how?" Claire asked.

"Most other men don't have you killed when they don't get what they want," Holt said.

"Would you be talking to me like this if I was wearing a detective's badge of a state trooper?" Claire said. "Or a man?"

"Dammit, Claire, if you were a man I wouldn't be trying to get you into bed," Holt said. "And I don't give a rat's ass what kind of badge you're wearing."

"Eat your noodles," Claire said.

*   *   *   *   *

They had taken Holt's car to the restaurant and it was dark when they returned to the station.

"You were right when you said I wouldn't talk that way to you if you were a man," Holt said. "I apologize for that remark."

"I'm really good at what I do, Matt," Claire said. "Don't let my pretty face and terrific pair of legs fool you. Okay."

Holt nodded. "About us?"

"I really don't have time for all that sweating and grunting right now," Claire said. "Let me finish what I've started and we'll talk about it. In the meantime you'll have to settle for this."

Claire leaned over and gave Holt a soft, very sweet kiss that lasted several seconds.

227

When they broke apart, Claire said, "See ya," and went into the squad room.

"Claire," Pederson said as Claire approached his desk. "Knox and Cole brought in a winner a little while ago. They're in the processing room."

Claire walked past the break room and opened the door to the processing room. Knox and Cole were fingerprinting a male of about forty.

"Hi, Claire. Meet Harry O'Day. Harry is a pickpocket," Knox said.

"That's a lie," O'Day said.

"You had eleven wallets and none of them yours," Knox said.

"I found them," O'Day said. "It's not my fault people lose their wallets and I happen to find them."

"Book him, lock him up and check him for priors," Claire said. "Mr. O'Day, I'm afraid you're our guest for the night."

"This is police brutality," O'Day said.

"Sure it is," Claire said.

"I want a phone call and a lawyer."

"Short, give him his call," Claire said. "I'm headed home."

"Night, Claire," Knox said.

* * * * *

Snowball purred loudly as Claire ran a cat brush through her fur.

"That was the first time I've kissed a man since my second husband," Claire said.

Snowball rubbed her head against the brush.

"Believe me it wasn't that big of a deal," Claire said. "We both tasted like Chinese noodles."

Snowball attacked the brush with her paw to signal Claire she had enough.

Claire set the brush on the nightstand.

"I agree, it's time for sleep," Claire said.

She rolled down the covers and Snowball assumed her position near Claire's stomach.

"How would you feel if you weren't the only one sharing my bed," Claire said.

Snowball looked at Claire.

"It was just a suggestion," Claire said and turned off the lamp.

Chapter Twenty-nine

CLAIRE SAT ON THE EDGE of Rose's desk and sipped coffee from her mug. Rose, dressed in uniform, was eating an almond cookie.

At his desk, Turley answered the phone. He said a few words and then turned to Claire. "Lieutenant Miller for you, Claire," he said.

Claire picked up Rose's phone. "This is Claire," she said.

"Claire, Lieutenant Miller. I thought I'd give you a heads up on the Disciples. Randall Boyd and eleven others took the ferry about an hour ago. They should hit Long Island around four this afternoon."

"Tate?"

"Wasn't with them my contact said, but a second group was mobilizing."

"Thanks for the heads up, Lieutenant," Claire said.

"I'll call you back about the second group when I know," Miller said.

"If I'm out use my cell number," Claire said.

She hung up and looked at Rose.

"I don't want to be cooped up today," Claire said. "Feel like some patrol time in your car?"

"I'm dressed for it," Rose said.

* * * * *

The amusement park was in full swing as Claire and Rose patrolled the fairgrounds.

"It's Saturday, Claire. We should be at the beach or shopping or doing whatever divorced, lonely women do on their days off," Rose said.

"I am doing what I do on my days off," Claire said.

"There's been some talk," Rose said.

"You mean gossip," Claire said as she approached a fried dough wagon. "Two with everything," she told the clerk inside the wagon.

"Just because it's gossip doesn't mean it isn't true," Rose said.

Claire handed the clerk twelve dollars and he handed her two plates with fried dough smothered in pineapple sauce and powdered sugar. She gave one plate to Rose.

"So what are the gossipers gossiping about?" Claire asked as she and Rose took a seat on a bench.

"That you're been dating a certain retired sheriff of late," Rose said. "God, how do you eat this mess?"

"Carefully," Claire said as she took a bite.

"So, are the rumors true?" Rose asked as she licked some pineapple sauce.

"I contacted Holt to ask him what he knew of the Shaw case and also about the motorcycle gang activity," Claire said.

"He's a handsome man," Rose said.

"He is," Claire agreed. "And if you ask if we did it I will smack you with this fried dough."

"I wasn't going to ask that," Rose said.

"Good."

"But as long as you brought it up."

"No, Rose, we didn't do anything except talk about Shaw, the Disciples and matters related," Claire said.

"And he feels?"

"As we do, that Shaw was dirty."

"But he wanted more?"

Claire shrugged. "He's a man."

Rose wiped pineapple sauce off her chin. "Those creeps will be here in a few hours," she said.

"That reminds me," Claire said. She set the plate on the bench and pulled out her cell phone and called Turley.

"Jim, it's Claire," she said when Turley answered the call. "Who is on right now?"

"Pederson and Ricard," Turley said.

"Call them and tell them to meet me at the entrance to the amusement park at three-thirty," Claire said. "What time does Short come on?"

"Six."

"Today it's five," Claire said. "Tell him to report to the squad room at five."

"Will do."

"Thank you."

Claire hung up and looked at Rose.

"Let's get some hamburgers," Claire said.

* * * * *

The cruiser pulled up beside Rose's car and Pederson and Ricard got out and walked to Claire.

"You sent for us?" Pederson asked.

"Head over to Twenty-seven East where the *Welcome to Smoky Point* sign is and pick a spot to watch the road," Claire said. "When you see a dozen idiots on Harleys headed to town, call me on my cell phone."

"Should we follow them?" Ricard asked.

"Yes, but from a distance," Claire said. "They'll be headed to the bars, so no hurry."

"Okay," Ricard said.

Pederson and Ricard returned to the cruiser and drove away.

Claire entered Rose's car where Rose was behind the wheel.

"Home, James," Claire said.

*   *   *   *   *

"What's going on, Claire?" Knox asked as he entered the squad room and found her seated on the edge of Rose's desk.

"The biker boneheads just got off the ferry and Pederson and Ricard called a few minutes ago from Twenty-seven and said they're headed east," Claire said.

"I'll head over to Alcoholics Alley," Knox said.

"We'll all go as soon as they arrive," Claire said. "Jim, get them on the radio and tell them to call in on the phone."

Turley called Pederson and Ricard on the radio. A minute later, the phone rang.

"Claire, Pederson," Turley said.

Claire took the phone. "Janelle, it's Claire. Are you in route to town?"

"Following the bikers from a safe distance," Pederson said.

"They're most likely headed to one of the bars on Alcoholic's Alley," Claire said. "Find a place to park and call back when they've entered a bar."

"Sure thing, Claire," Pederson said.

Claire handed the phone back to Turley.

"I don't get it," Knox said. "What are we doing, Claire?"

"Keeping the peace," Claire said.

*   *   *   *   *

Claire was in her office with Rose when Turley buzzed her.

"Pederson on line one," he said.

Claire picked up the phone. "Go ahead, Janelle," she said.

"We're parked at the end of the street," Pederson said. "The whole kit and caboodle are in the Palace bar. Know it?"

"I do."

"What do you want us to do?"

"Sit there until I show up," Claire said.

"That's it?"

"That's it," Claire said and hung up.

She looked at Rose.

"Let's give them enough time to get a few drinks under their belts," Claire said. "Where's Short?"

"I think he's in the break room eating almond cookies," Rose said.

* * * * *

Rose sat beside Knox and Claire rode in back as Knox drove the cruiser to Alcoholic's Alley.

"Park behind Pederson and Ricard," Claire said.

Knox parked directly behind them and Claire, Knox and Rose got out.

"Janelle, you and Ricard run a make on all the bikes," Claire said. "We'll be inside for a bit. Short, you and Rose stand back."

Claire led the way into the Palace bar. There was a good crowd and the music was loud and the beer and whiskey was flowing.

"This is like a bad country/western song," Rose said.

There was no missing Boyd. He was larger than he appeared in his photograph. He wore a white T-shirt, a sleeveless leather vest, dark jeans and snakeskin boots. His hair was longer than in the photograph and his face was covered by a neatly trimmed beard. The word Disciples was stitched on the back of his vest.

Several Disciples were at the bar with him. Others were at tables in the company of women. One was playing pool with a few of the regulars.

Claire walked to the bar and stood beside Boyd.

Boyd turned and looked at Claire.

"Have you come for the fireworks show?" Claire asked.

"What?" Boyd said. "The music."

Claire waved to the bartender and he approached her.

"Can you lower the music to say the level of a 747?" she said.

He nodded, walked to the end of the bar and lowered the music.

Boyd gave Claire the once over and then said, "I'm Randall Boyd, president of the Disciples motorcycle club."

"Claire Evergreen, sheriff of Smoky Point," Claire said.

"What happened to that other fellow?" Boyd said.

"He retired," Claire said.

"What can I do for you Sheriff Evergreen?" Boyd said.

"Ease my curiosity," Claire said.

Boyd tossed back his shot and reached for his beer. "About?' he said and sipped beer.

"Every year you screw-heads ride the ferry south, drive your hopped-up penises into town, get drunk, break up a bar, spend the night in jail, pay for the damages and then leave the next day," Claire said. "I'm curious as to why."

Boyd sipped more beer and then set the mug on the bar. "I'll bet you're a great chess player," he said.

"I was on my high school chess team," Claire said. "Won the state championship. So, what's the deal here?"

"It's no secret, Sheriff," Boyd said. "After a long cold winter, we take to the road and visit our brother clubs on the Eastern Seaboard. Renew old friendships and whatnot. We take the ferry because it saves us a day in the saddle and we get to let off a bit of pent up winter steam."

"I suppose you're too smart to bring weapons across state lines," Claire said.

Boyd moved his vest to display a multi-tool clipped to his belt. "Unless this qualifies as a weapon, all you'll find in our saddlebags are tools for making repairs to our bikes."

"Goddammit you son of a bitch," the Disciple playing pool yelled. "I hate cheating fucks like you."

Claire turned and looked at the pool table. The Disciple smashed his pool stick against the table shattering it into splinters.

"Is that some of the pent up winter steam you spoke about?" Claire said.

"Ross, get over here," Boyd shouted.

The Disciple waved a fist at the man he was playing pool with and then went to the bar.

"Ross, this is Sheriff Evergreen, the new sheriff of Smoky Point," Boyd said.

Ross looked Claire up and down and grinned. "I wouldn't mind being locked in a cell with you sweetheart," he said.

"Careful what you wish for," Claire said.

"Course, you ain't much in the tits department, but maybe if I fed and watered them they might grow a bit," Ross said.

Claire sighed. She turned to the bartender and waved him over.

"A roll of quarters and a bar towel," she said.

The bartender set a roll of quarters and a thin towel on the bar.

"Now Ross, I want you to watch carefully and I'm going to grant you your wish," Claire said.

Boyd looked at Claire with a tiny grin on his lips.

Claire picked up the roll of quarters and held it in her right fist. Then she wrapped the bar towel around her fist and looked up at Ross, who was about six foot two inches tall.

"Guess what comes next?" Claire asked Ross.

Ross squinted at Claire as she put all her weight behind a right hook and punched him in the jaw. His face snapped back and his entire body bent at the waist, but he was a large, heavy man and didn't go down.

Claire took a step forward and hit Ross under the jaw with an uppercut and he flopped onto his back and hit the floor unconscious.

Claire removed the towel and placed it and the roll of quarters on the bar.

"Bravo," Boyd said.

Claire looked at Knox and Rose.

"Short, put this idiot in the cage," Claire said. "I'll be along directly."

Knox and Rose stared at Claire.

"Short," Claire snapped.

Knox walked to Ross, got him to his feet and with help from Rose, took him outside.

"Sheriff Evergreen, may I buy you a drink?" Boyd said.

"I'm on duty," Claire said. "But I'll take a cup of coffee."

The bartender filled a mug with coffee, and then gave Boyd another shot.

"So, Randall, I would appreciate it if your boys didn't break up the place and cause me undue paperwork tonight," Claire said. "All the broken furniture and not to mention busted heads, who needs it? Do we understand each other, Randall?"

"Sheriff, my boys have been cooped up all winter," Boyd said. "They're going to let off some steam and we both know that. If not here, somewhere else. Tomorrow morning some more of my boys will show up and we'll be headed west and out of your hair."

Claire motioned to the bartender.

"Mr. Boyd has agreed to pay double for the damages and leave a

$1,000 tip, is that agreeable to you?" Claire said.

The bartender looked at Boyd. "If it is with him."

"How about it, Randall?" Claire said.

"I don't have a problem with that," Boyd said.

"Good. I have two cars sitting outside and when the fun starts I'll have them run your boys over," Claire said. "I wouldn't want them to get an OUI."

"That's right considerate of you, Sheriff," Boyd said.

"If you want to sit this one out, we have a chess set at the station," Claire said.

* * * * *

"It's your move, Randall," Claire said.

Boyd studied the chess board. They were in the break room at the table. Rose sat with them and watched.

"Don't rush me, Claire," Boyd said. He looked at Rose. "Deputy Bailey, is there anymore coffee left?"

"I just made it," Rose said.

She stood, went to the coffee maker and filled Boyd and Claire's cups, then returned to her seat.

"Thank you, Deputy," Boyd said.

"You're stalling, Randall," Claire said.

Boyd looked across the board at Claire.

"Don't think you have to pull your punches because I'm a woman, Randall," Claire said.

"That has never occurred to me, Claire," Boyd said.

The break room door opened and Turley walked in. "Claire, the prisoner is awake and he wants to see you."

"Be right there," Claire said. "Randall, make your move."

Boyd slid his queen across the board and snared one of Claire's pawns.

Claire stood. "Be right back."

She left the break room and went with Turley to the cage where a bleary-eyed Ross was standing at the bars.

"How do you like my tits now?" Claire said.

"Why am I in here?" Ross asked.

"I thought I'd save you some time," Claire said. "You buddies will be along shortly to keep you company."

"I ain't done anything 'cept get my ass knocked flat," Ross said.

"If I let you out do you promise to behave?" Claire asked.

"I think my jaw's broke," Ross said.

"Jim, let him wash up and then bring him to the break room," Claire said.

*　　*　　*　　*　　*

At the table, Ross held a bag of ice to his jaw and said, "What is this?"

"It's called chess," Boyd said. "And Claire appears to be quite good at it."

"You're not so bad yourself," Claire said. "It appears we're headed for a draw."

"Well my jaw is killing me," Ross said and looked at Claire.

"If you're looking for sympathy you'll find it in the dictionary between scumbag and suck," Claire said.

Boyd grinned at Claire.

Ross stared at Rose. "You're pretty," he said.

"Oh, please," Rose said.

The break room door opened and Turley poked his head in. "Claire, Short just called. They're bringing over the whole bunch."

*　　*　　*　　*　　*

Knox looked at Claire and said, "They're all shitfaced."

Claire looked at the ten bikers inside the cage. They were beat up and bleeding, but none appeared seriously hurt.

"Any need medical attention?" she asked.

"I don't think so."

"Any civilians hurt?"

"That's the thing, Claire; they were beating on each other."

"Boyd has agreed to double the amount for damages and leave a thousand dollar tip," Claire said. "Why don't you run him over to the bar."

Claire and Knox went to the break room.

"Randall, your babies are sleeping it off," Claire said. "My deputy will take you and jaws here to the bar where you can pay for damages. Tomorrow, I'll cut them loose and you can meet up with your second squad and be on your way."

"I appreciate your kindness, Claire," Boyd said.

Knox looked at Boyd and Ross.

"Let's go," Knox said.

*   *   *   *   *

"Go home, Rose, and don't come back until Monday," Claire said.

"What about you?" Rose asked.

"As soon as Short gets back I'll head home."

Rose nodded. "That was pretty amazing what you did in the bar."

"Is that how Holt would have handled it?" Claire said.

"He would have waited to respond to a call and half the place would have been smashed up by then," Rose said.

"Goodnight, Rose," Claire said.

Rose left Claire's office and a few minutes later, Knox entered the squad room and Claire went out to meet him.

"This is crazy," he said. "The bartender asked for thirteen hundred dollars in damages and Boyd paid that and gave him a thousand dollar tip."

"Tomorrow morning, cut the Little Rascals loose," Claire said. "We'll meet and greet the second shift and send them on their merry way."

"Headed out?"

Claire nodded. "Cole has dispatch, who are you on with?"

"Dawson."

"I hope the rest of the night is quiet," Claire said.

"Good night, Claire."

"Good night, Short."

"Hey Claire, I'm really glad you're here," Knox said.

*   *   *   *   *

Claire removed her holster and placed it on the nightstand. She flopped on the bed and immediately Snowball jumped on the bed, looking for a hug.

Claire wrapped her arms around the cat and stroked her ears.

Snowball yawned.

"I agree wholeheartedly," Claire said.

Chapter Thirty

HER RIGHT HAND WAS A bit sore from punching Ross in the jaw, so Claire took it easy on the push-ups and pull-ups and ran an extra twenty minutes instead. After a shower, she changed into slacks, white blouse and blazer and headed off to the office.

Turley was on duty as dispatch.

"Morning, Claire," he said. "I just made a pot of coffee."

Claire went to the break room, filled her mug and returned to the squad room.

"The Little Rascals give you any trouble?" she asked.

"Naw. I let them use the bathroom one at a time and made them a pot of coffee," Turley said.

"Who's on patrol?"

"Pederson and Cole. Short and Ricard on the late shift."

"I'll be in the office," Claire said. "Buzz me when Boyd gets here."

"Will do."

Claire went to her office and sat behind her desk. She opened her bottom desk drawer and pulled out the thick file on Patrick Shaw.

She read every word on every page searching the missing piece to the puzzle.

Shaw was dirty, of that Claire had no doubt.

But the word 'dirty' encompassed a great many things. Shaw could have been into anything from extortion to prostitution to drugs. There was no way of knowing until something broke.

The phone buzzed and she picked it up.

"Claire, Boyd is here," Turley said.

"Be right out."

Claire hung up and went to the squad room. Boyd was standing at Turley's desk.

"Well, look at you, Claire," Boyd said. "I like it better than the uniform."

"The uniform is for special occasions," Claire said.

"I hope the boys didn't give you any trouble," Boyd said.

"Calm as Hindu cows," Turley said.

"Good," Boyd said.

"Jim, let them out," Claire said.

Turley stood and walked to the door that led to the cage.

"Your other half on the way?" Claire asked Boyd.

"They should reach the Island by four," Boyd said. "We'll meet up and head west to the City. I'm going to take the boys to breakfast and I thought, if you didn't mind and we behaved ourselves, we'd kill some time at the beach."

"I have no problem with that," Claire said. "If everyone behaves."

"We'll be headed back this way in two weeks," Boyd said. "I'd like to stay overnight before we catch the ferry home. Will that be a problem?"

"None that I see as long as your little scamps stay in line," Claire said.

"A pleasure meeting you, Claire," Boyd said.

"Enjoy your pilgrimage," Claire said.

*　*　*　*　*

At her desk, Claire debated which was the more desirable way to spend the afternoon, hanging out with Snowball in the backyard, or hanging out with Holt.

Holt won out and she was about to pick up her phone when the cell phone in her pocket rang. She took out the phone, checked the number and hit *talk*.

"This is Claire," she said.

"Artie Wang, are you free?"

"I am. Why?"

"Wanna take a ride in an FBI jetliner?" Wang asked.

* * * * *

Wang ordered an ice cream sundae with extra whipped cream and nuts. Claire settled for a Coke with ice. They were at the Family Style restaurant on Route Twenty-seven.

"My wife won't let me near ice cream at home," Wang said as he spooned whipped cream into his mouth. "Or eggs, or cheese or anything else that tastes good since the doctor said my cholesterol was high."

Claire sipped some Coke.

"And salt," Wang said. "Zero salt. Do you know how dull life is without salt?"

"I can imagine," Claire said. "About this trip you mentioned?"

Wang ate a huge spoonful of ice cream, whipped cream and nuts, dabbed his lips with a napkin and said, "The birth certificate on the Harper's baby is false. So are the hospital records. Oh they're good. Top quality in fact, but fakes."

"So Mrs. Harper didn't have a baby?" Claire said.

"Not according to all records on file," Wang said. "From what my people have been able to trace, right around the time of the Burke kidnapping, Ben Harper withdrew $30,000 from his 401 and Melissa withdrew twenty thousand from hers. Shortly after that they moved to a suburb of Albany."

"They paid Alford for the baby," Claire said.

"Appears so," Wang said. "I want to talk to the Harpers first before I go after Alford. I figure I owe you ride on an FBI jetliner, want to go?"

"When?"

"Tomorrow."

"What time and where?"

"Ten o'clock at the private airfield in MacArthur."

Claire sipped some soda. "I'll be there, Artie. Your ice cream is melting."

Wang scooped up a spoonful. "You're to be congratulated, Claire. You cracked a ten year old case that the Bureau all but forgot."

"Alford?" Claire said.

"Once I confirm the baby is Burke's, I'll pick him up."

"I'd like to be in on that," Claire said. "It did happen in my town."

Wang nodded. "I don't have a problem with that."

The waitress stopped by the table.

"Is everything alright? Would you like something else?"

"A hunk of cheesecake with whipped cream," Wang said.

"Make that two," Claire said.

Wang looked at Claire.

"Nothing wrong with my cholesterol," she said.

*   *   *   *   *

As she drove past the beach, Claire made a sudden turn into the parking lot and parked next to the dozen motorcycles belonging to the Disciples.

She left her car and walked to the wall. Six of the Disciples were playing volleyball against six college girls. The others were sitting in the sand watching. Boyd was on a bench, drinking coffee.

Claire went through the opening in the wall and walked to Boyd. He noticed her, smiled and said, "My guys are getting their ass kicked."

Claire sat next to Boyd.

"I was driving by and saw your bikes," she said.

Boyd looked at Claire. "I'm afraid I don't have a watch. What time do you have?"

"Just after two."

"As soon as the girls are done beating my guys like a rug, we'll head over to the ferry and be on our way," Boyd said.

"Then I guess I'll see you in a few weeks," Claire said and stood up.

"Ever ride a bike?" Boyd said.

"All the time when I was on highway patrol duty in Rhode Island," Claire said.

"What the hell are you doing here?" Boyd asked. "In the one-horse town, I mean."

"Serving my purgatory," Claire said.

"Maybe you'd like to take a ride with me when we return?" Boyd said.

"I won't rule it out," Claire said.

*   *   *   *   *

Once Claire had driven off the parking lot, Boyd dug a crumpled pack of Camel cigarettes out of a vest pocket and lit it with a paper match. He inhaled deeply and blew smoke out through his nose. Then he took out his cell phone and dialed a number.

"It's me," he said when the call was answered. He listened for a moment and then said, "She's going to be a problem."

Boyd sucked in smoke, listened and then said, "Because she's smart. Too damn smart."

246

He listened for several more seconds and said, "She'll need to be dealt with when I return. Like I said, she's smart. And worse, she's curious."

Boyd listened, sighed, then hung up, stood up and tossed the cigarette to the sand.

*   *   *   *   *

Carl Walker sat in his easy back chair and looked across the coffee table to the sofa where Claire was seated.

"I will be flying to Albany tomorrow morning with the FBI to speak with the couple we believe have the kidnapped baby belonging to Michele Burke," Claire said.

"Is this some sort of… that happened ten years ago," Walker said.

"Yes, Carl, I know," Claire said.

"It appears I vastly underestimated your talents, Sheriff Evergreen," Walker said.

"Claire."

"Claire," Walker said. "How long will you be gone?"

"Just for the day," Claire said. "Rose will be in charge."

"And the kidnapper?"

"We'll deal with him when we return," Claire said. "It did happen on our beach, Carl."

"It did. Good luck, Claire. Fill me in when you return."

*   *   *   *   *

"Rose, Claire. I'm at the office," Claire said.

"Is something going on?" Rose said.

"No. I'm flying to Albany tomorrow with the FBI to speak with the Harpers."

"So they agree with us on the Harpers?"

"They do," Claire said. "You're in charge tomorrow. I probably won't be back until late, so if you need me call on my cell phone."

"Shouldn't Short take the reins?"

"He's needed in the field," Claire said. "You're calling the shots. Okay? And don't be afraid to put your foot down if you have to."

"Okay. Have a safe trip and I'll watch the store."

After hanging up with Rose, Claire gathered up all the reports on the Harpers and Alford and stuck it in her briefcase. She was about to stand and leave when she picked up the phone and called Holt.

"Claire, I was just thinking of you," Holt said when he answered the phone.

"Can I buy you a hot dog?" Claire said.

* * * * *

Claire wore a blue sundress with a thin white sweater and her Keds sneakers. She carried her gun and badge in her shoulder bag.

"I can't believe you found the Burke baby," Holt said.

They were walking the grounds at the amusement park.

"We'll see how it goes tomorrow, but I have no doubt it's Michele Burke's son," Claire said. "Let's get a corn dog."

Claire got two corn dogs from a food wagon and she and Holt took a seat on a bench.

"The kidnapper?" Holt asked as he took a bite of his corn dog.

"Agent Wang said we'll deal with him when we return."

"Amazingly good police work, Claire," Holt said.

"The trail of breadcrumbs was there to follow," Claire said.

"Don't sell yourself short, Claire," Holt said. "No one else saw the breadcrumbs, not even the FBI when the case was fresh."

"I got lucky," Claire said. "I didn't have the distractions they do.

Want to take a spin on the Ferris wheel before the fireworks start?"

"Why not?"

The Ferris wheel topped out at sixteen stories high and afforded a view of the town and the ocean. It was close to dusk when Claire and Holt went for a ride. The car had room for four, but it was just the two of them as the wheel took off to the top. Their bodies pressed shoulder to shoulder as the wheel spun slowly through its cycle.

"Matt," Claire said. "I won't lie to you. I do feel something for you."

"I'm glad, Claire," Holt said. "I'd hate to think I was making an old fool of myself for no reason."

"I haven't had… physical contact since my second divorce," Claire said. "I haven't felt the need."

"Maybe it's time for that to change?" Holt said.

"I think maybe you're right," Claire said.

"Can you take a weekend off?"

"Probably."

"I have a small cabin in the wetlands where I hunt rabbits, pheasants and turkey," Holt said. "We could spend the weekend alone and get acquainted so to speak."

"So to speak," Claire said.

"Well?"

"I think that sounds like a good idea," Claire said. "I'll arrange the time when I return from Albany."

"So when we get down, want to go to the parking lot and make out?" Holt said.

"Yeah, and it would be just my luck to have one of my deputies come by and bust us," Claire said.

* * * * *

Odd how the simplest things can register off the chart. At dusk,

Claire and Holt wandered over to the large bandstand to watch the fireworks show. It started just after dark.

Holt stood behind Claire and as the sky filled with dazzling skyrockets and waterfalls, he slipped his arms around her waist. The feeling was as if she'd been struck by a charge of static electricity. She folded her hands over Holt's and they didn't move until the show ended.

"I have to get up early," Claire said.

"Sure," Holt said.

They held hands as they walked through the parking lot to Claire's car. She gave him a soft, very sweet kiss goodnight that Claire could tell by the way his body tightened, left Holt wanting more.

*   *   *   *   *

Claire stroked Snowball's ears as the cat settled in on her stomach.

"Of course he wanted more, he's a man," Claire said. "Men always want more."

Snowball tilted her head to allow Claire to scratch behind her ears.

"But men are like puppies," Claire said. "They have to be weaned and properly trained and sometimes swatted on the nose with a rolled up newspaper."

Snowball started to purr loudly.

"What do you know about puppies, you're a cat," Claire said.

Chapter Thirty-one

"THIS IS A REALLY NICE jet," Claire said.

"Compliments of the American taxpayer," Wang said. "It's basically a flying command center. More coffee?"

"Please."

They were at the conference table in the center of the jet. Wang lifted the coffee pot off the table and filled Claire's cup, then his own.

"We land in about thirty minutes, give or take," Wang said. "Two agents from the Albany office will meet us at the airport."

"How long to their home?"

"Maybe twenty minutes," Wang said. "Ben Harper works in Albany and commutes. Mrs. Harper is a stay at home mom these days."

"What does he do for work?" Claire asked.

"For the last eight years he teaches high school science and chemistry," Wang said. "And coaches the football team."

"Jeez," Claire said.

"I know," Wang said. "We'll try to handle things as quietly as possibly for the boy's sake."

The pilot spoke over the intercom.

"Coming in for approach so you might want to return to your seats," he said.

Claire and Wang went to their seats and buckled up. She watched out the window as land, and then Albany came into view.

"Maybe we can get some cheeseburgers on the way?" Wang said.

Claire looked at him.

"My wife gave me tofu for breakfast," Wang said. "Ever had tofu? It's like eating wet chalk for God's sake."

"A cheeseburger would be nice," Claire said.

*   *   *   *   *

The Harpers lived in a small farmhouse in the country that was accessible only from a dirt road.

Melissa Harper was planting spring flowers in the front yard when the black SUV turned off the dirt road and onto the driveway.

She stood and watched as Claire, Wang and two agents climbed out of the SUV. Then she stumbled backward to the steps of the house, went weak in the knees and sat on the bottom step.

"I always knew this day would come," she said.

*   *   *   *   *

Claire, Wang and Melissa Harper sat at the kitchen table while the other two agents waited on the porch.

At forty-eight, Melissa was still an attractive woman although her dark hair had specks of gray in it now.

"We were only married a year when I was diagnosed with ovarian cancer," Melissa said. "Ben and I were crushed. We both wanted children. Our only hope was adoption. We waited for what seemed like forever. Than one day our attorney told us he could get us an infant for a fee. We..."

"How much of a fee?" Wang asked.

"$50,000. It was all that we had."

"Go on," Wang said.

"He said, our lawyer, that he could provide a birth certificate and hospitals records showing I gave birth," Melissa said. "Ben and I talked it over and after a decade of waiting, we did it. We paid our lawyer the money and he presented us with a beautiful baby boy."

"Did you know where he got the baby?" Claire asked.

"We never asked, but we suspected the black market," Melissa said. "As soon as we took possession, we moved here to Albany."

"What time does your son get home from school?" Wang asked.

"Normally the bus drops him off at three-thirty," Melissa said. "He has soccer practice today. Around five. My husband will be driving him home."

"Mrs. Harper, is the boy... I mean your son, is he happy?" Claire asked.

"God yes," Melissa said. "Ben and I love him more than life itself. He's an A student and plays baseball and soccer. He's a wonderful boy."

"Does he know he's... for want of a better word I'll say adopted?" Wang said.

"No. We never told him and planned not to," Melissa said. "I suppose he'll find out soon enough. Ben and I knew the risks and we discussed it many times what would happen if this day ever came. Well that day is here."

"You discussed this with your husband?" Claire asked.

"We know what we did is wrong," Melissa said. "We knew the day might come where we have to pay for what we did. We both knew if we got caught we'd go to prison, but for God's sake; please don't put our boy in a foster home."

Claire stared at Melissa.

"I love him more than anything and as much as I know it was wrong what we did, I don't regret one minute that we had him," Melissa said. "My husband feels the same."

Wang looked at Claire.

"Mrs. Harper, would you excuse us for a moment," Claire said.

With tears streaming down her face, Melissa nodded.

Claire and Wang went outside to the porch. The two agents from Albany were standing beside the SUV.

"Michele Burke is incapable of taking care of herself much less a ten-year-old boy," Claire said. "The boy will have to be sent to relatives he doesn't know if any even exist or a foster home."

"They purchased a human baby," Wang said. "And one where the mother was beaten and mentally damaged probably for life."

"Put the Harpers in prison for the next twenty years and at this point the only one who suffers is the boy," Claire said. "Michele Burke is in and out of the Twilight Zone from one minute to the next and the Harpers are willing to take their punishment. Besides the boy, who else suffers?"

Wang stared at Claire for several long seconds. He removed a cigar from his pocket and lit it with a lighter. "Goddammit," he said and walked down to the SUV where he pulled out his cell phone.

Claire sat in a chair and watched Wang talk on the phone. He puffed on the cigar and paced in front of the SUV as he talked. Finally he hung up and returned to the porch.

Claire followed Wang into the house back to the kitchen.

Melissa was still at the table, bleary-eyed and crying. She looked at Wang and Claire and wiped her eyes with a tissue.

"As soon as my husband arrives, we both will surrender the boy to you and take our punishment," she said.

"Mrs. Harper, in the best interest of the boy, we were never here," Wang said. "But I'm going to check back once in a while and that boy better be happy and on his way to college by the time he is eighteen. Am I understood?"

Melissa stared at Wang.

"I... I don't know what to say," she said.

"There's nothing to say, we were never here," Wang said.

* * * * *

As the jetliner took off, Wang lit a cigar and looked at Claire. "You were wrong about one thing," he said. "When you asked who else besides the boy suffers, you forgot to mention John Alford."

Claire watched Wang blow a thick smoke ring of cigar smoke.

"He's going to suffer a great deal," Wang said.

"Artie, when we land I'd like to buy you the best cheeseburger on the Island," Claire said.

"I'd like that," Wang said. "Claire."

"Can you smoke on a plane?" Claire asked.

"Who's smoking?" Wang said.

* * * * *

Wang bit into a double bacon cheeseburger and sighed with great satisfaction.

"So tonight when my wife serves me a veggie steak that tastes like burnt broccoli, I can look back upon this wonderful moment and not want to strangle her," he said.

Claire bit into her bacon cheeseburger and nodded. "Savor the moment, Artie," she said.

"Tomorrow morning, when we pick up Alford, I hope the bastard runs so I can shoot him in the leg," Wang said.

"I'd like to do it, Artie," Claire said. "You can have him, but I'd like to be the one to put the cuffs on him."

Wang took another bite of his burger and looked at Claire.

"It did happen in my town, Artie," she said. "I owe Michele Burke at least that much."

"How do you want to handle it?" Wang asked.

Claire put down her burger and pulled out her cell phone. "I already looked up and saved the number," she said as she scrolled and hit the auto dial button.

After a few seconds, Claire said, "I'd like to make an appointment to see Mr. Alford, please. Tomorrow if you can fit me in. My husband is being a real prick."

Wang grinned as he bit into his burger.

"Eleven o'clock would be fine. The name is Rose Bailey. Yes and thank you," Claire said and hung up.

"Who is Rose Bailey?" Wang asked.

"My deputy."

"I want to be like you when I grow up," Wang said as he popped the last bit of burger into his mouth.

"A twice divorced woman?"

"Let's get something really fattening for dessert," Wang said.

* * * * *

Turley was still on duty when Claire entered the squad room.

"Has Rose left for the day?" she asked.

"She's in the break room with Short and Pederson," Turley said. "They brought in a pair of winners a little while ago."

"Thanks."

Rose, Short and Pederson were drinking coffee at the break room table.

"You're back. How did it go?" Rose asked.

"Part two is tomorrow and then I'll fill you in," Claire said. "So I'm going to have to ask you to run the show again tomorrow. Turley told me you have occupants in the cage."

"Two boneheads fighting over a girl neither of them ever met before,"

Knox said. "Both claim the girl was giving them the eye."

"And the girl?"

"She was just waiting on her husband."

"Issue them desk appearance tickets and cut them loose," Claire said.

"Right."

"Rose, walk me out. I'm going home."

At her car, Claire said, "Did the boys and girls give you any trouble?"

"Actually, no," Rose said.

"Good, because when I'm gone you'll most likely be the one to inherit the star," Claire said.

Rose stared at Claire.

"Night, Rose," Claire said.

Chapter Thirty-two

CLAIRE MET WANG AND HIS team of four agents at a diner not far from John Alford's office in the Hamptons.

Claire watched in amazement as Wang shook an enormous amount of salt onto a platter of scrambled eggs with bacon and sausage. "My wife served me dry English muffins with wet tofu for breakfast," he said. "When she wasn't looking I gave it to the dog. He puked it up in the backyard. This will fix her."

Claire ordered pancakes and as she sliced into them, she said, "Your wife loves you, Artie. I think she wants you to stick around for a while."

"By feeding me garbage that makes the dog puke, ha," Wang said.

Claire ate some of her pancakes.

"So Claire, you go in alone but you go in hot," Wang said.

"I don't need to wear a wire," Claire said. "I doubt Alford could take my grandmother."

"You wear a wire or you don't go," Wang said.

"I'll wear a wire," Claire said. "Since your four-man team are all men, who wires me?"

Wang looked at Claire.

"We'll figure that out in the van," he said.

* * * * *

While two of Wang's men rode in the front of the van, the remaining two sat in back with Wang and Claire.

"We'll be at Alford's office in twenty minutes," Wang said to Claire. "Let's get you wired."

Claire removed her blue blazer to reveal a sleeveless white blouse. She unbuttoned the blouse and removed it. Under the blouse, she wore a frilly white bra.

"Jesus, Claire, your abs are amazing," Wang said.

"That's not all that's amazing," one of Wang's men said.

Wang turned to the man. "Close your mouth or I'll close it for you," he said. He looked at Claire. "Raise your arms, time to go live."

*   *   *   *   *

John Alford's office was on the top floor of a six-story building in a small office park in the Hamptons.

Claire stepped off the elevator with Wang and his crew behind her.

"We'll be in the hall," Wang said. "If we hear any sign of trouble we'll be in. Okay?"

"There won't be any trouble," Claire said.

"I'll determine that," Wang said. "We'll be right outside the door."

Claire walked to the door marked *John Alford Divorce Attorney*, opened it and stepped inside.

An attractive woman sat behind an ornate desk in a lavish reception office.

"May I help you?" she asked Claire.

"Rose Bailey to see Mr. Alford," Claire said.

"Yes, you're expected. Please follow me."

The woman stood and led Claire through a hallway to Alford's private office. She knocked once and opened the door.

Alford stood up from behind his large oak desk and smiled warmly at Claire as she walked to the desk. He was thin, boyishly handsome and showed no outward signs of his longtime drug abuse.

"Mrs. Bailey, I'm John Alford. Please have a seat," he said.

Claire took a plush leather chair opposite the desk.

Alford sat and smiled warmly at Claire.

"Now how may I help you, Mrs. Bailey?" he asked.

"My name isn't Rose Bailey," Claire said. "It's Sheriff Claire Evergreen and you are under arrest for the kidnapping of Michele Burke's baby from the beach at Smoky Point ten years ago."

The smile faded from Alford's face.

"I'm afraid I have no idea what you're talking about," he said.

"No? The Harpers do," Claire said. "I spoke with them only yesterday. They remember you real well. Shall I give them a call? We can reminisce about old times and things like $50,000."

Alford stared at Claire. She could see him shrink right before her eyes.

"Stand. Turn around. Let's do this the easy way," Claire said.

Alford stared at Claire.

"The hard way won't be pleasant," Claire said.

Alford slowly stood.

So did Claire. "Good boy," she said.

*   *   *   *   *

"Nicely done, Claire," Wang said.

Claire and Wang were riding in the center seats in the van. Two of Wang's men rode up front. Alford was sandwiched between two agents in the rear.

"She bullied me," Alford said.

"Shut up back there," Wang said.

"This is entrapment," Alford said.

"Obviously you don't know the meaning of entrapment," Wang said. "And still shut up."

"I want a lawyer," Alford said.

Wang turned around. "If I have to tell you to shut up one more time I'm going to pull over and let Sheriff Evergreen play kick the can with your face. Understood?"

Alford glared at Wang and his lips quivered.

"Go on, say something," Wang said.

Alford almost spoke, then lowered his eyes and looked at his shoes.

"Smart," Wang said.

"This wire is itching the hell out of me, Artie," Claire said.

"Take it off," Wang said.

As Claire unbuttoned her blouse, Wang looked at his men driving in the mirror.

"Eyes on the road, gentlemen," he said.

*　　*　　*　　*　　*

Federal Prosecutor Barbara Dix looked across the conference table at Wang and Claire in the Long Island Federal Building with an expression something close to astonishment.

"This is a ten year old case," Dix said.

"We know. Can you do it?" Wang asked.

"I'm quite frankly a bit amazed at your efficiency, Agent Wang," Dix said.

"It was all Claire," Wang said. "We were along for the ride."

"You're to be commended Sheriff Evergreen," Dix said.

"Look, Prosecutor Dix, I don't give a flip about commendations or even justice for that matter. I care about what's right. Can you present the deal we outlined or not," Claire said. "And call me Claire."

Dix looked at Wang.

He shrugged. "Yeah, she's always like that."

Dix looked at Claire.

"Ten years no parole in exchange for a written confession or twenty-five no parole for a trial at the age of forty-eight, he'll take the deal," Dix said. "Claire."

"Thank you," Claire said. "Barbara."

"You're welcome. Claire."

* * * * *

"They have a decent cafeteria on the third floor," Wang said. "Let's get some coffee and donuts."

"For God's sake, Artie, I don't want to have to explain to your wife that you died in my presence eating donuts," Claire said.

"Just coffee then," Artie said. "I want to talk to you."

* * * * *

Claire watched Wang shovel hot apple pie covered in warm cheese into his mouth and she said, "That's a bit more than just coffee, Artie."

"Here's my offer, Claire," Wang said.

"What offer?"

"Don't interrupt a senior FBI Agent," Wang said. "You come in on the ground floor but as part of my team. Inside a year you'll be my team leader."

"You're offering me a job?" Claire said.

"I did. I am, yes."

"I'm flattered, Artie, but in ten months I'll be in Rhode Island working homicides," Claire said.

"And kissing the ass of every corrupt politician in the state,"

Wang said.

"I like homicide, Artie."

"So you'll work homicide just on a federal level."

"Can I think about it before I give you an answer?"

"I expect no less," Wang said. "Take a week to think it over and give me a call."

* * * * *

Rose was laughing along with Mitzi in the squad room when Claire arrived. Turley was at his desk and said, "Some messages for you, Claire. I put them on your desk."

"Thank you," Claire said.

"We were just gossiping about Carl," Mitzi said as Claire approached Rose's desk.

"Last year at the 4th of July celebration he wore Bermuda shorts with black socks and sandals," Rose said.

"I wish you hadn't said that," Claire said.

"It sticks in your mind, doesn't it?" Mitzi said.

"So, tell me," Rose said.

"We picked up John Alford and charged him with the Michele Burke kidnapping," Claire said. "He'll do ten years no parole."

"That's... unbelievable, Claire," Mitzi said.

"It's a complicated deal, but it benefits the ten year old boy," Claire said.

"We should celebrate," Mitzi said.

"Not tonight," Claire said. "I'm too tired and my boobs are sore."

Rose and Mitzi stared at Claire.

"I had to wear a wire," Claire said. "It was too tight."

Mitzi gave Claire a warm hug and said, "Go home and soak in a hot tub. And have a glass of wine."

"I'll do exactly that as soon as I check my messages," Claire said.

"I'll walk you out," Rose said to Mitzi.

Claire entered her office, sat behind her desk, and checked the messages.

On top of the stack was a message from Cruz asking her to return his call.

Then one from Kellerman.

Holt called and asked her to call on his cell phone. It was after seven, but she picked up the phone and punched in his number.

Holt answered after three rings.

"Claire, I was hoping you'd call," he said.

"Matt, I was thinking about your suggestion about your cabin," Claire said.

"Are you getting cold feet?"

"Just the opposite," Claire said. "I'm looking forward to getting away for a few days."

"Good, because I'm at the cabin right now doing some housecleaning," Holt said. "It needed it."

"We will take it slow, won't we?"

"Like molasses in winter time if you want."

"Thank you, Matt," Claire said. "I'm tired. I'm going home and take a bath and get some sleep. I'll call you tomorrow."

"Good night, Claire," Holt said.

"Night, Matt."

Claire hung up and sat for a moment. She felt tired to the bone.

Rose walked in and sat on the sofa.

"Congratulations, Claire. This should get you back in homicide in no time," she said.

"The only thing that will get me back to Rhode Island before my suspension is up is an apology," Claire said. "And the more I think about it the more I want to tell the Congressman to fuck off."

Rose smiled. "Good, we get to keep you for another ten months," she said.

"If you have everything under control, I'm going home," Claire said.

"Go," Rose said.

Claire stood, picked up the remaining messages, put them in her pocket and said, "Night, Rose. See you in the morning."

*   *   *   *   *

Claire emptied her pockets at the kitchen table and remembered the messages. She looked at the top one. It was from prosecutor Barbara Dix. The next one was from Dugan.

The final message was from David Kleinfield.

It simply read to *return his call*. He left a callback number.

Claire took her phone and the message to the bedroom where she stripped down and ran the tub. Snowball followed her and hopped onto the toilet lid.

She inspected herself in the mirror. There were red marks above her waist to below her breasts from the wire.

Claire looked at Snowball. "He needs to learn how to put on a wire, the donut eating slob," she said.

Snowball meowed.

"Yeah, next time," Claire said.

She punched in the callback number and slipped into the tub. She lowered herself so that her neck was against the rim and waited for someone to pick up. On the fifth ring, David Kleinfield answered the call and said, "Hello Sheriff Evergreen."

"May I be presumptuous and assume that your father has some information for me," Claire said.

"You're invited to lunch tomorrow," David said. "My father likes to eat at twelve-thirty. Please be on time."

"What's on the menu?"

"I do all of my father's cooking," David said. "See you tomorrow."

"I didn't say that I was coming," Claire said.

"See you tomorrow," David said and hung up.

Claire set the phone on the tiled floor.

She looked at Snowball.

"I guess I'll see him tomorrow," she said.

Chapter Thirty-three

CLAIRE WORE A LIGHT GRAY pants suit with a sleeveless white blouse and wore her Glock under the jacket.

She carried a sixteen-ounce coffee with her when she entered the office.

Turley was on duty at his desk.

"Morning Claire," he said.

"Morning Jim. Who's on the schedule?"

"Pederson and Cole on the day, Short and Ricard on the late and Rose is on swing."

"I have a meeting at twelve-thirty," Claire said. "I'll be out of the office from eleven-thirty until around two I'd guess."

"I'll take your calls," Turley said.

Claire went to her office, sat at her desk and picked up the phone and returned Barbara Dix's call.

"This is Dix," she said when she came on the line.

"Barbara, it's Claire returning your call," Claire said.

"Well, haven't you caused quite a stir at the office," Dix said.

"In a good way I hope," Claire said. "Did Alford take the deal?"

"Under the advisement of his lawyer, he accepted," Dix said.

"The Harpers?"

"Wang explained your position on the matter and I agree, only the boy would be hurt," Dix said. "It bothers me they got away with this, but the welfare of the boy is at stake. The plea should include

267

paying for his medical bills."

"Good."

"So, Claire, there is an opening for a Special Investigator in the Prosecutor's Office," Dix said. "It covers all of Long Island and that includes Brooklyn and Queens. Interested?"

Claire smiled to herself. "Not two months ago I couldn't get hired dog catcher," she said.

"I checked with Rhode Island," Dix said. "Personally, if it was me, I'd a kicked him in the balls."

"Have you spoken with Artie?"

"He told me he offered you a Bureau position," Dix said.

"Can I think about it, Barbara? I have some unfinished business to attend to."

"Sure, but not too long."

"Thanks."

Claire hung up and sipped some coffee.

Then she picked up the phone again and called Dugan.

"How are things in the sticks?" he said when he picked up.

"There's more happening in this one-horse-town than half the state of Rhode Island," Claire said.

"The Congressman is worried."

"About?"

"His reelection come November."

"Why tell me?"

"He's afraid of losing the women's vote."

"I know one he can't count on."

"Do you want to hear this or not?"

"No, but go ahead anyway."

"The Congressman proposes a beer summit where he…"

"The Congressman has me confused with someone else. A fellow politician perhaps."

"Claire, would you shut up and listen?" Dugan said.

"I'm listening," Claire said.

"The Congressman wants to meet and have a mutual apology that the press will cover," Dugan said. "He makes up with the female vote and you go back to work with a promotion."

"A mutual apology? And I apologize for what exactly?"

"Claire, listen to…"

"He blew a 2.4 behind the wheel," Claire said. "Did he get an OUI like everybody else would? Did he pay the fine, take the mandatory course and lose his license for ninety days? If the answer is yes, I'll consider it."

"Claire, be…"

"Yes or no, did he?"

Dugan was silent.

"End of story," Claire said and hung up.

* * * * *

At exactly twelve-thirty, Claire knocked on the front door of the Kleinfield home and almost immediately, David Kleinfield opened the door.

"You look well, Sheriff Evergreen," he said.

David wore a pale blue summer-weight suit that seemed out of place for a man just answering the door.

"It's a warm afternoon. My father would rather eat in the breakfast nook with the air on. Is that alright with you?"

"It's your house. I'm just a guest," Claire said.

"I'll take the gun," David said.

Claire removed the holster and David hung it on the coat hook.

"Follow me please," David said.

The 'breakfast nook' was larger than Claire's kitchen with a table for ten and artwork on all four walls. The table was set for two with a carafe of coffee, hot water for tea, juice and glasses and mugs. Kleinfield wasn't at the table.

"Help yourself to coffee, tea or juice while I get my father," David said.

David left the nook and Claire filled a mug with coffee. She walked along the walls and examined the artwork as she sipped.

"Do you appreciate fine art?" Kleinfield asked when he entered the nook and found Claire examining a painting.

"To tell you the truth Abby, I wouldn't know a Rembrandt from paint by the numbers," Claire said.

"Neither would I," Kleinfield said. "My son believes artwork is an investment. He buys all this. Please, have a seat."

They both took chairs in front of the table settings.

"Lunch is my main meal of the day," Kleinfield said. "Dinner is usually soup and salad. Anything heavy after six and I'm awake all night with heartburn. It's part of growing old, I suppose."

The door opened and David wheeled in a serving trolley.

"My son does all my cooking," Kleinfield said. "It's not a task he enjoys but it's rather necessary I'm afraid."

Claire didn't ask and probably figured Kleinfield was afraid of being poisoned.

David served baked chicken breasts with dirty rice and green beans with roasted almonds. He filled the glasses with ice and water, nodded and left the nook.

"So tell me Claire, do you enjoy being a sheriff?" Kleinfield asked.

"No, Abby, I do not," Claire said.

"Then why do it?"

"It pays the bills."

"I don't believe that, Claire," Kleinfield said. "Twice married, an excellent record in homicide with the Rhode Island State Police, suspended over some pinhead incident that, if the police had any balls they would back you one hundred percent."

"You know a lot for a retired investor living on a pension," Claire said.

"Would you like to return to Rhode Island, Claire?" Kleinfield asked. "With a full apology in writing from the Congressman?"

"And you can make that happen?"

"I've been known as a man who can get certain things done from time to time."

"If it's all the same to you, Abby, I'll sit out my suspension."

Kleinfield grinned. "I'd be disappointed in you Claire if you didn't say that."

"So why am I here?" Claire asked.

"We'll discuss such matters over dessert," Kleinfield said.

*　*　*　*　*

David served coffee and fresh peach cobbler in the backyard. There was a large retractable awning that provided shade and a breeze off the ocean made it quite comfortable to sit at the table.

Kleinfield ate some cobbler, washed it down with coffee and said, "Your question was why are you here?"

Claire ate a spoonful of cobbler and nodded.

"You're here because you're that special breed of cop who is never satisfied," Kleinfield said. "Always prowling around seeking truth and willing to bend the law to do what's right. Before you're through you'll probably have two more marriages and those too will end in failure. The only time you are truly happy is when you're closing in on the bad guys. That you are here talking to me proves my point."

"So who's doing any talking?" Claire said.

Kleinfield smiled. "Sheriff Patrick Shaw was a mule," he said.

Claire took a sip of coffee, set the mug down and looked at Kleinfield. "A mule for who and carrying what?" she asked.

"The word from my friends in the City is that he grew overly greedy and had to be removed," Kleinfield said. "He was making a drop the night he was killed."

"Did your friends say anything else?" Claire said.

"They said to tell you good luck," Kleinfield said.

"Why did you tell me all this, Abby?" Claire asked.

"Tell you what, Claire?" Kleinfield asked. "You were never here."

"Is it time for me to leave?" Claire asked. "Isn't it, Abby?"

"I've enjoyed our chat," Kleinfield said. "Claire."

At the front door, David handed Claire her holster and a large brown paper bag.

"What's this?" she asked as she took the bag.

"Peach cobbler," David said. "It's still warm."

*   *   *   *   *

Claire entered the squad room and set the paper bag on Turley's desk.

"What's this?" he asked.

"Peach cobbler. It's really good."

Rose was at her desk and stood when Claire approached her.

"Office," Claire said. "Bring coffee."

Claire entered her office, removed her blazer and sat behind the desk. A moment later, Rose came in with two mugs of coffee and set one on the desk.

"Close the door," Claire said.

Rose closed the door and sat on the sofa.

"I have reason to believe that Shaw was transporting drugs to the City the night he was murdered," Claire said.

"We figured he was dirty, but transporting drugs?" Rose said.

272

"It explains a lot," Claire said. "The midnight run on the highway. Using the coolers as containers. Dress shoes for a fishing trip. Lack of bait. It all fits that he was on the road for something other than a fishing trip."

"Why was he killed?" Rose asked.

"My source tells me he got overly greedy."

"Your source?"

"It's reliable," Claire said.

"What do you want to do?" Rose asked.

"Get proof," Claire said.

"How?"

"Dig until something turns up," Claire said.

"This could turn Smoky Point on its ear," Rose said.

"Ears are not my concern," Claire said.

Rose sipped from her mug and said, "What now?"

"Basics," Claire said. Wear your uniform tomorrow."

Rose nodded.

"I need to make a call," Claire said.

Rose stood and walked to the door. "Closed?"

"Please."

Rose closed the door and Claire picked up the phone and called Holt. He answered after three rings.

"Hi Claire," Holt said. "I'm just leaving the…"

"We need to talk," Claire said. "Right away."

"Sounds serious."

"How long to get to your house?"

"Hour."

"I'll meet you there."

Claire hung up, went to the squad room, and stopped at Rose's desk.

"If you need me I'll be on cell," she said. "And what we spoke about is just between us."

"No problem," Rose said. "Anything you need me to do?"

"Check old records and log books going back ten years or more."

"Looking for?"

"The unknown."

"What does the unknown look like?" Rose said.

"You'll know it when you see it," Claire said.

*   *   *   *   *

Claire was sitting on Holt's front steps when he arrived in his pickup. It was covered in a layer of mud.

Holt exited and Claire stood as he approached her.

She looked at the pickup.

"Exactly where is this cabin of yours?" she said.

"Lots of rain on a dirt road," Holt said. "So what's up?"

"We need to talk privately," Claire said.

"Want to take the boat out? We can talk there. It's private."

"Okay."

*   *   *   *   *

Twenty minutes into the sound, Holt dropped anchor and turned off the motor. He left the helm and found Claire seated at the table. She had made coffee. There was a pot and two mugs. She filled one for him.

"Thanks," Holt said and took a seat. "So which hat are you wearing, Claire the woman or Claire the Sheriff?"

"It's about Patrick Shaw," Claire said.

"It doesn't surprise me, Claire. What about him?"

"He was a mule," Claire said. "He was transporting drugs the night he was murdered. He was getting too greedy and was killed for it."

"You know this how, Claire? How?"

"A reliable source," Claire said.

Holt stared at Claire for a moment. "Kleinfield. He's your reliable source, isn't he?" he said.

"And if he is?"

"Jesus, Claire, he's as big a mobster as the Italian Godfather," Holt said.

"So?"

"So why should he tell you anything, much less about Shaw?"

"He likes me," Claire said.

"He… for God's sake, Claire," Holt said. "The man would have you killed as soon as look at you if you got on his bad side."

Claire sipped coffee and then set the mug on the table. "I need eyes, Matt. Rose is learning, but she's still an amateur and besides, I'm not sure I want to take her any deeper. Will you help me with this?"

Holt stared at Claire.

"You're going to make me say it, aren't you?" Claire said. "Please."

"Dammit," Holt said.

Claire smiled. "Thank you," she said.

"We can't work on this at the office," Holt said. "Bring everything you have to my house tomorrow before breakfast. By the way, who else have you told about this?"

"Just Rose and she won't say a word."

"Good."

"Right now I don't want to think about it," Holt said. "I'm taking you back and then I'm going to take a twenty minute long hot shower and wash the mud off me, have a stiff drink and maybe watch a ballgame."

"Matt, nobody likes to think about a dirty cop," Claire said.

"Claire, when you go after a dirty cop, people get hurt," Holt said.

"It's just the nature of the beast."

*   *   *   *   *

Snowball tucked her paws under her as she settled in on Claire's stomach.

"What Matt said is true, there is no logical reason why a mobster like Kleinfield should care about or help me solve a decade old murder of a dirty cop," Claire said.

Snowball rubbed her head against Claire's hand and Claire stroked her.

"So why did he?" Claire said.

Snowball rolled onto her side and Claire rubbed her ears.

"There's a reason, what is it?"

As she continued to rub Snowball's ears, Claire looked up at the ceiling of her bedroom.

Snowball purred loudly and Claire felt her eyes grow heavy and close.

A little while later, her eyes snapped open and she sat up in bed.

"Kleinfield is not helping me," Claire said aloud. "He's helping himself."

Chapter Thirty-four

BEFORE SHE LEFT THE HOUSE, Claire phoned Rose at home and told her she would be in the field for several hours and to take charge of the office.

She arrived at Holt's house at eight-thirty with her briefcase stuffed.

"I'm making breakfast," Holt said as he led Claire to the kitchen. "Have a chair at the island and I'll get you coffee."

There were six bar stools at the chef's island and Claire set the briefcase down beside a chair and sat.

Holt set a mug of coffee in front of her and returned to the stove.

"I'm making omelets with roasted peppers, hash browns, bacon and sourdough toast," he said. "We can eat in here or the backyard."

*   *   *   *   *

From the backyard they could hear the waves crashing and gulls squawking at the beach. The patio table was in shade and the sun hadn't heated the air as yet.

Still, Claire was warm and removed her gray blazer.

"It occurred to me last night that what Kleinfield did wasn't to help me," Claire said. "But to help himself."

Holt sipped coffee and sat back in his chair. "Do you know what you're saying?"

"I think so, yes," Claire said. "That whatever operation Shaw was a part of ten years ago is still in operation today. If I can bust it open I identify and eliminate Kleinfield's competition."

"He's using you, Claire," Holt said. "To do his dirty work for him."

"That's one way of looking at it."

"What's the other?"

"I arrest a group of dealers, get some drugs off the street and find a murderer," Claire said. "If the peripheral damage is it helps Kleinfield, so be it. No one has been able to touch him anyway."

Holt nodded. "I like your attitude, but it can be risky."

"We're cops," Claire said. "What about our job isn't risky?"

"That depends entirely upon how far you are willing to go," Holt said.

"I've never been a girl to go half way," Claire said. "On anything."

Holt sighed. "Let's go inside and put our heads together and see what we come up with," he said.

* * * * *

Claire removed a legal pad and pen from her briefcase and set them on the kitchen table.

"Let's start with the known," Claire said.

Holt stood and walked to the counter and filled two mugs with fresh coffee. He returned to the table and sat.

"Thanks," Claire said. "We know that Shaw was murdered execution style in his car on the side of the road between midnight and one in the morning. He wasn't dressed for a fishing trip even though there were two rods in the car. He had no bait or coolers in the car that night. The coolers he won in tournaments were never found. He was seen at his retirement party with excessive flash money. He…"

"When was that?"

"His retirement party?" Claire said. "She dug through her notes. Right after Memorial Day eight years ago."

"I came aboard about a month or so later," Holt said.

"What else do we know?" Claire said. "We know that he didn't have any unusual activity in any bank accounts and what he left his ex-wife and children was right in line with what he earned. He probably had a slush fund that was lost with him."

"That's not a known, that's a guess," Holt said.

"I'll move that one to unknown for now," Claire said. "We know that he was involved in smuggling drugs and..."

"That's an assumption," Holt said. "Just because Kleinfield said Shaw was a mule doesn't make it true."

"That one gets a plausible," Claire said.

"Know what else is plausible?" Holt said. "That Shaw double dipped like I did. I collected my pension while I worked as sheriff and didn't spend a nickel of my sheriff's pay. How do you think I got the boat?"

"Say that's true," Claire said. "Eight years, about $200,000 in bankable pay, where is it? It wasn't in his known bank accounts and he didn't leave that kind of money to his family. Nor did he buy a boat, a house or any other damn thing that adds up to that kind of money."

Holt nodded. "I'll give you that. It's really difficult to hide money, especially from the IRS."

"I checked the old State Police and County sheriff reports and Shaw's finances," Claire said. "They found no hidden bank accounts or safe deposit boxes, but that doesn't mean he didn't have one or more than one under an assumed name."

"I'll give you that one, too."

"Let's look at some unknowns," Claire said.

"Start with it's unknown if Kleinfield was telling the truth or not," Holt said.

"Granted," Claire said. "It's unknown what Shaw was doing on the shoulder of the highway after midnight dressed in casual clothes with two fishing rods in the car and without bait or a tackle box."

"It's possible Shaw was one of these fishing nuts that always carries a rod just in case they get the urge to wet a line at some stream they've never tried. An impulse fisherman," Holt said.

"Would an impulse fisherman carry his rods but not his tackle box?" Claire asked.

"No."

"It's unknown why Shaw pulled off the road. A check of his car showed nothing wrong. There were no skid marks on the road to indicate an emergency stop. His window was down and the shooter had a clear path to shoot him in the head. Question, if you were involved in a road rage incident and a man approached you with a weapon, would you lower your window?"

"I would not."

"If you were involved in such an incident and were armed, wouldn't you pull your weapon?"

"I would."

"So, why didn't Shaw?"

Holt looked at Claire.

"I've rolled that question around in my mind a thousand times," Claire said. "I always come up with the same answer."

"That Shaw knew his killer," Holt said.

Claire nodded. "Not only knew but was expecting him."

Holt sipped coffee and then sighed. "Maybe I could go back and look at Shaw's friends and known associates?" he said.

"Let me swear you in so it's official," Claire said. "Raise your right hand. I have an extra badge in my briefcase."

"You're kidding?"

"No, I'm not."

Holt held up his right hand and Claire swore him in as a deputy.

"Dress as you like, but start carrying your gun," Claire said.

"This doesn't change our plans for the cabin?" Holt asked.

"I don't see why it will," Claire said.

"Maybe we could...?"

"Sure, when we go to the cabin," Claire said. "Right now I have to get to the office. A good place to start is with Shaw's drunken ex-wife."

* * * * *

"You swore Matt Holt in as your secret deputy?" Rose said.

"Emphasis on the word secret," Claire said. "He's going to look into Shaw's past friends, associates and whatnot. How are you doing with old records?"

"Something interesting," Rose said. "Prior to sixteen years ago arrests for drugs were almost nonexistent. After that we hit a boom, then a peak and we've held it steady ever since."

"Shaw was sworn in sixteen years ago, wasn't he?"

"He was," Rose said.

"Rose, besides our bonehead bikers, check how many names made the sixteen year list as repeat offenders," Claire said. "Shaw may have had a partner he used as a mule or even a distributor."

"I hadn't thought of that," Rose said.

"I need to make a call," Claire said.

Rose stood, left the office and closed the door.

Claire picked up the phone and called Cruz.

After three transfers and a five-minute wait on hold, Cruz picked up and said, "Does it always take you this long to return a call?"

"I'll be at your office in one hour," Claire said. "See if you can get a hold of Kellerman."

"Maybe if you told me why I would..."

"Thanks, Bill," Claire said and hung up.

*   *   *   *   *

When Claire was escorted into Cruz's office, Kellerman and Cruz were at the conference table.

Claire carried her briefcase and a large bag from Donut World.

"Are you aware that it's almost six o'clock?" Kellerman asked Claire.

"I have a watch," Claire said.

"My wife is expecting me home for dinner," Cruz said.

"I need thirty minutes, Bill," Claire said. "And then you can rush home to your nice tofu steak and green beans dinner. I brought a dozen donuts I thought we could munch on while we talk. They're still warm."

Cruz and Kellerman eyed the paper bag.

"Damn," Cruz said.

*   *   *   *   *

"The question is not do we believe Kleinfield was being truthful about Shaw, but to what extent?" Kellerman said.

Cruz dipped a pumpkin flavored donut into his coffee and took a bite. "And his motives are questionable," he said.

"Of course they are," Claire said. "But that doesn't mean they don't serve a useful purpose."

Kellerman and Cruz exchanged glances.

"Kleinfield is a…" Cruz said as he took another bite of his donut, chewed and swallowed. "Shrewd and calculating son of a bitch. If his story is to be believed and we pursue it he gets the police to get rid of his competition for him."

"I don't deny that Kleinfield benefits," Claire said. "But so do we. We get a murderer and get to put away some dealers. I've asked Matthew Holt to assist me with investigative work. He knows New York City and I don't."

"You think this stretches that far?" Cruz asked.

"Shaw was a City cop and he was driving west the night he was murdered," Claire said.

"You'll need investigative manpower," Cruz said.

"Why do you think I'm here?" Claire said.

"They'll take direction from me, Claire," Cruz said. "I won't budge on that one no matter how many donuts you bring."

Claire looked at Cruz.

"I'll assume the homicide end of this," Kellerman said. "My guys will run with the murder aspect and Claire, no more working independently. I call the shots and if you can't handle that you're out. We work as a team with a pecking order. Understood?"

"Are you boys done spraying testosterone on the walls because if you are I'd like to say something?" Claire said. "If you ever condescend to me again I will tell the both of you to fuck off and go my own way. Understood?"

"We didn't…" Cruz said.

"The next time you scamps want to play let's see who has the biggest dick in the room, remember it's not the size but how well you use it that counts," Claire said.

She stood and walked to the door and opened it.

"Claire, wait a minute," Cruz said. "Are you part of the team or not?"

"Who said I wasn't," Claire said and walked out.

Cruz and Kellerman looked at each other.

"She has quite the temper," Kellerman said.

"How would you feel if you broke your ass to resurface an old case that nobody else wanted or made and at the last minute a couple of assholes showed up and snatched it away from you?" Cruz said.

"Are we the assholes?" Kellerman asked.

Cruz sighed. "Any more donuts in the bag?"

*   *   *   *   *

Claire was soaking in a hot tub, her head against the rim and a washcloth on her eyes when her cell phone rang.

She removed the cloth and looked at Snowball who was seated on the lid of the toilet. "Want to get that?" Claire asked.

She reached down and picked up the phone, checked the incoming number, pressed *talk* and said, "Have you run out of donuts?"

"And testosterone," Cruz said. "Look, Claire, we got carried away. We were out of line. Our thought process was… is a bit different than yours."

"If this is an apology, it really sucks," Claire said.

"Let me finish," Cruz said. "You're thinking Shaw and his drug connection. We were thinking of the bigger fish Kleinfield."

"Now Bill, do you really think Kleinfield would have told me what he told me if every one of his bases wasn't totally covered?" Claire said. "He'll only let you get close to him if he wants you to and he doesn't. And your apology still sucks."

"Help me out here, Claire, I'm sinking," Cruz said.

"You said we were a team," Claire said. "We'll sink or swim as one."

"Thank you, Claire."

"You're welcome, Bill," Claire said. "Call me when you have everything in place."

"Give us a few days," Cruz said.

"Night-night. Enjoy your tofu steak," Claire said and hung up.

She looked at Snowball. "Men," Claire said and the placed the washcloth over her eyes.

Chapter Thirty-five

CLAIRE ARRIVED AT THE OFFICE to find David Kleinfield standing beside a black Lincoln Town Car in the parking lot.

"Good morning, Claire. Get in," David said.

"Why, are we going somewhere?" Claire asked.

"Please get in, Claire," David said. "My father wishes to see you."

David opened the rear door. Barbara Dix was seated behind the driver's seat.

"I need to tell my dispatcher," Claire said.

"That's what cell phones are for," David said.

Claire got in next to Barbara and David closed the door.

"Hello, Barbara," Claire said.

"Nice to see you again, Claire," Dix said.

"We're going for a ride," Claire said.

"Appears so," Dix said.

*　*　*　*　*

David served warm bagels with cream cheese or butter, scrambled eggs, sausage and hash browns, juice and coffee.

Claire and Dix took seats at the backyard table.

"My father will be out in a few minutes," David said. "Enjoy your breakfast."

Once David was inside, Dix said, "Polite bastard isn't he?"

"Might as well eat," Claire said.

"Any idea what this is about?" Dix asked.

"Yes," Claire said.

"And?"

"It's complicated and I'm sure Abby will fill you in," Claire said.

"Abby?" Dix said. "What have I missed?"

The kitchen door opened and Kleinfield emerged and walked to the table.

"Nice to see you again, Claire," he said.

"You too, Abby," Claire said.

Kleinfield took a chair and looked at Dix.

"Prosecutor Dix, I have followed your career closely," Kleinfield said. "Very impressive."

"You follow my career?" Dix said. "Why?"

"Some follow sports teams or the horses, I follow promising attorneys," Kleinfield said. "Call it a hobby. I predict you'll make federal judge one day. How is your breakfast?"

"Wonderful," Claire said. "But I don't think you sent for us to break bread in your backyard."

"Do you know my son David makes the bagels from scratch?" Kleinfield asked.

"I didn't know that," Claire said.

"Do you remember our prior conversation, Claire?" Kleinfield said.

"Every word."

"Then this should interest you, both of you," Kleinfield said. "I've spoken to some of my retired investor friends in the City about our deceased sheriff in question. I asked them to continue to make some discrete inquiries into the matter. What they found out was that shortly before his death, Shaw took out a ten-year lease on a safe deposit box at the First Savings and Loan of Brooklyn."

"Brooklyn falls under my jurisdiction," Dix said.

"Amazing coincidence that you're here enjoying breakfast on this lovely morning," Kleinfield said.

"Safe deposit boxes require identification and keys," Claire said.

"A search warrant and key should suffice," Kleinfield said. "Wouldn't you agree Prosecutor Dix?"

"I would," Dix said.

"Enjoy your breakfast. My son will see you on the way out," Kleinfield said and stood up.

* * * * *

At the front door, David handed Claire her holster and a brown paper bag. He gave Dix an identical bag.

"What's this?" Dix asked.

"Bagels," David said. "Still warm. I'll bring the car around."

* * * * *

Once they were underway, Claire opened her bag and mixed in with the bagels was a long key marked FSLB #232.

She looked into the rearview mirror at David.

"David, if you don't mind, I'd like to get out with Barbara at her office," Claire said.

"No problem, Claire," David said.

* * * * *

Cruz ate a dry bagel as he looked at the key in Claire's hand.

"Is this on the level?" he said.

"I was there, Bill," Dix said.

Al Lamanda

"Now you're with the Bill, huh," Cruz said.

"We're waiting on a search warrant signed by a federal judge and then we're going to Brooklyn," Dix said. "The bank closes at five and we intend to be there before it closes. Are you coming with us? Bill."

"What about Kellerman?" Cruz asked.

"He's invited to the party," Dix said.

*   *   *   *   *

Kellerman and Cruz sat in front while Kellerman drove his unmarked State Police car. Claire and Dix occupied the back seats.

"Pass me one of those bagels," Kellerman said.

Cruz opened the bag and handed Kellerman a bagel.

"Thanks," Kellerman said.

"It's three o'clock," Dix said.

"Plenty of time," Kellerman said.

Cruz turned in his seat and looked at Claire. "This Kleinfield has a plan," he said. "And I think it's more than he's being a good citizen. There must be something more in this for him than getting rid of some competition."

"He's playing us is what he's doing," Kellerman said. "The man went to a great deal of trouble to help us who would jump at the chance to lock his ass up. Why?"

"You're assuming Kleinfield went to a great deal of trouble," Dix said. "For all we know it was pick up the phone and make one call."

"Maybe so, but Kleinfield doesn't have to do anything at all," Kellerman said. "So why is he?"

"Let's focus on one thing at a time for now," Dix said.

"Claire, what do you say?" Cruz asked.

"Anymore of those bagels?" Claire said.

*   *   *   *   *

The bank manager read the warrant and then said, "Follow me please."

He led them down a flight of stairs to the safe deposit box room and unlocked the steel door with a key.

"Each box requires two keys," the manager said. "Mine and yours."

The room held one thousand boxes with a dozen viewing stations. The manager led them to box 232 and said, "We put the keys in together and turn at the same time."

Claire handed the key to Dix and she and the manager inserted their keys, turned them and unlocked the box.

The manager removed his key and slid the long box from its sleeve.

"Follow me please," he said and took the box to a private viewing station and set it on the desk. "Ring when you are ready."

After the manager left the viewing station, Dix reached for the cover of the yard-long box and slowly flipped it open.

Dix gasped softly at the sight of the rows of twenty dollar bills bound with rubber bands. She counted twelve rows and lifted one stack. It was three inches thick.

"Christ, how much is in there?" Cruz said.

"What's that?" Claire asked and reached between the last row and wall of the box and withdrew a thin black book.

Claire opened the book and looked at the first page. "It's a list of some kind, but it seems to be written in code."

"Let me see that," Kellerman said and took the book.

"We can look at it later," Dix said. "Right now we need to get this money and book to my office."

"Your office?" Cruz said.

Dix looked at Cruz. "Let me know when your office outranks mine," she said.

* * * * *

"That's the last of it," Dix said as she set a stack of bills on the conference table in her office. "The total is $400,000."

Claire picked up the thin black book. "These codes are more than eight years old," she said. "They are probably all obsolete by now, but if we could crack them they might tell us who and what Shaw was involved in and we possibly could update them."

"Anybody here know shit about code breaking?" Kellerman asked.

"No, but the FBI does and I happen to have made a new friend," Claire said.

Kellerman looked at her. "Artie Wang," he said.

"Yup, Artie Wang," Claire said. She looked at Cruz. "You two have a lot in common. Neither of your wives can cook."

"Call him," Kellerman said.

"It's ten o'clock at night," Claire said. "I'll call him in the morning. Right now I need a ride home."

"I can arrange that," Dix said.

"Me, too," Claire said.

* * * * *

"I'm simply amazed," Holt said.

"It is a lot to soak in, isn't it?" Claire said.

"Once you bring in the FBI this is theirs," Holt said. "Not county, state or local."

Claire nodded. "I know," she said. "To be honest, this is about as far as I can go with it given my resources. The FBI has an army of code breakers and the means to trace the cash if it is traceable."

"Am I relieved of duty yet?" Holt said.

"Depends on the type of duty you're talking about," Claire said.

Holt glanced at Claire. "So that's what gets your motor running," he said. "A little danger, a murder or two, a few mobsters and you purr like a kitten."

"Even kittens have claws," Claire said.

"Ouch," Holt said.

"There's my car," Claire said.

Holt parked alongside it. "I could follow you home?" he said.

"You could," Claire said.

Holt looked at her.

"Oh for," Claire said and took Holt in her arms.

He was amazed at how physically strong she was and after several deep, long kisses, Claire broke them apart.

"Are you wearing a gun?" she asked.

"No."

"That's enough kissing then," Claire said. "Save it for the cabin."

"Jeez, Claire."

"Night-night."

*   *   *   *   *

Randall Boyd watched the bonfire on the beach as burning cinders rose up and took flight on the ocean breeze. The rally was large with about 500 bikers and their women scattered along the beach in Virginia.

His cell phone rang and he checked the number and stepped away from the noise to answer it.

"This is Boyd," he said.

He held his left finger in his ear as he listened.

"What the fuck do you want me to do about it?" he said. "I didn't hire the bitch."

He turned and looked at the bonfire as he listened, then said,

"Yeah, Goddammit, yeah. You created the monster, now I gotta fucking deal with it. I'll be there in three days."

Boyd hung up and walked to the bonfire where his guys were standing.

He found Tate with the others. "Find Ross," he said. "We're leaving."

"Leaving? We just got here," Tate said.

"Business," Boyd said.

"Well, where are we going?" Tate asked.

"Smoky Point," Boyd said.

Chapter Thirty-six

WANG FLIPPED THROUGH THE THIN pages in the little black notebook. "It's code alright. No doubt," he said.

"If you could break it, even though it's eight years old or more, it could lead to some heavy made guys from back in the day," Dix said.

"Where's the $400,000?" Wang asked.

"My evidence room," Dix said.

"We have an entire division that traces crime-related money," Wang said. "I'll have it picked up later today."

"We feel that whatever his motive is for leading us to Shaw's safe deposit box, we'll never learn what that is," Dix said. "Kleinfield is too smart to expose himself and you can believe that he didn't do this without covering every square inch of his ass."

Wang looked at Claire who was seated across the conference table from him. "How do you see this, Claire?"

"Kleinfield is using us, no doubt," Claire said. "Whatever his motives are, I don't believe we'll find them out unless he wants us to."

Wang nodded. "I'll take the book. A team of agents will stop by in a while for the money. Claire, let me buy you lunch."

*   *   *   *   *

"I want you to back off on this, Claire," Wang said. "It belongs to me now."

"I know," Claire said.

"How quickly I've learned that when you say, 'I know' you're most likely to do as you damn well please," Wang said. "I mean it, Claire. Back off."

"Consider me backed," Claire said.

Wang sighed, nodded and said, "Let's order."

*　*　*　*　*

Over dessert and coffee, Wang said, "Have you considered my job offer?"

"I was giving it some serious thought when this popped up," Claire said. "Can I have a few more days, Artie?"

"One week," Wang said. "And while you're mulling things over, if anything else should pop up concerning Patrick Shaw or Kleinfield you call me first before you do anything else."

"Promise," Claire said.

"You're a helluva cop, Claire," Wang said. "I'd really love to have you on my team. Don't fuck this up and go cowboy on me and ruin it all."

"Why, Artie, I've never even been on a horse," Claire said.

*　*　*　*　*

"Good God, Claire," Knox said.

"So what now?" Turley asked.

"I've taken it as far as I can go," Claire said. "The FBI assumes responsibility for it now."

"And we do nothing?" Rose said.

"No, we keep the peace in Smoky Point and enforce the law as its sheriff's department," Claire said. "Starting right now."

Knox and Turley stood up from the sofa.

"Rose, stay for a second," Claire said.

After Knox and Turley left and closed the door, Claire said, "Kleinfield wouldn't have bothered to initiate this if there wasn't something in it for him."

"Something like what?" Rose asked.

"Good question," Claire said. "No answer. I called the town council together for a meeting. I want you to go with me."

* * * * *

Claire and Rose sat in folding chairs and faced the town council who sat at the same long table they sat at the day of Claire's first interview.

No one interrupted Claire as she gave a full report. Claire watched faces as she spoke. The three council members that were in the dark showed shock, dismay and concern on their faces.

Mitzi ran the entire gambit. Her face registered surprise, shock, disappointment and anger.

Except for Carl Walker. He sat stone-faced the entire time Claire made her report.

"So it's in the hands of the FBI and they will do with it what they can," Claire concluded.

Walker sat back in his chair, sipped from his water glass and looked at Claire. "If this goes public, which it will in the event the FBI is successful, our town will fall off the map. Tourists will…"

"This isn't about tourist season, Carl," Mitzi said.

"Miss Maxwell, eighty percent of our budget comes from tourist season," Walker said. "Without a healthy season what are we but just another dead town on the Eastern Seaboard."

"Carl, you're overreacting." Mitzi said.

"Claire, you and Rose are excused," Walker said. "The Council and I wish to hold a private meeting."

Al Lamanda

* * * * *

"What do you think?" Rose asked as she sat on the sofa in Claire's office.

"I think Carl is correct," Claire said. "This town will be turned on its ear."

"It's not the town's fault if a dishonest sheriff was involved in… whatever the hell Shaw was involved in," Rose said.

"Remember your history?" Claire asked.

"Some."

"Remember Harry Truman?"

"Along with millions of Japanese."

"That aside, he said, 'The buck stops here'," Claire said.

Rose nodded.

"And so it does," Rose said.

* * * * *

"That's it then, Claire," Holt said. "There is no more to be done on your end. Let the FBI pull their hair out over it."

Claire sliced into her steak and ate a small piece.

Holt sighed. "You're wearing that look again."

"What look?"

"The one that says I should leave well enough alone but I just can't help myself," Holt said. "That look."

"Would you?" Claire asked.

"I'm not the cop you are, Claire," Holt said. "I never was. If I had been I would have done on my watch what you did on yours."

Claire ate another small piece of steak and washed it down with a tiny sip of wine. "Do you think Carl is correct about the tourists?"

"I think the way things are today that tourists will flock here by the tens of thousands out of morbid curiosity," Holt said. "Especially after cable news runs the story twenty-four-seven for weeks on end."

"Ya got a point," Claire said.

"Want to go down to the beach and swim naked?" Holt said.

"There's like a thousand people on the beach, Matt," Claire said. "And then there is the issue of sand in your butt."

"We could go back to your place?"

"My cat doesn't play well with others."

"We could go back to my place then?"

"We could."

"But?"

"I'd rather wait for the weekend."

Holt nodded. "Want dessert?"

"The way to a girl's heart is through the dessert menu," Claire said.

*　*　*　*　*

Ross was watching cartoons on the motel room television while Boyd did his best to ignore the ignorant bastard and read a paperback book.

Tate was in the room next door. They flipped a coin to see who shared a room with Ross and Boyd lost. It didn't occur to either of them to share a room and let Ross bunk alone.

Boyd lit a cigarette and took a sip from the fifth of bourbon on the night stand. As he set the bottle down, his cell phone rang. He checked the number and answered the call.

"This is Boyd," he said. "Hold on."

Boyd covered the phone and looked at Ross.

"Do you mind?" Boyd said.

"Do I mind what?" Ross said.

"Could you mute that please?" Boyd said.

"Oh. Sorry."

Ross used the mute button on the remote to silence the television. "Go ahead," Boyd said.

He listened for a few seconds, and then said, "By tomorrow night."

Boyd glanced at the television. The coyote had fallen off a cliff, and as he hit the ground, an anvil fell on his head.

On his bed, Ross burst out laughing.

"Just remember," Boyd said. "We don't work for free."

He hung up, tossed the phone on the nightstand and looked at Ross.

"You can un-mute that now," he said.

Chapter Thirty-seven

AT HER DESK, CLAIRE ANSWERED the buzz from Turley and said, "Yes, Jim?"

"Special Agent Wang on line one for you, Claire," Turley said.

"Thank you," Claire said and picked up line one.

"Artie, how are you?" Claire said.

"I'm free for lunch," Wang said. "Are you?"

"As I have been twiddling my thumbs for the past two days and nights, the answer is yes," Claire said.

"Meet me at the diner near the Federal Building at one," Wang said.

"I'll be there," Claire said.

Claire hung up and went to the squad room. Except for Turley, the squad room was empty. Rose was off as she agreed to cover the weekend so Claire could spend it with Holt at his cabin.

"Jim, I'll be meeting with Agent Wang for a few hours," Claire said. "Short is backup until I return."

"No problem," Turley said.

* * * * *

"Why are you in uniform?" Wang asked as Claire entered the diner and found him at a booth by the window.

"My second-in-command has the day off," Claire said. "I'm backup on calls."

"Let's order," Wang said. "Then we'll talk."

A waitress approached the table.

"I'll have two Philly cheese steaks with a double order of the seasoned fries and a large Coke," Wang said.

"House salad with iced tea," Claire told the waitress.

After the waitress left, Claire said, "You're as bad as Cruz."

"Life is short and it's better with salt," Wang said.

"But longer without it. So why am I here, Artie?" Claire asked.

Wang dipped into his jacket pocket for his well-worn notebook. He flipped pages. "With regard to the $400,000, the bills are all between ten and twenty years old. Some are marked with various proof pens that they use to swipe a bill as real. Nothing interesting about that at all. However the lab boys will keep plugging away at it and maybe they can trace some of the money to an end. What does this tell you?"

"Professional all the way," Claire said. "About the little black book."

"Now here is where things get interesting," Wang said. "The boys over in code have made a bit of progress. TFB mean anything to you?"

"Sounds like a burger restaurant," Claire said.

"How about TFB 0.45?" Wang said.

"0.45? That's the metric system," Claire said.

"That's right, the metric system," Wang said. "We believe TFB is Three Finger Brown, a notorious drug dealer in Harlem. He passed away about five years ago, but his son took the mantle. Our Manhattan office thinks they can run a sting and finally shut them down."

"So Shaw was transporting drugs the night he was murdered," Claire said. "Which would explain the clothing, lack of bait and it makes sense to me he was using his coolers to contain the drugs."

"Judging from the $400,000, Shaw got overly greedy and was killed for it," Wang said.

"So who took his place and is the operation still active?" Claire asked.

"When you ride the money train you just don't hop off over a casualty," Wang said. "The code boys believe each set of initials is a buyer and the weight in kilos. They also think certain numbers mean dates. As far as they can tell the dates are all between Memorial Day and Columbus Day."

Claire stared at Wang. Her ears buzzed as her hearing dimmed. She knew Wang was still talking but she heard not one word.

"Claire! Claire!" Wang said. "What?"

"Memorial Day and Columbus Day, is that what you said?" Claire said.

"I did, yes."

"Artie, every Memorial Day and each major holiday after that until Columbus Day, motorcycle gangs from Rhode Island take the ferry to Smoky Point," Claire said. "The reason they claim they do this is that it saves them time on their way to visit sister clubs. This has been going on for close to twenty years now."

"You're sure?"

"Of course, I'm sure," Claire said. "The Disciples just a few weeks ago raised hell in a bar and I locked them up overnight."

Wang thought for a moment. "What's their rep?"

"Suspected of just about everything," Claire said. "Including drugs, selling black market guns and murder for hire."

"So, if they run true to form, they should return around or on the 4th."

"Correct."

"And if they run true to form they should have drugs with them to pass off to the new mule."

"Also correct."

"So, Claire, wanna be part of a joint operation task force?" Wang asked.

Claire closed her eyes for a moment. Then she opened them, looked at Wang and said, "How did I miss that?"

"Miss what?" Wang asked.

"The obvious."

* * * * *

Claire rushed past Turley into her office, sat at her desk and rummaged through stacks of printed reports.

She found the files on Kleinfield and read through them. His youngest son was killed in a head-on collision with a motorcycle on Route Twenty-seven, twelve years ago at the age of twenty. The cyclist was identified as a member of the Disciples Motorcycle Club.

Claire closed the file. "Abby, you brilliant son of a bitch, you got me to do your dirty work for you. Didn't you my man?"

She picked up her phone and called Holt's cell phone. His voice mailbox picked up.

"Matt, get back on the clock. Things just reached critical mass. Meet me at my place as soon as you can," she said and hung up.

* * * * *

Claire didn't turn on the lights and waited for Holt in the living room. She made coffee and sipped from a cup at the window. She still wore her full uniform, including holster.

Shortly after dark, around eight-thirty, Claire heard a vehicle approach. She looked out the window and watched Holt's pickup stop next to her car.

She went to the front door and when she heard footsteps, opened the door and said, "It's about time you…" and was knocked backward when Holt was flung into the room.

Boyd, Tate and Ross rushed in and closed the door. Boyd and Tate held Glock pistols in their hands, aimed at her.

Claire looked at Holt. His ankles and wrists were bound by duct tape and a long piece covered his mouth. He'd been worked over pretty good before being bound. His nose was mashed and eyes were swollen nearly closed.

"Sorry about your little boyfriend, Claire," Boyd said. "He resisted the idea of loaning us the use of his truck."

"Did it make you feel like a big man, three against one?" Claire said.

"Me and Tate never laid a finger on him," Boyd said. "It was all Ross."

Grinning, Ross stepped forward. "Your turn, sweetheart," he said.

Claire assumed an attack position.

Boyd shook his head. "Take your medicine, Claire," he said.

On the floor, Holt screamed through the duct tape.

"Hush," Boyd said and kicked Holt in the jaw.

"Watch the birdie," Ross said and lurched forward and punched Claire on the left side of her face with tremendous force.

Claire hit the floor on her stomach.

"What, nothing cute to say," Ross said and kicked her in the stomach. "You fucking bitch."

Ross kicked Claire several more times, grunting with glee as his heavy boot made contact. "I'll beat your fucking brains in," he said. "And then I'll just plain fuck you."

"Ross, enough," Boyd said.

"I ain't paid her back yet for that roll of quarters," Ross said.

"Later," Boyd said. "Pick her up and let's go."

Chapter Thirty-eight

THE DARKNESS OF HER CONFINEMENT was as if she had suddenly gone blind, it was that dark.

The first instinct was to panic. No amount of training can overcome that initial response. What the training does, however, is help you fight through the panic and allow clear thinking to emerge.

She could feel the sides of her confinement with her hands. They were made of wood. The air was damp and smelled stale. She slowed her breathing to sips because she didn't know how much air was available and needed to conserve what there was or risk suffocating.

She reached up and touched the ceiling. It was also made of wood and maybe a foot above her face.

She swallowed the terror in her chest and tried to remember how this came to pass and couldn't. The last thing she remembered was...

Her utility belt, it was still around her waist.

She felt for her weapon and it was in the holster on her right hip. On her left hip was the palm-sized Maglite she always carried and she withdrew it from the sheath. Her hands shook a bit as she clicked it on.

Immediately she recognized her confinement.

She was inside a cheap pine coffin.

Jesus Christ, she had been buried alive.

Sip. Don't gasp for air because if you hyperventilate you're done.

Claire took in small amounts of air through her nose. Her face felt swollen and her ribs and stomach ached from being kicked. But she was alive and that was curious that she should be so.

She touched the lid on the coffin again and pressed against it.

It moved slightly.

They hadn't nailed it shut. Yet.

Claire moved the lid a few inches and looked up at the night sky overhead and sucked in the fresher air that flowed in.

She strained her hearing but heard nothing but the slight breeze flowing into the coffin.

She moved the lid enough so that she could crawl out of the coffin. Her sides were on fire and he mouth was full of blood. She crouched beside the coffin and quietly replaced the lid.

She was in a deep patch of woods, where was anybody's guess. She stayed crouched beside the coffin and let her hearing adjust and she heard a sound in the distance.

Maybe fifty yards to the east.

Claire slowly stood and grabbed her right side as a sharp pain knifed through her. She had bruised if not broken ribs.

Then, slowly, she followed the sound.

She paused when she heard voices.

"That's enough," Mitzi Maxwell said. "You're not digging a fucking well here."

"You want the body to be found or what?" Boyd said.

"Have it your way," Mitzi said. "After she's in the ground, meet me at my place. We have next month's shipment to discuss."

Claire hid behind a tree. She heard a car start and drive away.

She heard Boyd say, "Okay, that's enough. Tate, make sure she's out and nail the box shut. I want to get her in the ground and get the fuck out of here."

"I'll do it," Ross said. "I'd like a crack at her little snatch first."

"No you won't," Boyd said. "Tate, go nail it shut."

"What if she wakes up?" Take asked.

"Then kill her. What did you think?" Boyd said.

Claire hid behind the tree in shadow as Tate walked past her to the coffin. He was a large man, nearly as big as Ross. She looked around and picked up a round stone that weighed about a pound and followed Tate from a safe distance.

She paused when he reached the coffin. He was smart enough to pull his gun before opening the lid.

There was a flashlight in Tate's back pocket and he pulled it and held it in his left hand. He stuck his Glock into his belt and as he slid the lid of the coffin out of the way, Claire raced the ten paces between them and smacked him on the back of his head.

There was a loud thud and Tate collapsed to the ground. He was alive but unconscious. Claire removed the cuffs from her belt and cuffed his hands behind his back.

Then she pulled her Glock and walked toward Boyd and Ross.

She stopped at a tree around ten feet from where Ross was still in the hole digging with a shovel.

Boyd stood over the hole, watching.

Claire took out the flashlight and aimed it at Boyd with her left hand while aiming the Glock with her right.

She clicked on the flashlight.

Boyd's back and part of Ross was caught in the powerful Maglite beam.

"I didn't hear any nails hammering," Boyd said.

"That's because your man Arlo is not looking so good with his head split open," Claire said.

Boyd sighed. "Oh, Claire," he said.

"Toss your weapon, put your hands on your head and turn around," Claire said.

"I can't do that, Claire," Boyd said.

"Don't test me, Boyd," Claire said. "I'm no doll."

"No, Claire, you're no doll," Boyd said.

"I told you we shoulda killed this bitch," Ross said.

"Shut up, Ross," Boyd said.

"Yeah, shut up, Ross," Claire said. "Last chance, Boyd."

Claire waited for the moment she knew would come. Boyd's body tensed as his right hand moved to his belt.

"Don't, Boyd. You won't make it," Claire said.

She heard Boyd suck in air, pause and then he spun around with his gun in his right hand.

Claire's first shot hit Boyd square in the chest. His body absorbed the impact and snapped backward as if pulled by a rope.

He screamed and aimed his gun at Claire.

Her second shot put a hole in his chest just a few inches from the first. Slowly, he sunk to his knees.

"You play a good game of chess," Boyd said.

Still holding the gun, Boyd aimed it at Claire.

Her third shot struck him in the neck and he looked at Claire and she saw the light go out in his eyes and he fell backward into the hole at Ross's feet.

"And you don't," Claire said.

Ross looked down at Boyd. Then his eyes slowly rose up and his face was a twisted rage. He held the shovel above his head and charged out of the hole screaming at the top of his lungs.

Claire shot Ross in the chest and the bullet slowed him down as blood squirted from the hole.

"That's for the punch in the face," Claire said.

Ross staggered forward and Claire shot him in the chest a second time.

"That's for the kick in the ribs," she said.

The shovel fell from Ross's grasp.

"And this is for wanting to rape me," Claire said and put a third hole in Ross's chest.

Ross fell over, dead before he hit the ground.

Claire took a deep breath and replaced the Glock into the holster. Then she pulled out her cell phone and called the office.

Pederson answered the phone.

"Janelle, no time to explain," Claire said. "Call an ambulance and send them to my house right away. And call Short and Rose and tell them to meet the ambulance. I'll explain later."

With her flashlight, Claire guided herself about one hundred yards to where Holt's truck was parked behind a large tree just off a deserted dirt road.

They keys were in the ignition.

Chapter Thirty-nine

CLAIRE PARKED HOLT'S PICKUP A block from Mitzi Maxwell's house and walked to it in the dark.

When she reached the house, she walked around to the side, staying in the dark but looking through the windows.

Mitzi was on the sofa with a drink.

Claire went to the back of the house. The rear door led to the kitchen. She tried the doorknob. It was unlocked.

Slowly, Claire opened the door and stepped into the kitchen. There was a swinging door that led to the living room. She walked to the door and pulled her Glock and switched out the magazine.

Claire placed her left hand on the door, pushed it opened and stepped into the living room.

"I'm here, Mitzi," she said.

With her back to Claire, Mitzi took a sip of her drink.

"Would you care for a drink, Claire?" Mitzi asked.

"No I would not," Claire said.

"Not even a little one?"

"So how does it all work?" Claire asked. "The Disciples bring the dope smuggled in their bikes and pass it off while they pretend to get drunk and break up a bar. Then you send a mule to make deliveries?"

"More or less," Mitzi said.

"Shaw?"

"He served his purpose," Mitzi said.

"And when he wasn't useful anymore you had him killed?"

"More or less."

"You're not in this alone," Claire said. "Carl Walker?"

"That silly little man."

"Who?"

"I've told you all I'm going to tell you, Claire," Mitzi said.

"Mitzi, put your hands on your head and stand up," Claire said.

"Do you know why I pushed for you for the job?" Mitzi said. "Because I thought you were just another pretty face looking to kill a year. I underestimated you, Claire. I won't make that mistake twice."

"Hands on your head and stand up, Mitzi," Claire said. "I won't tell you again."

"I can't go to prison, Claire," Mitzi said. "I'm too old and too spoiled."

"Do you think I'm just going to let you walk?" Claire asked.

"No, I suppose not," Mitzi said. "Ever been in love, Claire? I mean real head-over-heels in love so much you're willing to die."

"Not really," Claire said.

Mitzi stood and turned and aimed the cocked revolver in her right hand at Claire.

Claire shot Mitzi in the chest an inch above the heart. As she fell over backward, the revolver fired one shot into the ceiling.

Claire walked to Mitzi and kicked the revolver away.

Mitzi looked up at Claire as the life drained from her body. After a few shallow breaths, Mitzi's chest went still and her eyes closed.

"Dammit, Mitzi," Claire said.

She sat on the sofa and looked at the lifeless body.

In her pocket, Claire's cell phone. She pulled it out, checked the number, hit *talk* and said, "Go ahead, Short."

"What the fuck, Claire?" Knox said.

"Is Holt alive?" Claire asked.

"He's beat to shit, but yeah. He's in the ambulance right now."

"Call for another one to Mitzi Maxwell's house and call the county sheriff's office," Claire said. "No, wait, I'll do that."

* * * * *

As paramedics carried Mitzi's body out to an ambulance, Wang and Cruz looked at Claire.

She was seated on the sofa with a glass of bourbon over ice.

"Are you okay?" Cruz asked.

Claire took a small sip from her glass and nodded.

"My men found the three bodies in the woods," Wang said. "One of them is alive but has a severe concussion. Looks like they were all set to bury you alive."

"Jesus H. Christ," Cruz said.

"You look pretty beat up yourself," Wang said. "Let's get you to the hospital and have you checked out."

"Have you ever been in love?" Claire said.

"What?" Cruz asked.

"Those were her last words," Claire said.

Cruz sighed. "Let's get you to the hospital."

"Can we stop for some donuts on the way?" Claire said.

Chapter Forty

CLAIRE WALKED INTO HOLT'S HOSPITAL room after being checked out by an emergency room doctor.

Holt was in bed, awake and hooked up to an IV.

"Claire," he said. "Are you okay?"

"Fine," Claire said as she approached the bed. "You?"

"I'll live," Holt said. "I heard you took down the three plus Mitzi Maxwell."

"Boyd and Tate, they're just hard-core criminals in it for the buck," Claire said. "Mitzi was the brains and used Shaw's contacts in New York to mule the drugs. At first I thought Shaw was killed because he got too greedy. But that wasn't it, not at all."

"Claire, I don't know what you're..." Holt said.

"You see, Matt, Mitzi found a new boyfriend and was head-over-heels in love," Claire said. "So much so she died to protect him."

Holt stared at Claire.

"Nice touch having them beat you up before bringing them to my place," Claire said.

"I don't know what you're..." Holt said.

"That day I asked you to pick me up at home, remember?" Claire said. "I never told you where I lived."

Claire turned and walked to the door, paused and turned around.

"There's a very nice FBI Agent named Artie Wang and the County Sheriff Bill Cruz waiting in the hall to talk to you," Claire said.

"Barbara Dix will be along shortly. You crazy kids play nice now, you hear."

Claire opened the door and walked out.

* * * * *

"I'm absolutely dumbfounded," Carl Walker said.

He was seated on the sofa in Claire's office.

"With the main players dead the FBI may never get full closure, but the gravy train has stopped rolling through Smoky Point for now," Claire said.

"Mitzi Maxwell?" Walker said. "And Matt Holt?"

"Sometimes the obvious is so obvious you don't see it," Claire said.

Her phone buzzed and she picked it up.

"Claire, the reporters are lining up outside," Turley said.

"Tell them Town Manager and Mayor Carl Walker will be giving a press conference at noon," Claire said and hung up.

She looked at Walker.

"Your fifteen minutes of fame is waiting, Carl," Claire said.

Walker stood up. "I best prepare," he said.

"You best," Claire said.

"Mitzi Maxwell and Matthew Holt," Walker said.

"It's what makes the world go around, Carl," Claire said.

Walker nodded and left the office.

Claire sat in silence for a few moments. Then there was a knock on the door and Rose and Knox entered. Knox held a coffee mug.

"Would you like some coffee?" Knox asked. "Claire."

Chapter Forty-one

"HOW DO YOU LIKE THE scones, Claire?" Kleinfield asked. "David baked them fresh just this morning."

"He should open up a bakery," Claire said.

They were at the table in Kleinfield's backyard.

"Revenge is a dish best served cold," Claire said. "But you know all about that, don't you? Abby."

"Vichyssoise is best served cold, Claire," Kleinfield said. "So is ice cream."

"I suppose it's all just a big coincidence that you helped me and in doing so took out the motorcycle gang that killed your son?" Claire said.

"I saw this T-shirt once," Kleinfield said. "It said, *Shit Happens*."

Claire nodded. "Thank you, Abby."

"It was nice seeing you again, Claire," Kleinfield said.

At the door, David handed Claire her holster and a paper bag.

"And this is?" Claire said.

"Scones. Still warm," David said.

Claire nodded. "Of course."

＊　＊　＊　＊　＊

Driving east on Route Twenty-seven, Claire grinned as she passed the *Welcome* to *Smoky Point* sign along the road.

Her cell phone rang and she pushed the button on the dashboard to put it on speaker.

"This is Claire," she said.

"Claire, it's Dugan. Have you been watching the news?"

"No, what's it say?"

"Don't give me that," Dugan said. "The boss wants to see you right away."

"Tell the boss thanks, but no thanks," Claire said. "I already got a job."

"Claire, wait a…" Dugan said as Claire hung up.

About the Author

AL LAMANDA WAS BORN AND raised in New York City. For his work, he has been nominated for the Edgar Award, the Shamus Award, and won the Nero Wolfe Award for Best Mystery of the Year for his novel, *With 6 You Get Wally*, book five in the John Bekker Mysteries. The series continues with *Who Killed Joe Italiano?* (2018), *For Deader or Worse* (2019), and *The Case of the Missing Fan Dancer*, published by Encircle Publications in March 2022.

In addition to his many mysteries, Al also writes Western novels under the name Ethan J. Wolfe, which have been highly received by the Western Historical Society. He served in the United States Marine Corps, and worked as a private investigator and professional bodyguard in New York, Massachusetts, and Florida. He also served as a security and loss prevention consultant for many large corporations. In his free time, Al studied boxing, mixing it up in many amateur fights, and still trains today.

His historical fiction novel set in New York City in the late 1940s, *City of Darkness*, was published by Encircle in January, 2021. He has published two Rollie Finch Mysteries, *Once Upon a Time on 9/11* (April 2021), and *Rollie and the Missing Six* (August 2022). Al is always working on his next novel.